CW00938454

It Always Rains
On Sunday

It Always Rains On Sunday

Arthur La Bern

With an introduction by Cathi Unsworth

LONDON BOOKS CLASSICS

LONDON BOOKS
39 Lavender Gardens
London SW11 1DJ
www.london-books.co.uk

First published 1945 by Nicholson & Watson
This edition published by London Books 2015

London Books would like to thank Arthur La Bern's nephew,
Peter Wickins, for sharing his memories of his uncle and for
permitting us to publish this and future works.

A catalogue record for this book
is available from the British Library

ISBN 978-0-9568155-5-2

Printed and bound in Great Britain by
CPI Group (UK) Ltd, Croydon, CR0 4YY

Typeset by Octavo Smith Publishing Services in Plantin 9.75/12.5
www.octavosmith.com

INTRODUCTION

In the opening chapters of Arthur La Bern's *It Always Rains On Sunday*, a trio of nefarious characters gather at the bar of The Two Compasses public house in Marcus Street, just around the corner from Petticoat Lane. All are wearing 'ten-and-elevenpenny imitations of Anthony Eden hats, white silk mufflers, quite smart fifty-shilling suits and patent shoes' – the standard tailoring of the late-1930s East End wide boy. The gang appears to be led by Whitey Williams, a once promising lightweight boxer, whose height and remarkably fair complexion lend him an aura of power. Whitey considers himself to be a bit of a mastermind; it is a result of one of his hot tips that they have assembled in this location, awaiting the arrival of someone a little higher up the distribution chain.

Whitey's cohort Dicey Perkins, by contrast, has decaying teeth set into the slack jaw of a sallow face, and is displaying the unsavoury habit that has earned him the nickname of Pick Nose Perkins from his enemies. Dicey slouches against the counter, using his good leg to relieve the pressure of its gammy twin, the legacy of a 70mph car crash and subsequent hospital treatment which, he claims, was deliberately rendered substandard by order of the local police. For all his outward imperfections, Dicey is still considered the best getaway driver east of the Aldgate Pump.

But it is the third, and least conspicuous of these characters, who is actually the most interesting. Here's how the author describes him:

> Alfie Price, the shortest of the trio was a dapper little chap, with his hat tilted forward so that it shaded his small, bird-like eyes. He wore a thin, Ronald Colman moustache, and had a habit of sucking one of his back teeth when deep in thought. He had a semi-circular scar just below his right cheekbone, souvenir of a

Derby-day fracas, when one of the Birmingham boys had tapped a half-pint glass in two and thrust the jagged edge hard into Alfie's face, saying, 'Here's luck, Alfie!'

Alfie is the man who has organised a meet with Lou Hyams, local face and proprietor of the amusements on Whitechapel Road, to see if he can't help them get rid of the unexpected grand haul of the job they did the night before. Not the £800 Whitey claimed would be inside the empty safe at Mackay And Holden's warehouse in Great Mansell Street, but the consolation gross of roller skates that were inside the van they nicked from the yard instead. Alfie is the only one of them who is smart enough to think of this contingency, fruitless though it turns out to be. Similarly, when Detective-Sergeant Fothergill replaces the regretfully unhelpful Lou Hyams at the bar, it is Alfie alone who has the mental agility to sidestep the copper's line of questioning about a stolen van, found minus its cargo of roller skates, on Hackney Marshes that morning. Alfie Price, though the real leader of this mob, is not the central character of the novel, which, like a wonderfully noir soap opera, revolves around one particularly fraught day in the life of the Sandigate family of Coronet Grove. But he is the one who most closely resembles the man who wrote it.

Arthur La Bern, as he is pictured in the author photo that originally graced the inside jacket of the 1975 edition of his novel *Nightmare*, was a dapper little chap all right, although the Colman moustache he continued to sport three decades later actually gave him more of a resemblance to the other Ron of classic British cinema, Mr Fraser. La Bern is pictured sitting on the sort of Chesterfield sofa you'd expect to find in the sort of Soho drinking club where a sometime crime reporter, war correspondent and novelist might like to spend his leisure hours. One of those places where all the faces, coppers and hacks mingle and the raw materials for a man in the writing trade hang on the air as thickly as the smoke. Not that Arthur looks very comfortable being photographed here. He is still wearing his tailored camel overcoat over his smart suit and silk tie, one hand in his pocket, the other leaning against the arm of the sofa as if he is just about to push himself up and away from the intrusive glare of the lens. His 'bird-like eyes' stare past the photographer with a poker player's expression of inscrutability. Perhaps it's not the location. Perhaps he just doesn't like being photographed, full stop. Even as the shutter clicks, La Bern is leaving the frame, leaving his readers none the wiser.

It's like the story of his life.

Arthur La Bern is known these days, if he is known at all, by aficionados of British pulp fiction and cult cinema, for two books that were turned into landmark movies, both remarkable in very different ways. One of them is the book that you hold in your hand, *It Always Rains On Sunday*, first published in 1945 by Nicholson & Watson, which became Robert Hamer's 1947 Ealing classic – one of the few pictures from this period to portray life in the community around Whitechapel with real veracity. The other is his 1966 novel *Goodbye Piccadilly, Farewell Leicester Square*, the story of a sadistic killer which became Alfred Hitchcock's controversial 1972 *Frenzy*, a film La Bern hated so much he wrote to *The Times* to denounce Hitchcock and his choice of scriptwriter, Anthony Shaffer, in no uncertain terms.

'The result on the screen is appalling,' he wrote. 'I would like to ask Mr Hitchcock and Mr Shaffer what happened between book and script to the authentic London characters I created.' He ended his letter: 'Finally: I wish to dissociate myself with Mr Shaffer's grotesque misrepresentation of Scotland Yard offices.'

It is telling that it is misrepresentation and lack of authenticity that got Arthur so riled. From what slim traces remain of the life he left behind in London in 1990, at the age of eighty-one, it can be discerned that when it came to police and thieves, wide boys and hacks, racetrack gangs and the voices of the London streets, La Bern knew with great authority and detail of what he wrote. Even if he was a bit evasive about his part in it all.

On the short biographical blurbs printed on the jackets of his books, La Bern would often describe himself as a Gallic Cockney, sometimes claiming Huguenot ancestry. In fact, he was the son of Lionel and Lizzy Labern, née Charlotte Colombo. His father came from Holborn and his mother from Clerkenwell, a third-generation Londoner of Italian descent. Arthur Joseph Labern was born in the Islington of 1909, to multicultural streets buzzing with hives of enterprising criminal families and gangs, some of whom may now be familiar to viewers of the BBC's *Peaky Blinders*.

His mother's family were doll-makers in an area made notorious by the razor-wielding trio of brothers led by Ollovia Sabini, who called himself Charles and was more commonly known as Darby. Before his current incarnation as the sharp-suited, Brummie-baiting 'King Of The Racetracks' played by Noah Taylor, Darby Sabini had previously inspired Graham Greene's *Brighton Rock*, both as the character Mr Colleoni, living it large at the Cosmopolitan Hotel, and in the depiction of gang violence that was based on an incident involving the Sabini firm at Brighton racetrack on the South Downs in 1935.

As well as their Midlands rivals, the Sabinis' many London adversaries included: the Hoxton Mob, who came to grief in a 1936 battle on Lewes racecourse that ended in mass incarceration; The Broad Mob from Camden Town; the mainly Jewish Aldgate Mob; and the Yiddishers of Whitechapel, whose numbers included the bookie-turned-protection-racketeer Jack 'Spot' Comer, who would team up with his Camden Town rival Billy Hill to run the rackets during the Forties and Fifties. All of which rich aroma of roguery swirls vividly around the description of the three would-be hoods at the bar of The Two Compasses.

The young Arthur was left fatherless before he was a year old, when Lionel died in 1910, and an older brother went to an early grave three years later, aged only twelve. Arthur and his sister Lizzy grew up in the kind of poverty that infuses the pages of *It Always Rains On Sunday*, with its all-too-plausible descriptions of Spry's Hotel dosshouse and its miserable denizens; and the day-to-day drudgery of cooking, cleaning and mending that dominates the life of the women in the Sandigate household: sisters Doris and Violet and their stepmother Rose. This was Arthur's first novel, so it is perhaps telling that his fictional teenagers have also grown up without one of their parents.

The twenty-four-hour cycle of the book begins with Rose imperiously ordering Doris out of bed to make tea 'for your father', but actually meaning for herself. The girls' resentment of their dad's second bride, herself the former barmaid of The Two Compasses, soon boils over into scenes of brutality sufficient to shock the normally amiable patriarch George – not to mention the contemporary reader unfamiliar with the use of stair-rods as instruments of punishment. In the world La Bern depicts, however, there is very little out of the ordinary about this. Indeed, there is barely a domestic scene within the milieu of Coronet Grove and Marcus Street that is not infused with violence, or the threat of it.

Arthur, who was close to both his mother and sister, writes the squabbling Sandigate sisters – hormonal hellcat Vi and moody, melancholy Doris – with empathy and verisimilitude. The other female characters of this populous novel are equally well-drawn. Rose, who comes face-to-face with her past in the form of the runaway convict Tommy Swann hiding out in her garden shed, may be forever etched on the memory of the cineaste as the luminous Googie Withers, who played her so effectively in Robert Hamer's film. But the Rose of La Bern's novel is a character losing her glamour in a different manner to her screen incarnation. The world she inhabits is those last peacetime days of 1939, before the devastation of the Blitz and the lingering privations of rationing that fashioned the film's wearier, more sympathetic presentation of her.

This Mrs Sandigate has let herself cushion into plumpness after ten years of marriage and the birth of son Alfie, and, though still proud of her creamy skin and copper hair, she has accepted that the brief flashes of decadence she knew in her youth are now behind her. Which is why, when she reads on the front page of the *News Of The World* that Doris brings her along with her Sunday morning cup of tea, that her former lover Tommy Swann has escaped from Dartmoor, the veneer of domestic content she has steadfastly created for herself starts to crumble so dramatically. For it was Tommy, intoxicating Tommy, who gave Rose that long-ago glimpse of the high life. Tommy to whom she might have been married now – had he not got himself pinched first.

Twelve years after La Bern's father Lionel died, his mother Lizzy remarried. She had another son called Charlie, mirroring perhaps the role of Alfie Sandigate in *It Always Rains On Sunday*.

But Arthur was little older than this boy by the time he had left school, at the age of thirteen, and began to live the shifting, itinerant existence of the wide boys at The Two Compasses bar himself. His nephew Peter, son of the younger Lizzie, remembers Uncle Arthur as 'a bit of a spiv' – always snappily dressed and wearing his trademark moustache – and able to attract plenty of female interest. However else he was earning money, he accrued enough of it to buy a typewriter, which he kept at his mother's house.

According to his book blurbs, Arthur worked as a journalist for a number of newspapers, including the *Evening Standard*, the *Evening News*, the *Daily Mirror* and the *Daily Mail* in the Thirties. During the Second World War he was a war correspondent for the *Evening Standard* and flew with the Fleet Air Arm in the Pacific. During his time on Fleet Street he worked as a crime reporter – although his biographies of two of Britain's most notorious bogeymen, Brides In The Bath murderer George Joseph Smith and Acid Bath killer John George Haigh, while partially researched during this time, would be published only after he had made his mark as a novelist, in 1967 and 1973 respectively.

His third novel, 1948's *Paper Orchid*, displays an insider's knowledge of Fleet Street hierarchies and methodologies and the characters that populate the grand newspaper offices, print rooms and surrounding warren of alleys and pubs that is as authentic as the familiarity with East End life depicted in *It Always Rains On Sunday*. It was adapted for cinema in 1949 by a Roy Ward Barker cutting his teeth on gritty post-war noir before his move into television history with *The Avengers*, *Department S* and *The Saint*. Arthur is credited alongside screenwriter Val Guest for providing additional dialogue, and it's worth seeking out for the performance of a young Sid James as the crime reporter Freddy C Evans who, despite lacking a pencil line of bristles on his upper lip, has a certain Arthurbiographical quality about him. However, Guest's inexplicably clunky dismemberment of his source material's corkscrew plot renders it no real match for the first and best of all Arthur's film adaptations.

Interestingly, *It Always Rains On Sunday* was brought to the big screen by another outsider. Although Robert Hamer's affluent background could not be more different from La Bern's hard way up, there are nonetheless strange parallels in the trajectories of both their lives. Born to a wealthy family, Hamer was a child genius who won a scholarship to Cambridge and went on to direct the film that is often cited as the jewel in Ealing's crown, 1949's *Kind Hearts And Coronets*. Yet he would end his days an alcoholic wreck, hallucinating he was being stalked by vengeful lobsters.

Hamer's rise up the ranks was as dramatic as his subsequent fall from grace. He began as a cutting-room assistant at Gaumont-British studios in 1934 and a year later, at London Films, began working for the brilliant Brazilian director Alberto Cavalcanti, whom he followed to Ealing in 1941. Hamer had his first credit as a director in Cavalcanti's 1945 horror portmanteau *Dead Of Night*, with the story of a haunted mirror that turns its owner into a homicidal maniac – an allegory for sexual repression that reflected back its creator's closeted circumstances. Hamer had been sent down from Cambridge amid the whiff of scandal and his work would continue to pick up further Wildean threads, despite his two marriages. The same year came his debut in the director's chair, *Pink String And Ceiling Wax*, a Victorian melodrama set in Brighton, that starred Googie Withers as a vengeful pub landlady plotting the murder of her husband – and marking her out as Hamer's perfect leading lady.

The Ealing Studios template was the 'group story', which was deployed in all its classic comedies and is a forerunner to what we would recognise today as the standard soap-opera format of multiple characters with interconnecting stories centred on a particular street and the pubs and businesses run there. La Bern's novel, which spirals out from the Sandigate household into the Petticoat Lane plots of Lou Hyams and his brother Morry, along with the attendant market, the bar of The Two Compasses and Spry's Hotel, was therefore perfect source material.

Hamer's cast did do credit to the authenticity of most of Arthur's characters. John Slater's Lou Hyams looks like he swaggered straight out of a spieler, but still more inspired is the choice of Sydney Tafler as the upwardly mobile Morry, the self-styled 'Man

With Sax Appeal', who leads a swing band under the Anglicised surname of Higham and runs a record shop on Petticoat Lane; and Betty Ann Davies as his long-suffering wife Sadie, wearily wise to all Morry's 'little *shiksas*' – including his current squeeze, Vi Sandigate. Unsurprisingly, after this showing, Tafler would go on to take the lead role in Ken Hughes' 1952 spivsploitation flick *Wide Boy*.

Jack Warner, still three years away from the pivotal role in *The Blue Lamp* that would cement him forever in the mind of the British populace as Dixon of Dock Green, naturally takes the role of Detective-Sergeant Fothergill. Jimmy Hanley – who, in an interesting London Books connection, took the lead role in Penrose Tennyson's 1939 adaptation of James Curtis' *There Ain't No Justice* – plays Whitey, while East Ender Alfie Bass is a natural for Dicey. But – perhaps because of the other character named Alfie (Sandigate, played by David Liney) – Alfie Price evaporates between the book and the screen. A character named Freddie replaces him, played by John Carol and sadly not Ronald Fraser.

There are other departures that are obviously expedient to the tighter plot required in a film – for instance, Lou Hyams' love interest Bessie Weinbaum here becomes his sister, taking the place of Fay in the novel and rendering poor Lou girl-less. Others are perhaps fashioned more to Hamer's comedic taste. Crime reporter Slopey Collins, as played by Michael Howard, is an unrecognisably camper creature than the skirt-chasing, hardbitten hack readers will encounter in this book.

The central performances of the film belong to Googie Withers and the man who was about to become her husband, Australian actor John McCallum as Tommy Swann. The reason *It Always Rains On Sunday* became Ealing's box office hit of 1947 would largely be down to the empathy aroused in every female filmgoer by Withers' mesmerising portrayal of a conflicted woman whose life is as drab and relentless as the drizzle that enfolds her world and who will end up risking all for one backwards glimpse of what might have been. The tangible chemistry between Withers and McCallum heightens the frisson between the past and the present, the golden-haired, silk-suited girl seen in flashback with whom Tommy Swann fell in love and the Utility-dressed brunette Rose has become since marrying George.

What it wasn't possible for Hamer to translate from the novel was the sheer beauty of La Bern's spare, evocative prose – but he had a good enough analogy for it in the employment of Douglas Slocombe as his director of photography. Slocombe, like La Bern, was a former journalist who had only become a cameraman because of the war and had also served with the First Air Fleet. He photographed the German invasions of Poland and Holland before returning to England, where Alberto Cavalcanti convinced him to divide his time between work for the Ministry of Information and Ealing films. His footage of the Atlantic convoys ended up being used by both his employers, on propaganda films for the former and in *The Big Blockade* (1941) and *San Demetrio London* (1943) by director Charles Frend, for the latter.

Like Hamer, Slocombe cut his teeth in his eventual profession as DP on *Dead Of Night* with the distinctive noir lighting that would be the hallmark of *It Always Rains On Sunday*. In a similar fashion to Carol Reed's contemporaneous *Odd Man Out* (1947) and *The Third Man* (1949), he turns the East End itself into the eyes through which we view the action, from every conceivable angle between the children splashing about in the gutters and the pigeons sheltering in the eaves above. From the roar and buzz of the market on Sunday morning to the climactic night-time chase through a Stratford railway yard, all the excitement, danger and melancholy of the novel is conveyed by Slocombe's lens. And yet, as you will soon discover, nothing can quite recreate the piquancy of lines such as these:

Thus a Sunday night in Stepney. Rain falling. Cinemas crowded. Public houses crowded. Cymbal-banging, red-jerseyed Salvationists. Grey-haired apostle of the Lord tramping the gutters between sandwich boards. Warm odour of good food from *Strictly Kosher* restaurants, the double triangle of the House Of David in gilt stencil on the steam-clouded windows. A hundred tattered communists, rain-soaked but still vociferous, marching back from Hyde Park yelling '*Arms for Spain!*' Youths playing on pin-table machines. Lovers in dark doorways. Trams and buses thundering and screaming down the main roads. Roads garish with neon and a hundred different sights, sounds and smells. And back of the main roads a wilderness of grey streets, little dwelling-houses, rows and rows and rows of them, intersected by gaunt blocks of tenements. Against the sky a filigree tangle of swaying aerials.

Following the success of his debut, Arthur's pen continued to flow. The novels *Night Darkens The Streets* (1947), *Paper Orchid* (1948), *Pennygreen Street* (1950), *It Was Christmas Every Day* (1952), *The Big Money Box* (1960), *Brighton Belle* (1963), *It Will Be Warmer When it Snows* (1966), *Goodbye Piccadilly, Farewell Leicester Square* (1966), *A Nice Class Of People* (1969), *Hallelujah* (1973) and *Nightmare* (1975) followed.

The most engaging subsequent celluloid rendering of his work is David Macdonald's 1948 adaptation of *Night Darkens The Streets* for Gainsborough Studios as *Good-Time Girl* – what is lost in the retitling is made up for in getting straight to the point. Producer Sydney Box and his scriptwriting wife Muriel adapted their source material in a way that was supposed to be socially conscientious – the story of the titular Gwen Rawlings is told to a runaway, played by the sixteen-year-old Diana Dors, by Flora Robson's juvenile-court magistrate. Her message is stark in its simplicity and can be best imagined coming straight from the mouth of Mr Cholmondley-Warner in *Harry Enfield's Television Programme*: 'Girls – do not go out with wide boys. Otherwise you will go to reform school – and then die!' However, the film does boast a wonderful cast, led by Jean Kent as Gwen, Herbert Lom as nightclub owner Max and Dennis Price as jazzer Red Farrell. Best of all is Griffith Jones as Danny Martin, cornering the market in satanic spivs begun with his portrayal of Narcy in the previous year's Alberto Cavalcanti-directed *They Made Me A Fugitive*.

La Bern's novels were interspersed with the two aforementioned true-crime works, *The Life And Death Of A Ladykiller* and *Haigh: The Mind Of A Murderer*, through which La Bern attempted to 'walk in the footsteps' of his deviant subjects in order to understand their motivations. During his research for both, which began in his Fleet Street days, La Bern drew on the experience of a great many highly respected detectives, barristers and forensic scientists who had worked on each case. The dedication of his Haigh book to Robert Fabian makes it plain how au fait he actually was with Scotland Yard's top brass.

Arthur's fascination with George Joseph Smith, who murdered three of the string of eight women he bigamously married for money; smooth-talking John George Haigh, who dissolved the bodies of his 'business associates' in an acid bath and went to the gallows with a quip on his lips; as well as the equally spivvy former pilot Neville Heath, who brutally murdered two young women in 1946, is deployed throughout the plot of *Goodbye Piccadilly, Farewell Leicester Square*. The psyches of these real-life killers weave their way into Arthur's fictitious depiction of both the stealthy sexual predator Bob Rusk and his compromised friend, former RAF bomber Dick Blamey, who is haunted by his participation in the firestorm of Dresden.

At the time La Bern's second most famous novel was published, there had also been a spate of unsolved murders in London that find further echoes in this fiction. Between 1959 and 1965, eight working girls were murdered by a fiend the press named Jack The Stripper, after victims were found stripped and strangled with their own stockings in and around the stretch of the Thames between Hammersmith and Acton. Despite the biggest manhunt in Metropolitan Police history, the murderer was never caught and appeared to vanish into thin air after the final body was found. The parallels between this phantom killer's MO and that of the necktie strangler of the book were obviously too good to miss when Alfred Hitchcock, who also nurtured something of an obsession with Haigh and Heath, got his hands on it.

Frenzy begins with a scene in which a naked, strangled woman's body is found bobbing in the waters by Tower Bridge, and Hitch went on to promote the film with a trailer that featured himself floating along the Thames. One of the most obvious changes he and Shaffer made to the plot of the novel was its shifting from the immediate post-war into a contemporary setting. They also changed

Blamey's name to Blaney, which was the name of the man who owned Hitchcock's family home before his father. Following the release of the film, the book was rebranded under the title *Frenzy*, stripping La Bern's novel even of its original, evocative moniker.

La Bern was not alone in his abhorrence of Hitchcock's adaptation – for many of the director's detractors, the scenes of rape and attendant asphyxiation typified his worst misogynistic tendencies. With its kipper-tied leads Barry Foster and Jon Finch wearing the worst excesses of a lurid colour palette and a dirty sense of humour running throughout, *Frenzy* definitely reflected the brutal swing of the Sixties into the Seventies – though the scenes shot in the now defunct Covent Garden fruit and vegetable market also preserve a London treasure that has since been lost, in a similar way to Douglas Slocombe's rendering of Forties Petticoat Lane.

It does seem eerily prophetic that La Bern's career should be bookended by two films that could not have been a more different experience for him, nor have presented his original vision in such an opposing way. For the darkness that infused Hitchcock's production and La Bern's reaction to it seems in hindsight to have been part of a cloud that was beginning to encroach upon the author himself.

Like so many of the characters in his novels, Arthur enjoyed the high life but found it impossible to keep control of the money that had flowed in at the start of his career as a novelist. According to his nephew Peter, La Bern travelled the entire arc from living in Chelsea to sewing mailbags in prison, serving time as an undischarged bankrupt.

His last novel, *Nightmare*, presented a bleak story of the civil-rights abuse of psychiatric patients, as narrated by a suicidal, alcoholic QC. This was one of the few books that did not translate to the screen, and it is quite possible the grim theme is a reflection on the author's own personal circumstances. Arthur continued to work as a journalist – revealingly, one of his last leader columns is from *The Times* in 1982, wherein he berated the stingy unfairness of the newly launched Public Lending Right for authors in comparison to the vastly more generous and stringently enforced

Performing Rights Society rates for musicians. One of the many great changes he had known in his lifetime must have been the dramatic reduction in earnings that even a successful writer could expect to make.

By the time he was in his seventies, Arthur was on his uppers. Once he was arrested for vagrancy after sleeping on Brighton beach and wrote angrily to the local paper, comparing his current circumstances to the glory days he once knew, drinking champagne outside the Grand Hotel. Like Rose Sandigate looking back over her shoulder, it is tragic to imagine this forgotten old man, surrounded now only by the ghosts of those halcyon days at the seaside: Darby Sabini, Gwen Rawlings, the razor gangs, good-time girls and wide boys et al. Of Arthur La Bern getting up from his seat at that afterhours club where they all used to know him so well, ready to exit the frame.

Far better to replace that vision with the magic of his own words, conjure back that lost world he made so mesmerising and alluring, right down to the description of the ever-present rain. Watch instead how Alfie Price steps out of the pages of this book:

Alfie tilted his hat forward, then pushed it back, raised an eyebrow, then sucked a back tooth long and thoughtfully. His next action was to swallow his beer with all possible speed.

'Let's get out of 'ere,' he said.

So they went, leaving behind them a cloud of cigarette smoke and three froth-patterned, empty glasses.

Cathi Unsworth
London, December 2014

CHAPTER I

I

The houses in Coronet Grove were originally constructed in yellow brick, but in the course of half a century the factory fumes and domestic smoke of East London have transformed this bright ochre rash into a grey smudge, which is only relieved by the six white steps in front of each house, the bright colours on the advertisement hoarding at the end of the street and the white lace curtains at the windows, here and there parted to reveal the dark-green plumage of an aspidistra plant.

Walking through this mean thoroughfare any weekday morning, the passer-by would be unable to avoid noticing a rounded and broad part of the anatomies of the housewives of Coronet Grove as they kneel on frayed scrubbing-mats energetically whitening the steps. Gaze up higher at the surrounding houses, and here and there this same passer-by would again see the same rotund portion of the human body, decently covered, of course, as the owners thereof sit on windowsills, their feet dangling safely inside, left hand gripping the window frame, right hand industriously polishing the panes.

If a more animated view of Coronet Grove is desired, it should be visited any Friday evening when the children are playing on the pavements, and it is almost certain that one of the paint-blistered doors will open and a woman in an apron, sleeves rolled up to the elbow, will appear and call out so shrilly that the rest of the street can hear: 'Alice! You Alice, come and be barfed!' Or it may be Teddie or Elsie, or even Shirley, and sometimes a Deanna – for in these days the all-pervading influence of the cinema plays its part in the choice of names for backstreet offspring . . .

There were no bathrooms in Coronet Grove, but it would take more than this typically Victorian oversight to prevent its womenfolk keeping their families clean. In this case, cleanliness is certainly next to Godliness, or almost. For just around the corner is Coronet Square and St Saviour's Church, against the railings of which many a local-boy-and-girl romance has begun on a dark night, to receive its celestial blessing at some later date inside the church itself. In fact, one Easter no fewer than twenty-three couples were married at St Saviour's – there was a picture commemorating the event in the *Star*.

Many is the anecdote that could be recounted of couples who began their blissful courting by the church railings in Coronet Square. Caleb Beasley, a spoilsport of a councillor, did once bully the council into erecting a lamp-standard by the railings, but as the lamp at the top of it was smashed with astonishing and persistent frequency, the council eventually decided to let it stay smashed and the church railings unlit.

Then there was the summer when the Rev Philip Black decided that it was high time the church railings were repainted. He decided on a bright green, and, despite all the white chalk warnings to *Beware Of Paint*, the local laundries and dry cleaners were faced with the problem of getting paint marks out of an incredible number of best Sunday frocks . . .

Two thoroughfares lead into Coronet Square. One is Coronet Grove. The other, Marcus Street. Now, the people who live in the Grove are no better financially or socially than the people who live in Marcus Street. More or less, they all do the same kind of job, fill in the same football coupons, breed the same kind of children, and those children all go to the same yellow-brick council school, have teeth and tonsils extracted at the same welfare centre, and when they leave school go to the same labour exchange, where their subsequent careers are decided by whatever vacancies appear on the books. The women who have just had, or are just going to have, babies all go to the same maternity clinic.

Despite this similarity in appearance, habits and general mode of living, the Grove people always considered themselves slightly superior to the Marcus Street folk, although this superiority once had a rude shock in view of the startling, not to say scandalous, events that took place in the Grove, putting pictures of one of its little houses on the front pages of national newspapers, and the inner and most intimate history of which I am about to relate.

Perhaps it was something about the architecture of this unpretentious street, with its amber-stained glass fanlights over paint-blistered doors, that gave it an air of not belonging to the vicinity, as if the makers of the London jigsaw had dropped this piece in the wrong place, gone away to look for the right piece and never bothered to return . . .

For one thing, there were no shops in Coronet Grove to debase its residential atmosphere, although there was of course the hoarding at the end of the street and the card in the window of number 13 which announced *J Potts* to be a *Chimney Sweep And Rat Catcher*, surely the strangest combination of professions. In Marcus Street, however, there were two public houses, a pawnbroker's, a sweetshop, a dining-room which was a *Good Pull-Up For Drivers*, an old clothes shop proudly announced to be a *Dress Agency*, where *Wardrobes* were *Bought And Sold*, and where it was possible to obtain *Outsizes Up To 64 Hips*. There was a fried-fish shop, an ironmonger's and a *Certified Midwife*.

Coronet Grove was detached from all this, and to have known the Grove at its most detached, it should have been visited early on a Sunday morning in the pre-Blitz days, when the nearby church bells used to ring; and when the ringing of those bells meant what church bells had meant for centuries – a call to the faithful. Not that anybody in Coronet Grove ever responded to the call, except old Mrs Willis, and she was generally acknowledged to be slightly 'mental' . . .

It is a Sunday morning I have selected to open this tale of East End streets, in the days before these same streets became bomb-scarred and devastated, when war was still so much paper talk and nobody had ever seen an Anderson shelter . . .

On this Sunday morning the church bells were ringing as usual, and a pale-faced girl of seventeen, with straight, yellow hair tied in paper curlers, raised herself from the brass-knobbed bed and pulled the blind aside to look out at the weather and the backyard. It was raining . . .

So great was her chagrin that she flung herself down on to the mattress with a bump that awakened her sister, eighteen-year-old Vi, who slept in the same bed. She opened her eyes for no more

23

than a fraction of a second, and then, aggravated at having a pleasing dream disturbed, kicked out viciously, and as she closed her eyes again growled drowsily, 'Kee' still, can't yer?' then promptly went to sleep again.

The bedroom would not have formed an inspiring subject for a picture illustrating a woman's page article on 'A Young Lady's Boudoir'. The bed took up nearly a third of the available space. The linoleum on the floor was bright and well scrubbed, but the pattern of the entwined daisy-chains had long since worn away. There was a ragged piece of red carpet on each side of the bed, and two wooden chairs draped with stockings and various pieces of underwear. There was a table near the window covered with a piece of blue-and-white-check American cloth, on which stood a heavy mahogany-framed mirror; two hairbrushes, each with wisps of fair hair adhering to the bristles; a Tokalon powder-box; a scent spray that didn't work; an eau-de-Cologne bottle; a minute bottle labelled *Ashes Of Roses*; two face flannels, one bearing an ornate letter V, the other an equally ornate letter D; one glass containing two toothbrushes and a tube of Colgate's; tablets of soap, one pink, the other mauve; an empty chocolate box; a cracked vase containing a pathetic spray of wax flowers; a blue tissue package of cotton wool; a scattering of needles, pins and lengths of cotton; a bottle of nail varnish; a pair of curling tongs.

The monotony of the faded pink-and-green wallpaper was stressed rather than enlivened by a framed print of disconsolate sheep perpetually lost on disconsolate moors; pictures of film stars torn from illustrated weeklies; and some old Christmas cards decorating a marble clock, the hands of which pointed perpetually to five minutes past three . . .

For quite ten minutes Doris Sandigate lay face downwards on the pillow, listening to the swish of the rain, the bells tolling mournfully, her sister breathing heavily at her side; and from the next room her father snoring. Rain. Rain. Rain. It was always the same on a Sunday . . .

It was a shrill voice, wheezy with asthma, that brought her abruptly from her thoughts. A voice from the next room calling, 'Doris, yer father wants a cuppa tea.'

Doris was so accustomed to this Sabbath-morning request that she never saw the humour of it. Mr George Sandigate, snoring peacefully, was oblivious to any need he may have had for the cup that cheers. The fact was that it was *Mrs* Sandigate who wanted a cup of tea. It was just her way of putting it. Just as in the evening Mrs Sandigate would sometimes say, 'Doris, yer father wants a bottle beer,' when actually it was Mrs Sandigate herself who fancied the bottle of beer. Mr Sandigate preferred his alcoholic beverage standing at the counter.

'Doris!'

Mrs Sandigate cleared her phlegm-encrusted throat and called once more, louder this time.

'Doris, yer father wants a cuppa tea.'

'All right,' replied Doris crossly. 'I 'eard.'

She slipped out of the bedclothes, pulled her Marks And Spencer's pyjamas off and paused for a second to look at herself in the wardrobe mirror, the door of which hung lopsided on one hinge. She stretched her arms. She was pleased with the reflection of her body. She was beginning to look more like a woman.

Then she heard the harsh, familiar sound of her stepmother clearing her throat again. The whining, husky voice drifted from the front bedroom.

'You Doris, yer father wants a . . .'

'All right,' said Doris. 'I 'eard you first time.'

Dressing quickly, she pattered down the stairs in the two-and-elevenpenny pair of slippers John had bought for her last Christmas. She collected the *News Of The World* from the front-door mat and opened the door to get the quart bottle of milk from the doorstep.

Then she went down to the kitchen. It was chilly after the bedroom. The grate was strewn with the ashes of the previous night's fire, and a ball of greasy paper on the hearth betokened the Saturday night supper of fish and chips.

A big black cat, its yellow eyes beseeching and tail erect, was rubbing its arched back against the door that led to the wash-house and the backyard. It was meowing plaintively.

There was some dirty crockery in a bowl in the sink; eggshells, potato peelings and an empty cocoa tin in a bucket on the floor, and in the middle of the straw mat by the table were the remains of a mouse.

She unbolted the door to let the cat out, and a gust of wind and rain blew in, this sudden contact with the outside elements making the cat less anxious to explore the backyard. The animal just turned its tail against the weather and rubbed its fur against the girl's bare shin.

Doris slammed the door somewhat violently. She did not know that one of the panes was loose. It was one of those typical backyard doors, mass-produced for working-class homes, the upper half of which consists of four panes of glass. The previous afternoon little Alfie Sandigate (who had a snub nose and his mother's red hair) had had his playmate in from number 13. Both being proud possessors of new penknives, they had driven away boredom for half an hour by picking the plaster surround of one of the lower panes.

So, when Doris slammed the door, this pane of glass shattered to the ground, and in came the wind and rain. Doris swore. The cat jumped up on to the gas stove, yellow eyes startled in its black face. From upstairs drifted a shrill, wheezy and indignant voice . . .

'Is that yer temper, young lady?'

Doris ignored the petulant voice from above and filled the kettle and lit the gas. She found that the draught from the broken window blew the flame out, so she screened the gaping aperture with a page torn from the previous night's newspaper. Even then the corner flapped up and down, but it was better than nothing.

Waiting for the kettle to boil, she lit a cigarette from one of the packets of five Player's she had won playing on the machines in the amusement arcade in the Whitechapel Road. She often dallied there on Saturday afternoons on her way home from work, and she was quite lucky at the various games.

The tough-looking, unshaven attendants in their white smocks, rattling keys and bags of coppers, grinned when they saw her trip in. Not one patron in fifty went out winning, so they did not object to a pretty bit of stuff like Doris Sandigate winning a few packets now and then. Yesterday afternoon she had won seven packets with a shilling's worth of coppers, and the attendants had not even looked annoyed. The proprietor, Lou Hyams, had even walked over to congratulate her.

He was a youngish man, in the early thirties. He had impudent, smiling eyes, flawless white teeth and shiny black hair parted in the middle. He wore smart striped suits, tailored silk shirts and spotted ties. He wore small-brimmed American hats and suede shoes; smoked Abdulla cigarettes and sometimes cigars.

His elbow touched her arm as he leaned against the machine on which she had been playing.

'What are you gonna do now?' he grinned. 'Smoke yourself to death?'

'Oh, no; I'm goin' to give some of them to my boyfriend.'

'Lucky boyfriend!'

The wireless amplifier overhead was booming forth a crackling version of 'The Chestnut Tree'.

'Oh, well, I suppose I must go 'ome now.'

'Got far to go?' he asked.

'Coronet Grove.'

'That's quite a good walk. I'm going that way. I'll give you a lift, if you like.'

And he nodded towards his flash American automobile parked in the kerbway, a streamlined terraplane affair, all blue and silver. The very idea of riding in it made her catch her breath, but she shook her head and said, 'Oh it's ever so nice of you; but not today, I couldn't.'

He laughed. A harsh but fascinating laugh.

'Some other time, eh?' he said. 'Okay; I'll be seeing you . . .'

Doris kicked open her stepmother's bedroom door and took in the tray of tea and the *News Of The World*. Rose Sandigate sat up in bed and extended a fat, white hand to the tray. She was a woman in the middle forties, a good deal younger than her husband. At twenty no doubt she had been very attractive. Her skin was still very white, and her hair a burnished copper hue, thick and long. Her eyes were green-blue. Her lips were slack but sensual. She was getting very fat.

'Been long enough, ain't yer?' she demanded, grabbing the tray. 'What you smashed downstairs?'

'Back-door winder pane fell out,' said Doris briefly over her shoulder, going out quickly and closing the door.

She then took a cup of tea in to her sister. Vi had the bedclothes pulled up around her ears, revealing only her very fair hair and the tip of her nose. She opened her eyes as Doris entered the room, her lashes blinking. She yawned, sat up and stretched out an arm for the tea. Doris stared at her.

'You've still got your dance frock on!' she exclaimed.

'All right, you don't have to shout,' hissed Vi.

'You'll ruin that frock.'

'That's my lookout,' growled Vi. 'Why don't yer put more sugar in the tea?'

'I put three lumps in. Did you go to the dance?'

'Course I went to the dance. I got so drunk I couldn't undress meself. The chap who brought me 'ome opened the front door for me. I couldn't see the key'ole . . .'

Vi broke off to take several hurried gulps of tea.

'Good job Rosie didn't hear you come in,' said Doris.

Among themselves the Sandigate girls always referred to Mrs Sandigate as Rosie.

'Well, she didn't,' retorted Vi, her nose in the teacup. 'And I wouldn't care if she did. I'm fed up wiv 'er trying to boss me.'

She drank the rest of the tea noisily, handed the cup back and settled down to sleep again. Doris went downstairs, feeling slightly shocked, slightly disgusted at her elder sister. She was always feeling slightly shocked at Vi, but she envied her greater measure of freedom.

She sipped her own cup of tea and then relit the cigarette which she had crushed out prior to going upstairs. Mr and Mrs Sandigate were so narrow-minded. All the girls Doris knew made up their faces as naturally as combing their hair. Doris had to put her make-up on secretly in the lav and then run out of the house before she was seen. When she came home at night she paused on the step to wipe it off. It was all very undignified.

All her girl friends belonged to perm clubs. Doris had to be satisfied with what waves and curls she could impart into her straight, yellow hair with the aid of an old pair of irons and paper curlers – and even this operation was frowned upon by Rose Sandigate, whose own hair was naturally wavy. The first time she had seen Doris curling her hair she had snatched the irons from her hand and hit her across the mouth with them. Doris had a swollen lip for a month afterwards.

By the time Doris had finished her cigarette the monotonous dirge of the church bells had ceased. It was very quiet except for the swish of the rain and the sound of a milkman whistling as he clattered up and down the steps along the Grove. She kneeled down at the grate, preparatory to cleaning it and lighting the fire . . .

Upstairs, Mr George Sandigate, brewer's drayman and darts player, father of five children, came back to consciousness by slow degrees with each succulent sip of his morning tea. He never spoke on a Sunday morning until he had finished that first cup of tea, a cup of tea to which Mrs Sandigate always added two spoonfuls of whisky from the small bottle they kept under the pillow.

Mr Sandigate was rather a short man, but broad in the shoulder, slightly bald, with small blue eyes under a hairless brow. He had a ruddy, weather-whipped complexion, a squarish chin and small, protruding ears. You would certainly not take him for the father of four daughters, who were all more or less easy on the eye – the eldest two now married. Perhaps they derived their good looks from their mother, his first wife, who had died one rainy Sunday in the London Hospital, where they had taken her after she had caught pneumonia hanging up the washing in the backyard in Coronet Grove.

Sandigate had a throaty chuckle, a ponderous manner, but an alert readiness to 'see through' anybody or anything which he termed as being 'not genuine'. He had a deep distrust for new-fangled notions, had not been to a cinema more than twice in his life, but went to a music hall regularly every Friday night, usually the Hackney Empire, and the Holborn Empire on special occasions. He didn't like swing bands or scat singers, or ballroom dancing acts; preferred comics like the late lamented Billy Bennett and Florrie Ford. He knew all Florrie's songs off by heart.

He was not an educated man, but he was not entirely an ignoramus. On some subjects he could talk with a sort of downright authority. His was not a particularly enlightening form of conversation, but he spoke as a man always sure of his facts. And he got by. An inveterate reader of newspapers (which he nevertheless termed as being full of 'tripe'), he could tell you the date of every sensational murder trial within his own lifetime. He could tell you the name of judge, counsel, accused and victim. Without hesitation he would tell you the jury's verdict, and he could recall whether there was a subsequent appeal or a strong recommendation to mercy. He would tell you, almost with pride, that he had been born on the very day Charlie Peace was hanged, February 25th, 1879. Yet he had never been in a police court in his life, let alone the Central Criminal Court.

He could tell you the winner of every Derby and classic race since the beginning of the century. He had a bet regularly every day. He had never been on a racecourse.

He wore a collar and tie only once a week – on a Sunday night. He detested and distrusted rich men and 'toffs'. He had never called a man 'sir' in his life. He was a staunch Conservative.

Ten years ago he had married for the second time – two years after his first wife, Angy, had died. He had married Rosie, the buxom, copper-headed barmaid at The Two Compasses, in Marcus Street. She was just turned thirty and he just turned fifty when they married, and their union caused quite a lot of comment in the neighbourhood. The women in the Grove weren't too pleased about it, either. Rosie, however, more than held her own.

She rapidly acquired the reputation of a terror, and had a disconcerting habit of 'showing up' any woman who talked idly or disparagingly about her by going to that person's house and shouting foul oaths, not infrequently resorting to physical violence. Coronet Grove was not used to that sort of thing. It belonged to Marcus Street and the purlieus of the Commercial Road. Two years after the register-office wedding a son was born. They called him Alfred George Sandigate.

Little Alfie was now eight years of age. He played with knives, threw stones, swore and, in general, was a very naughty child. With his half-sisters he was not popular, but he had an all-powerful ally and protector in his mother . . .

Mr Sandigate put the cup and saucer down with an unsteady hand, yawned and turned his head to look at copper-headed Rosie, who was sitting up in bed, a pink, loosely knitted bed-jacket round her fat, white shoulders, reading the *News Of The World*.

'Let's 'ave a bit of the paper, Rose,' he said.

Rose, for the moment, did not reply. Her literary accomplishments did not permit her to read and to carry on any kind of conversation, however brief, at the same time. When she read the newspaper, and she read little else – except *True Love Romances* – she did so slowly and methodically, her stubby index finger travelling along the lines of type, her lips silently repeating the words.

Mr Sandigate yawned again, stretched himself, put one arm round Rose and squeezed her. She shook him off irritably. Her powers of concentration when reading did not even permit that kind of distraction. Mr Sandigate yawned again and looked round the bedroom. He surveyed it with quiet pride.

It was a fairly large room, surprisingly so when you remembered that the houses in the Grove were very small, with two windows looking on to the street. It was scrupulously clean and thoroughly dusted. The furniture, being paid for at the rate of three and nine-pence a week, was comparatively new – a light-oak suite set out on a green carpet in almost the identical position it had occupied in the shop window in Bishopsgate. The eiderdown was green and gold, purchased with Providence cheques. Mr Sandigate's trousers, his long pants inside them, were hanging over the dressing-table mirror, the black-and-white check braces dangling in a soap dish. His shirt and socks were on the floor. His white muffler dangled from a brass hook on the door. Mrs Sandigate's OS corsets were spread out like a pink concertina across a small basketwork chair, together with stockings, suspenders, petticoat and various other items of underwear.

There was a sharp, wheezy hiss as Mrs Sandigate breathed quickly and looked up from the paper.

'Tommy Swann's escaped from Dartmoor!' she exclaimed.

'Tripe!' retorted Mr Sandigate, with the air of an authority. 'Nobody ever escapes from Dartmoor.'

'No?' said Mrs Sandigate, and she jabbed a fat thumb at a two-column headline and a picture of a narrow-lipped, narrow-eyed man with large ears. 'Read that, then.'

Mr Sandigate reached across his wife for his steel-framed reading glasses. He read the report slowly, frowning like an expert witness whose testimony has been doubted.

'They'll catch him again,' he said at last. 'Nobody ever escapes from Dartmoor. I bet they've got 'im already.'

'It takes pluck,' said Rosie. 'It takes pluck, but 'e's a mug to try it . . .'

'All crooks are mugs,' said her husband, staring up at an early fly that was pursuing a lonely course across the ceiling. 'Bloody mugs, that's what they are . . .'

'I dunno,' said Rose. 'Some of 'em do all right.'

George Sandigate made a sound that indicated contempt, reached under the bed, paused for a moment, and then spat. Then he relaxed again.

'Bloody mugs, that's what they are,' he repeated, gazing up at the ceiling again.

Rose made no reply. She did not even hear what her husband said. She was engrossed with the photograph of Tommy Swann, comparing it with her recollections of the Tommy Swann who had danced the tango like George Raft, and who made the kind of love she had never had, or ever expected to have, from Mr Sandigate.

Rose had her memories of Tommy Swann. He was one of those flashy, small-time rogues who lack even the intelligence to be systematic in their roguery. Always dreaming of pulling off a job big enough to enable them to retire gracefully and luxuriously from the ceaseless guerrilla warfare between law and lawlessness, they lived for the most part on the fruits of petty thefts and cadging from more prosperous colleagues. Occasionally, very occasionally, they pulled off something that yielded as much as fifty pounds. Then they would buy another suit, stand prolific drinks in the saloon bar, go racing every day and generally have a good time, until they were forced to put the new suit in Uncle's and look around for another soft job. Something as sweet as a nut.

It was after one of these easy, sweet-as-a-nut jobs that Rose first met Tommy Swann. Rose had been working at The Two Compasses for a fortnight when in walked Tommy in a new light-blue suit, a tan-shade trilby hat, a coloured silk shirt with a floral-patterned tie and a new black herringbone overcoat neatly folded over his arm. You could see your face in his pointed, black patent shoes.

She had half-a-dozen gin and limes with Tommy that night. No customer had ever bought her more than one, or at most two, drinks in the same evening. She consented to go to the pictures with him on her next half-day, which happened to be the following day. In the pictures he caressed her thigh with one hand and gave her a diamond brooch with the other. (He told her he had bought it wholesale, although actually he had got it much cheaper than that – much cheaper.) They went to the pictures several times afterwards, and each time he caressed her thigh, although naturally he didn't give her a diamond brooch each time. She wasn't quite a gold-digger. But he did confess his ardent love for her. He did not propose matrimony as, unfortunately, he still had a wife living in Leeds or somewhere. But he did make the suggestion that Rose might as well come and live with him as slave her guts out in a public house for next to nothing a week. Rose said she'd think it over . . .

The next afternoon Tommy was picked up outside Aldgate station for a job he swore he knew nothing about. Nevertheless, all his protestations of innocence did not save him getting three years' penal servitude, and Rose married Mr Sandigate.

When the news leaked into Tommy in his prison-enforced celibacy, he became so furious that he knocked a warder down and kicked his teeth out because he happened to look like George Sandigate. For this little outburst Tommy got another two years on his sentence.

On release from prison, he did not reappear on the East End scene, however. He joined up with the Notting Hill boys, some of whom he had met in chokey. With these lads he enjoyed a brief run of freedom, sometimes breaking into a shop, sometimes stealing a landlady's bed linen; stealing motor-cars, stealing bicycles; once 'blagging' a firm's payroll from a middle-aged cashier on his way from the bank; on hot days sleeping all day in Hyde Park, or sunbathing on the Serpentine Lido; hanging round coffee stalls during the long, warm nights. The easy-come, the easy-go existence of small-time crooks.

Then Tommy fell again. He went up the steps to be confronted with no fewer than five charges, his past record and a judge who on one occasion had been lenient to him. On this occasion the judge was not so lenient. He happened to be suffering from rheumatism, and Tommy got five years' penal servitude and five years' preventive detention. Ten years. Ten bloody years. Even Tommy blenched . . .

Rose had not been heartbroken at the fate of her ex-lover, although the thought of him always awakened memories of a kind that Mr Sandigate could never awaken. George Sandigate had given her a home, independence; a kind of respectability and security; had delivered her from the drudgery of beer-pulling. Things that Tommy Swann could never have given her, but it was to Tommy that she was indebted for her one brief taste of life. The life that appealed to her. The joy of spending money, of going up to West End clubs and mixing with swells and gang chiefs, racing heads and mobsmen.

Vividly she remembered the night Tommy had taken her to a club in a yard at the back of Gerrard Street. You had to go past a men's green-painted iron urinal to get to it. She remembered that because a drunken man came out with his trousers all unbuttoned. In the club, which was up a flight of stairs over a garage, Tommy had given her a handful of silver and said, 'Try yer luck on the fruit machines.'

The first shilling she inserted won the jackpot. Nearly four pounds in hard, bright, tinkling shillings came pouring out into her hands, cascading on to the floor – more money than she had ever earned in a week's hard work as a barmaid. Say what you like, it was a thrill. There was drinks all round. They danced till four o'clock in the morning, and took a taxi home, and in the taxi . . .

She put down the paper. Outside it was still raining hard. She could hear it pattering on the tin roof of the shed in the backyard. She wondered where Tommy Swann was now. Soaked to the skin, hiding in some ditch, perhaps. Or perhaps already back in his cell. A punishment cell.

'That Doris broke the back-door window,' she said suddenly.

'How she manage that?' inquired Mr Sandigate, taking up the paper she had dropped and turning to the sports pages.

'Temper, the little bitch,' said Rose.

'Ah,' said Mr Sandigate.

'You oughta do something about 'er temper,' said Rose.

George Sandigate grunted.

'Cor blimey,' he said, 'ol' Joe Potts won the silver darts this week.'

At this apparently innocent remark, Rose Sandigate gave vent to one of her high-pitched and vociferous outbursts that were the talk of Coronet Grove. With one fat, flabby hand she knocked the paper out of her husband's grasp.

'Darts!' she screamed. 'That's all you bloody well think abaht.'

Mr Sandigate pulled the pink bed-jacket off and kissed her wetly on her fat shoulder. He caressed her voluminous breasts . . . A cup slithered off the bedstead, spilling tea on the green carpet. The one-and-fourpenny size whisky bottle also slithered to the floor . . . Outside it was still raining . . . Rose gazed up at the ceiling, thinking of Tommy Swann . . .

II

Vi was getting out of bed and pulling last night's crumpled finery over her fair, tousled head. She shook it out, a shimmering cascade of Whitechapel Road splendour, and draped it over a hanger in the darkest corner of the wardrobe. The new dance frock would have to be ironed in secret to avoid awkward questioning.

Standing in her knickers and brassiere, she looked at herself in the mirror. Funny. She didn't *look* any different. She didn't even look more experienced. Yet she knew she wasn't quite the same

Violet Sandigate who had powdered and scented her body from sixpenny boxes and bottles before this very mirror only last night.

At the recollection a warm flush crept up her slender neck and suffused her face. It probably wouldn't have happened if she hadn't been so tight. Never before in her life had she had so many drinks, or drinks of such golden and throbbing variety. Not common pale ales or even the more finicky gin-and-its, but champagne cocktails and John Collins. She remembered the John Collins because it seemed so funny for a man's name to be a drink. It wasn't so much the drinks she had during the interval of the dance at the People's Palace as those she had when she went to the roadhouse with Morry Higham afterwards. Before her mental blackout set in she felt like an entirely new being, and it was during those ecstatic moments it had happened.

In Morry Higham's car at three o'clock in the morning, parked in the moonlight in Epping Forest. Morry Higham had a dance band. He played at a lot of the local dances, and had a music shop in Petticoat Lane. Of course, she knew the correct spelling of his name was H-y-a-m-s, and that he was the younger brother of Lou Hyams, who had an amusement arcade in the Whitechapel Road. But he was much better looking, she considered, than his brother, who by comparison was common and showy. Morry Higham's fiddle was a Klotz (so he said), and his dress clothes were by Kratzky. Both suited him admirably.

Last night, driving out to Epping Forest, the rain pattering down on the hood, she had been flattered by his frank confessions, the way he talked about his ambitions. Intentions, perhaps.

He was going to clean up in the dance-band world, like Ambrose, he said. He was going to get on the air, get regular sessions, take the dropsy from the music publishers, make them pay and pay big and like it, because by that time he'd be a big name. Then he'd make films, and he'd name his own price, and they'd be real musicals. Oh, yes, he'd got it all lined up. He knew he was going places, and nobody was going to trip *him* up.

Half of it might have been Greek to Violet, being wrapped up in a musician's phraseology she didn't even begin to understand. But it was wonderful just listening to him. He talked of a new world of enchanted achievement. He talked glibly of the great ones of the radio just as casually as she might talk about the forewoman in the factory where she worked. Of Ambrose . . . 'Bert said to me only the other day . . .' Of Hylton . . . 'Jack offered me fifty nicker a week to join him, but I said, "No, thanks, Jack. I'm paddling my own canoe."' And Roy Fox, Joe Loss, Geraldo, Jack Payne and many more. He knew them all by their first names (so he said), and had drinks with them, joked with them, played golf with them. So it went on and on, until her head was beginning to spin just a little and the car stopped under the trees in Epping Forest and he turned off the engine.

It was very quiet, except for the pattering of the rain on the canvas hood. He put his arm round her. She saw his white tie was lopsided and a wisp of dark hair hanging over his eyes. She straightened it. His arm tightened round her. 'My word, you're beautiful,' he said softly . . . And the rain pattered on the canvas hood . . .

III

Old Timothy came slowly down the steps of Spry's Hotel wiping his mouth with the back of his gnarled hand. Last night a poor woman, unable to afford money, had given him a herring from her own shopping bag. He had just cooked and ate it in the kitchen at Spry's. (Wrapped in a piece of newspaper, he had kept it beneath his pillow all night for safety.) It had tasted good. The succulent juice of it was still upon his lips . . .

It was Sunday morning. The church bells were ringing and not many people were about yet. But there would bound to be one or two by the bus stop. He heard footsteps approaching and fumbled in the pocket of his khaki overcoat. His fingers closed in on the matchbox.

'Box o' matches,' he whined. 'Spare a copper fer a poor blind man. Box o' matches . . . Box o' matches . . .'

But the footsteps approaching were only those of Ali, the lascar, who had come out of Spry's only a few minutes after Timothy. In his bright-blue ship's overalls, much too short for his long, thin body, he was walking to Petticoat Lane. In his knuckly brown hand he carried a battered suitcase, full of ties, socks, handkerchiefs and scarves.

He was chewing a piece of bread which he had dipped in the blackened frying pan in which Timothy had fried his herring. The oil on the bread tasted good . . .

He paused at the kerbside, tapping his stick, as a police car whirled past and pulled up abruptly outside Spry's . . .

Spry's Hotel, in Stepney, will not be found in any of the guide-books or railway timetables. It is not recommended by any auto-mobile associations or travel bureaus. Yet it is known the world over. A large Regency-style house, no doubt at one time the town house of some affluent maritime gentleman, its spacious windows are now curtained by cobwebs and bits of dirty rag. It is sometimes visited at odd hours by burly, red-necked young men in mackin-toshes and trilby hats, who keep well away from the walls, not being anxious to pick up any bed bugs, being more concerned with the identities of the human habitués of the place where Good Clean Beds can be obtained for as little as 8d a night, or 4s for the week. It is quite possible that when the beds were first installed at Spry's Hotel that they were both good and clean, but as that was many years ago, those two virtues in the bedding have been modified by the march of time and the equally insistent march of lice. Spry's Hotel, you will have gathered, is a common lodging house.

Theoretically speaking, it is owned by a Mr Ned Spry, but the fact is that in this flourishing establishment of squeaking mattresses, creaking floorboards, peeling wallpaper, grimy windows, nocturnal snores, gastric rumblings and odious smells, Mr Ned Spry's position amounts to nothing more than a maker of beds and maid of all work. A dwarf-like little man with a large head and a withered left arm that dangles in front of him like a broken wing, he shuffles pigeon-toed up and down the bare, unwashed stairs; a sullen, grunting monstrosity, perpetually sniffing and snuffling, mucous running continually from his nostrils, which he sometimes wipes with the cuff of his greasy sleeve or the tip of his lolling tongue.

The only person who really mattered at Spry's Hotel was Maria Spry – whether she was Spry's legal wife was a matter for heated conjecture. She was at least five times as big as Spry, and the subject of their conjugal felicities had for years been an inspiration for bawdy jokes and obscene laughter on the part of the patrons. Grossly imaginative pictures of Ned and Maria Spry embraced in moments of connubial bliss were scratched on the walls of the toilet, and much coarse laughter could be heard at winter nights in the large, old-fashioned kitchen in the basement, where the bedraggled guests dried stinking socks and grilled penny bloaters over the same fire range.

Tinkers and tailors, beggars and boozers, old lags and chocolate-faced lascars, army deserters and wife deserters, collar-stud pedlars and garbage-rakers; the blind and the near-blind; the maimed, the diseased and festering; human mysteries of all colours, creeds and nationalities came from all corners of the globe to sleep amid the bugs, the sounds and smells of Spry's Hotel.

Not all of the patrons were entirely indigent. There was, for instance, old Timothy, the blind beggar. (He was not entirely blind, still having a glimmer of light left in one eye.) Clutching his one and only box of matches, he could be seen almost any day shuffling up and down Stepney's highways and byways, calling out in his thin, querulous voice, *'Box o' matches! Spare a penny fer a poor blind man! Box o' matches! Spare a copper fer a poor, blind man . . .'*

Old Timothy always slept at Spry's. He had been known to pick up crusts of bread from the gutter and masticate them between his toothless gums. Yet some of the lodgers would tell you that his greasy Post Office book showed that he had between six and seven hundred pounds deposited, and next to his unwashed body, pinned to his ragged flannel shirt, was another fifty pounds in Treasury notes, so the story went. His hair was long and white, the ends of it being hidden beneath the greasy khaki overcoat, which on more virile shoulders had seen blood spilled in Flanders mud, but now trailed down past infirm ankles, sweeping the East End gutters . . .

A dark-blue car pulled up in the kerbway outside Spry's, and two men in mackintoshes got out. The uniformed driver stayed at the wheel.

'Won't be long, Bert,' one of them said to the driver, and they walked quickly through the rain up the grey steps of Spry's Hotel.

Ned Spry, who had seen them coming, went to his wife's room, opened the door and said succinctly, 'It's the cops, Maria.'

Then he continued with his Sabbath-morning duties, an enamel pail swinging in his hand as he climbed the creaking stairs. Maria always dealt with the cops.

She got out of bed, pulled a faded green coat on over her flannel nightdress, and padded bare-footed into the passageway. She saw them standing just inside the front door. Detective-Sergeants Leech and Nicolson.

'Morning, Mrs Spry!' said Leech cheerfully, shaking the rain off his black, soft hat.

'What the bloody 'ell d'you want?' Her voice was thick and husky.

'Mind if we look at your visitors' book?'

Without a word she thrust a tattered exercise book towards him. Smiling, cocky little Leech flicked over a few pages, looked at the most recent entries, then handed the book back.

'Extraordinary the number of Smiths and Browns who stay here, isn't it?' he said pleasantly.

'I don't give 'em their bleedin' names,' said Maria.

'Mind if we have a look at your guests?'

'All the same if I do, I suppose,' said Maria. 'Go ahead. It's a bleedin' liberty, all the same. This is a respectable 'ouse, this is . . . '

'We're sure it is,' said Leech, smiling. 'Aren't we, Freddy?'

Nicolson nodded, but he did not smile. He was gazing with a sickly fascination at an insect that was crawling down the neck of Maria Spry's nightdress. It disappeared as she drew the faded green coat closer about herself.

'I ain't catchin' my death o' cold standin' 'ere all day,' she sniffed. 'I'm goin' back to bed.'

'One minute,' said Leech. 'Have you ever seen this man before?'

He held out two photographs, one full face and one side face of a narrow-lipped, narrow-eyed man with large ears and upturned nostrils. She gazed at them with seeming lack of interest.

'No,' she said dully, 'can't say as I 'ave. Who is it?'

'Tommy Swann. I knocked him off here once . . .'

'Well, what abaht it?' said Maria. 'I can't remember the face of every bleedin' bloke what stays 'ere. 'E ain't 'ere now. 'Sides, I 'eard Tommy Swann was in prison . . .'

'He was until yesterday,' said Leech genially. 'But the naughty man ran away . . .'

'Bleedin' good luck to 'im,' said Maria Spry, and padded back to her bedroom, a vast, shapeless creature with uncombed hair around her shoulders, two jade earrings dangling from her ears, the torn lining of the green coat hanging down her bare calf. Her bedroom door closed with a bang that reverberated over the whole building.

'Better have a look round, Freddy,' said Leech . . .

He opened the first door on the right and the stench hit them full in the face. There was a growling murmur of voices. Awakening coughs and spitting. Two or three men sat up in their beds. Others turned over again, pulling the grey sheets closer over their heads. The rain made patterns on the grimy windows . . .

'All out! All out!'

Ned Spry went about his rousing-out round of the lodging-house rooms rather like a park-keeper at closing time. Dirty as the beds might be, infested with lice, it was as difficult to get some of the sleepers out as it is to get lovers to leave a park bench on a summer's evening or the alcoholic to leave a comfortable saloon bar.

During weekdays the sleepers were expected to be out of their beds by eight o'clock. On Sundays they were granted a concession and were allowed to stay until nine. If they wished, they could stay another hour or so in the big basement kitchen, where they had facilities for boiling tea, cooking breakfast, adjusting their mysterious parcels or washing their hands under the tap just outside by the backyard door. If they wished . . .

'All out!' shouted Ned gruffly, dropping the enamel pail with as much noise as possible, pushing up the windows so that the rain-threaded wind came blowing through the rooms in lively gusts.

From many of the recumbent forms under the red-and-grey blankets there was no movement. One of them growled, 'Shut the winder, you ol' sod,' and another one made a rude noise. Here and there a grimy, tousled head appeared from the cocoon of blankets, and cigarette stubs were lighted and puffed at with the obvious enjoyment of the day's first smoke. An old man sat on the side of his bed threading a piece of string through one of his boots.

'All out!' grunted Ned, grunting with the exertion of pushing up another window.

'Jest 'ark at the ol' bleeder!' A long, scarecrow of a man with greying hair and a strawberry mark over his right cheek sat up in bed and leered angrily at Ned Spry. 'Jest 'ark at 'im. Jest 'ark at 'im . . .'

'All out!' shouted Ned imperturbably, and flung up another window.

By this last window a street tipster, wearing a grey top-hat, had been sitting on his bed writing the names of horses on tiny slips of paper. As the window opened the slips of paper rose gaily in the air, the wind blowing them in all directions.

'You ol' bastard!' screamed the tipster. 'Look what you done!'

'All out!' grunted Ned Spry. 'All out!'

The little, red-faced tipster was on his hands and knees picking up his precious slips of paper. Ned Spry emptied a chamber into his enamel pail.

'All out!' he shouted.

The blankets on the bed at the end of the room parted and a shining black face appeared. The negro grinned as he scratched his woolly hair.

'Sa-ay, ain't you got no other toon on yuh record but yuh mus' keep singing "All out," Mistah Spry?' he asked.

'All out!' grunted Ned Spry, and wiped his nose, first with the tip of his tongue, then with the back of his hand.

'What did the coppers want?' asked the man with the strawberry mark. 'Bleedin' nice kip-'ouse this is, I must say. First we git our sleep disturbed by a lot of Ds turning us over, and then this silly old bugger comes round bleating "All out! All out!" That's what we pay our money for, I suppose. Nice kip, I don't fink.'

'If yer don't like it yer know what yer can do!' a voice suddenly bawled from the door.

Maria Spry was standing there, her arms folded over her vast bosom, her hair straggling round her shoulders, a cigarette drooping from the gash that was her mouth, the smoke drifting from her nostrils.

'All out!' shouted Ned Spry. 'All out!'

Ding, dong, rang the bells of St Saviour's. *Ding, dong.* In the kitchen of the house in Coronet Grove, Doris Sandigate was smoking a cigarette. Upstairs, Vi Sandigate gazed in the wardrobe mirror and thought about her lost virginity. Out in the backyard rain pattered on the tin roof of the shed. In the front a milkman clattered up and down steps. A mile away, outside the lodging-house in Stepney Causeway, two young detectives got back into a dark-blue car. 'Did you see the lice crawling down her neck?' said one, and the other laughed as he pulled out his cigarette case. An empty tramcar clanged past. A bus thundered. Smoke was beginning to drift from a myriad grey house-tops, curling towards the Sabbath sky like a million cat tails . . . *Ding, dong,* rang the bells of St Saviour's. *Ding, dong* . . . Old Mrs Willis, at 17 the Grove, was putting on her best black Sunday hat. *Ding, dong. Ding, dong* . . .

A blind beggar turned into the Mile End Road tapping his white stick against the kerb. *'Box o' matches!'* came his chant. *'Spare a copper fer a poor blind man.'* An old woman fumbled in her shabby purse . . .

IV

Mr George Sandigate got out of bed and walked to the window, pulled the blind aside and looked out. Rose watched him through half-closed eyes.

''As ter go and rain every bloody Sunday,' he growled.

He let go of the blind and walked to the dressing-table. He was naked except for a short cotton undershirt. His legs from the thighs down were covered with hair. His feet were shapeless, the big toes crossed over the smaller toes. He took the long pants from out of the trousers hanging over the dressing-table mirror, and then went to the wardrobe to get out his best trousers. He teetered about on one foot as he pulled his pants on.

'What we got fer breakfus', Rose?' he asked.

''Addicks,' replied his wife.

She got out of bed and walked to the door, scratching her buttocks.

'You, Doris!' she called down the stairs. 'Put the 'addicks on . . .'

The rain was playing a tattoo on the tin shed in the backyard. Some restive fowls a few doors up were clucking noisily. Round the corner in St Saviour's the Rev Philip Black cleared his throat and announced, 'Hymn 301.' Old Mrs Willis stood up and opened her hymn-book at *page 301*. Mr Caleb Beasley, at the organ, pressed his black-trousered leg down on the pedals and plucked at the stops with his claw-like hands. The shivering, sweet moan of organ music swelled through the church. Tremulously, the congregation sang the praises of the Lord. It was Sunday morning . . .

CHAPTER 2

I

Mr George Sandigate pushed back his plate, took a swig of tea, belched and reached for his pipe. He had finished breakfast. Doris was collecting the dirty plates. The bowl of hot water was steaming in the sink. Vi was upstairs making up her face. She was going out.

Doris was also going out. She had arranged to meet Johnny Price at Aldgate Underground station. She was going to look nice today, because she would be wearing the new pair of dark-blue shoes she had bought for five shillings at the Bata sale. They were just right for her guinea two-piece, and her blue hat matched the colour of her eyes. She would put just a touch of rouge to her face and scarcely any lipstick at all, and if she had time she would put just one or two waves in her yellow hair, just where it would show under the brim of her hat. Yes, she would make herself look nice if she had time, but she would have to hurry with the washing up, although being careful not to break anything.

It had become a sort of tradition in the Sandigate household that Doris did the washing up when she was home. She was the kind of girl who volunteered to do things like that. She derived a definite sentimental pleasure by doing things for other people. She was the kind of girl who liked helping blind people across busy roads. As a schoolgirl, during summer holidays, she had pushed pramloads of children to London Fields, or to the Tower Of London gardens. At Christmas-time she bought dozens of greeting cards and as many presents as her slender resources would permit. She saved up all the year for those Christmas cards and Christmas presents, and nobody whom she knew was left out. While if anyone showed her an unexpected kindness the deed almost brought tears of gratitude into her eyes.

Like most girls of her age, she dreamed of a wonderful love. A love that would surpass all other loves ever known. She was incapable of reading a Shakespearian play, but when they had done Shakespeare's plays at school she had always imagined herself as the heroine. One week she could imagine herself as a twentieth-century Rosalind. The next week she could experience all the emotions of Beatrice. In the privacy of her bedroom she knew just how Desdemona felt, and she could be Juliet at any hour of the day, although she had considerable difficulty in imagining a suitable Romeo.

Johnny Price was certainly no Romeo. He was her only regular boyfriend, but from a romantic aspect he was somewhat disappointing. He was the younger brother of the notorious Alfie Price. John, unlike Alfie, was respectable. He worked in Spitalfields Fruit Market as a junior clerk, and earned thirty-seven shillings and sixpence a week. He was also a voluntary messenger in the newly created AFS. He was clean-living and decent, and got boils on the back of his neck at regular intervals. He did not tell her dirty jokes like other boys she had met. She had a great admiration for his athletic prowess. As a schoolgirl she had seen him win the East London Schools' Mile. They had very little in common, however. He was a football and speedway fan, and his heroes were Bryn Jones and Bluey Wilkinson and Stanley Wooderson. She liked him, but she knew he could never be her lover. His conversation she found tedious, but if she had been asked what she would prefer a boyfriend to talk about she would have had no idea. She herself rarely used a sentence with more than six words in it.

Her romantic aspirations, unlike those of her sister Vi, were not entirely sensual. Scraping the fishbones off the dirty breakfast plates this Sunday morning, she was not depressed by the drudgery of washing up. She imagined herself washing up in a sunlit kitchen like the kitchens one saw in the films, all gleaming white and full of labour-saving devices and a refrigerator, while a handsome young husband came in to kiss her goodbye before going off to the office. Of such pretty-coloured texture were her daydreams fashioned, but not for the world would she have told of those dreams.

She was submerged in one such daydream when she dropped a cup. It splintered into three pieces, and her dream was destroyed simultaneously by the sound of the breakage and by the sound of Mrs Sandigate's voice shouting, 'Little bitch! There she goes again.'

The vision of the smart suburban residence faded. She was back again in the subterranean kitchen in Coronet Grove, E1, with the vague mixture of smells that emanated from the faulty drains and the more distinct smells that emanated from within the house. The most distinguishable of these indoor smells was that of Mr Sandigate's pipe, which permeated every corner of the house. Its pungency was ever present, even when Mr Sandigate was not smoking. It met you when you entered the front door and it lingered with you when you had left the house. It was like Mrs Sandigate's voice. There was no escaping it. Even when you were in the lavatory you could still hear Mrs Sandigate talking, and when Rose Sandigate raised her voice it could be heard at the other end of the street. Rose Sandigate was raising her voice now. She strode heavily into the kitchen, her face flushed, her eyes bright with anger.

''Ow many more things you goin' ter smash today?' she demanded.

'It slipped,' said Doris.

'Slipped!' Rose Sandigate scorned the excuse. 'I've a good mind to slip you one across yer face, careless little bitch you.'

For a moment the placid Doris felt a surge of anger within herself. She felt bitter and sick and humiliated. Her small mouth tightened, but remained mute as she plunged her hands into the greasy water and continued with the washing up.

'And don't you scowl at me, my lady,' Mrs Sandigate continued.

'I wasn't scowling.'

'That's it, make me out a liar,' said Mrs Sandigate.

And she swung round on her husband.

'Why don't you keep your kids in order?' she demanded. 'You sit there and 'ear her answering me back and making me out a liar and you don't say a bloody word.'

'I didn't say you was a liar,' said Doris from the sink. 'I said I wasn't scowling. Nor I wasn't.'

'You're scowling now, you little bitch.'

'I'm not.'

'D'you 'ear that?' Mrs Sandigate demanded of her husband.

47

'She says she's not scowling. Jes' look at her face, jes' look at it?'

'What's the matter with you, Doris?' said Mr Sandigate irritably. 'You want a dose of salts or something?'

'A bloody good 'iding, that's what she wants,' said Mrs Sandigate . . .

Upstairs Vi Sandigate was feeling superior to all this mean squabbling, and as she delicately shaped the red Cupid's bow on her mouth she raised her voice in song. Soon, she thought, I will be free from all this sordidness. Already she had made her plans. What a surprise they would have when they heard her voice coming over the wireless, singing with the new radio dance band, Morry Higham's Swingers! As it was, they had to be content with her voice as it drifted down the kitchen stairs –

'Somewhere, over the rainbow, far up 'igh . . .'

And her song mingled with the sounds of the squabble from below, a squabble in which she did not feel the least bit interested. And Mrs Sandigate's voice became more shrill and more shrill, and the tears at last brimmed into Doris Sandigate's eyes and mingled with the greasy water that swirled over the dirty fish-plates. And the black cat prowled around the bucket for the fishbones, and the smell of Mr Sandigate's pipe permeated every corner of the little house. At noon Mr Sandigate would take his set of darts off the mantelpiece and he would make his way towards the public bar of The Two Compasses. At noon the public-house doors would be unbolted, and from within would come the familiar thud, thud as the barmaids pulled up the frothing pints. It was Sunday. Even the teashops would be crowded today. Every table in Lyons' at Aldgate was occupied. Petticoat Lane was filling up, becoming a babble of voices. From Aldgate and from Aldgate East, by tramcar and omnibus, Sunday-morning shoppers, touts and curiosity seekers came from all parts of London and beyond. From the new raw, red housing estates that fringed the arterial roads, from places as far apart as Southend and Croydon.

The newsvendors bawled, *Sunday speshull! London 'unt for escaped convict. Sunday speshull!* And an old blind man rattled his white stick on the kerb and whined, *'Box o' matches! Box o' matches!'* Crowds of youths and young girls pushed into the amusement

arcades in the Whitechapel Road . . . A hundred tattered communists in khaki shirts and long hair distributed pamphlets as they
marched through the rain with their tattered crimson banner
towards Hyde Park and some kind of demonstration, shouting
out *'Arms for Spain!'* as they splashed through the puddles and
held up the traffic . . . A young woman in a red-and-black straw
bonnet stood on a street corner amid a circle of young women in
red-and-black straw bonnets and cried out, *'I am saved – saved
through the blood of our Lord!'* Street organs jangled 'September In
The Rain'. Loudspeakers blared. It was Sunday. Tomorrow was
Monday. There was a vast peace and a vast relaxation and a vast
noise . . . Doris Sandigate cried over the sink, and Vi Sandigate
sang happily as she put the finishing touch to her lips. She had
just remembered. Morry Higham had promised to give her some
gramophone records.

II

Higham's Music Emporium in Middlesex Street had a modernistic
black-and-silver façade, and, like most of the shops in the
surrounding labyrinth of alleyways commonly known as Petticoat
Lane, always opened on Sunday morning.

In fact, Sunday was the only day in the week in which Higham's
did any noticeable business. For the rest of the week the black-
and-silver cash register did little more than record sixpenny sales,
a box of gramophone needles, a sheet of popular music; and even
these transactions were at infrequent intervals.

The public demand for sheet music was not sufficient to pay
the rent of a kiosk, let alone a large shop, but Higham's, like most
East End shops, had a wide variety of stock. It included children's
bicycles and scooters, radio sets, piano-accordions, portable
gramophones, gramophone records, harmonicas, roller skates,
boxes of tin soldiers, trap drums, tin whistles, resin, table-tennis
balls, catgut, saxophone mouthpieces, false whiskers, books of
humorous monologues, French chalk, balls of twine, hairpins and,
of course, sheet music . . .

Morry Higham had just opened his shop and was standing in the doorway smoking a cigarette and exchanging backchat with some of the rain-soaked traders who were erecting their stalls in the gutter preparatory for the Sunday harvest. No matter how hard it rained, Petticoat Lane on Sunday was always thronged with shoppers.

'Got any Brylcreem?' he asked Solly, the little hunchback, whose head was deep inside a packing case, whilst both his hands pulled out bottles of hair oil, packets of razor blades, bottles of eau-de-Cologne, scent sprays, combs, hairbrushes, shaving soaps and packets of shampoo powder.

Solly The Hunchback jerked himself up, revealing a large head of curly black hair, two red-rimmed eyes and a cadaverous chin covered with ginger bristles. He spat into the gutter.

'Course I got Brylcreem,' he said, breathing thickly. 'I got everything.'

'Good,' said Morry. 'I want a bottle.'

Solly crossed the sidewalk in amazingly long strides for so small a man, the rain dripping from his glossy black curls and teeming down his ragged raincoat. He thrust a white-filled, black-topped, red-labelled bottle into Morry's hand.

'How much?' asked Morry.

'Shilling to you,' said Solly.

'What?' protested Morry. 'Is that what you call cut price? I can get it for elevenpence anywhere.'

'Not genuine stuff you can't,' said Solly, shaking his curly head vigorously. 'Not genuine stuff. Oh, no! Oh, dear me, no! Shilling's the price, and a shilling I want.'

He held out a determined palm. The rain pattered on it.

'I tell you it's the genuine stuff,' said Morry. 'Same label, same bottle.'

Solly shook his head. The rain splashed on his work-soiled palm.

'Oh, dear me, no!' he said. 'Oh, dear me, no! Shilling a bottle Brylcreem.'

'I tell you I can get it for elevenpence at Riskin's,' yelled Morry.

'Oh, dear me, no you can't!' said Solly. 'Riskin gets his stock from the same place as me.'

'Tell you what,' said Morry. 'I'll toss you double or quits.'

Solly shook his head. He spat into the gutter.

'Do me a favour. Go elsewhere for your hair cream. Come on, give me the bottle back. I'm a busy man.'

Morry smiled and counted out a shilling in coppers. Solly thrust it into his hip pocket, strode back across the pavement and once more dived his head into the packing case.

The shopkeeper-cum-band-leader sauntered back into the shop humming, sprinkled some cream on his hair and began combing it carefully. He was thinking of last night's pleasant aftermath to the dance. He turned on the radio amplifier and a programme of dance music from Luxembourg went booming forth, filling the shop and the rain-soaked street outside. *'My own,'* wailed a woman crooner. *'Let me call you my own.'* Morry swayed to the rhythm as he combed his hair.

'Morry!' a woman's voice drifted from upstairs, almost drowned by the noise of the amplifier. 'Your breakfast is ready, Morry!' . . .

'Okay, Sadie,' he called out. 'I'm coming.'

His feet clattered up the stairs. Whilst Morry breakfasted on scrambled eggs, hot rolls and coffee, Sadie, his wife, went down to look after the shop. She was a slim, tired-looking woman with an ivory skin, dark sorrowful eyes, full lips and a peaky chin. There was all the patience of all womankind in her eyes. Once she had loved Morry; loved him to distraction. His ambitions were her ambitions. But long ago she had realised that he no longer cared for her. For him she had sacrificed everything. Her money had opened the music shop. Her money had paid for the modern-istic black-and-silver façade. Her money had paid for the car in which he went riding around with strange girls. Her money had financed him in starting a dance band. Now she had no money, and when she asked for some to buy food or clothes for the four children he lost his temper and swore; told her she was extra-vagant. Where did all the money go to, he wanted to know. He was always giving her money, he said. Other women had to manage on half what she got, less than that, and with larger families, too.

51

Whenever there was a few shillings in the till in the shop he would ring up *No sale* and put it in his pocket.

She stood at the shop door watching the bustling activity of the market. Her youngest baby was asleep in her arms. The next youngest was clinging to her skirts. Across the road, in the bakery shop, Lizzie Burstein was pouring a trayload of hot rolls and *bigles* into the front window counter. A chocolate-faced lascar in bright-blue overalls had opened a battered suitcase and was shaking out a gaily coloured armful of scarves and neckties. Moisheh Goldberg, at the sweet stall, was having a violent row with Freedman, the butcher, swearing at him in Yiddish. Sadie smiled as she listened to the argument. It seemed that Freedman had been plucking a row of plump, yellow chickens, and the tiny white feathers had been blown by the breeze like a cloud of white spray to settle on and adhere to Moisheh Goldberg's beautifully arranged show of boiled sweets. Young Sammy Morris was hanging up ladies' knickers as if he loved the task, and with the superb artistry of the born salesman. Herschell Pulvermacher, at the fruit stall, was opening a case of apples, shouting, 'They're lovely, they're juicy, they're lovely!' Mannie Sokolof was standing on a chair examining the waterproof covering of his stall, fearful that the rain would ruin his stock of snow-white, black-eyed Baby Pandas. Two cockney costermongers, caps aslant over their eyes, came pushing a barrowload of young daffodils, like a moving rectangle of golden sunshine between the grey houses.

'Mind yer backs there, please! Mind yer backs, nah, *please!*'

Sadie loved daffodils. Each nodding bloom was a note of music, a murmuring golden, silent symphony. She went to the edge of the pavement. 'How much the daffs, Bill?'

'Tanner a bunch,' said Bill, and pulled up the barrow with a jerk.

A wild extravagance seized her. She could not resist the sudden throbbing hunger to grasp at that fragile beauty, the beauty that was slowly and surely slipping from her life.

'Give me four bunches,' she called out.

Bill came across with four generous bunches of golden blooms nodding on pale-green stalks. He was a hulking, fresh-faced youth with flashing white teeth, curly blond hair escaping from the peak of his check cap.

'Did you go to the dance at the Palace last night, Bill?' Sadie asked as she handed him a florin.

Bill Higgins, after nine o'clock on Saturday nights, discarded cap and muffler, put on his best bib and tucker, and stepped out at the local dances, and quite a nib at it he was, too. You wouldn't think it to look at him, but he had once won a local jitterbug contest, accompanied by a lady friend, of course. He grinned as he nodded.

'Yes; I took Minnie Wallace, the Scotch tart out of Fielding Street,' he said.

'Nice girl,' commented Sadie. 'She comes in sometimes to buy gramophone records. You'll be getting married one of these times, no?'

'Me and Minnie!' ejaculated Bill. He laughed. 'None of that now, missus! Nothing like that abaht us. Still, we enjoyed ahselves.'

'I bet you did,' smiled Sadie. 'You had a late night, no?'

'Not too late,' said Bill. 'I never stay late if I'm grafting the next day. 'Sides, the dance was all over at twelve. Your old man seemed ter be enjoying hisself.'

'Yes, he likes his work,' said Sadie slowly.

'He's got a good band,' said Bill.

'Yes, he's got a good band,' said Sadie slowly.

She went back into the shop and toned the volume of the wireless amplifier. So the dance had finished at twelve! Morry had arrived home at four o'clock in the morning, complaining that there had been an extension until three. He had been tired. The supper she had left in the oven had been spoiled. She threw the flowers down on to the shop counter.

A fit of coughing seized her. The baby woke up and began to howl. The other one tugged at her skirts and whimpered for sweets . . .

Hoarse voices drifted in from the street. 'Lovely apples, tanner a pound. Tanner a pound, apples.' 'What about a nice tender chicken, lady?' 'Look at 'em, girls; just look at 'em, two bob a pair – pure silk, any colour yer like. My own girl wears them. Look, that's where the elastic cut my finger.' 'Here yah, mother, the Baby Panda, the latest novelty, keep the kid quiet for hours.' 'A safety razor, packet of Sheffield blades, and a stick of shaving soap – all fer a bob. Can yuh beat that?' The voices gradually blending to a roar. The market was on. Sunday was in full swing. A dance tune boomed from the amplifier. Sadie toned it down still more. Her head aching. The baby was howling. The other one was tugging at her skirts.

The dance music suddenly stopped and a distorted Oxford voice said, '*May I remind you that this programme comes to you with the compliments of Doctor Little's Little Liver Pills . . .*'

Out in the street a red-faced tipster had suddenly hurled a grey top-hat into the middle of the wet, greasy roadway.

'That's my tit-fer,' he bawled. 'And if I 'aven't got the winner of the National I'll eat it right 'ere in this marketplace . . .'

'*For indigestion, discomfort after meals, flatulence . . .*'

'I'll eat it right 'ere in this marketplace,' repeated the tipster hoarsely.

'The horse or the hat?' shouted Sammy Morris, holding up a pair of black lace knickers . . .

'*And always remember to look for Doctor Little's trademark . . .*'

Morry came trotting down the stairs to the shop, wiping his mouth on a small pocket handkerchief with an ornate black MH stitched on it.

'Coffee was cold,' he grumbled.

'You could have made some more,' said Sadie.

'I like that!' ejaculated Morry. 'Me, a busy man, working all night, working all day. Then I'm to make my own coffee. You'll be expecting me to wash the napkins next. Hullo, where they come from?'

He picked up the daffodils and turned them round and round in his hand, staring at them as if they were some strange plant from the depths of a primitive jungle.

'And how should you think I came by them?' asked Sadie. 'That I grew them in our garden?'

'Now don't be silly,' said her husband. 'Where did you get them? Can't answer a civil question now?'

'All right. I bought them.'

'Bought them?' he repeated as if he didn't quite comprehend.

'Yes, I bought them.' She soothed the baby in her arms. 'Hush, darling. We're going upstairs now. Hush!'

Morry was still turning the flowers over.

'But why did you have to buy flowers?' he asked.

'Because I like flowers,' said Sadie. 'They brighten the place up. Hush, darling! Hush!'

'How much were they?'

'Two shillings.' She turned her head away from the baby and coughed.

Morry's gaze wandered from the flowers to Sadie and then back to the flowers.

'Did you say two shillings?' he said.

'Yes, I said two shillings. Sixpence a bunch.'

He looked at her strangely, threw the flowers back on to the counter, and said, 'Have you gone mad?'

'No. Why? Hush, darling.'

Morry could not talk fast enough, and when he got excited he lisped.

'You mean to tell me that you've paid two shillingth for flowers and you're not mad? Why, you muth be mad.'

With one baby howling in her arms and another pulling at her skirts, Sadie picked up the flowers and walked silently to the stairs. On the first stair she paused to look at her husband. He was still staring at her.

'I'm not mad yet, Morry,' she said. 'But unless I have a little something to brighten my existence I will go mad. Do you grudge me a few flowers, do you?'

'Certainly not. But two shillings!'

A sudden rage seemed to seize the usually passive Sadie, and a dark flush suffused her oval face. Her black eyes blazed. She raised her free arm and hurled the four bunches of daffodils at her husband. They hit him across the eyes and fell around him like posies around a May Queen.

'Yes, two shillings!' Sadie shouted. 'I could have told you I got them for nothing – if I'd been a liar like you.'

Morry stood there with daffodils clinging to his jacket and spread out around his feet.

'Liar like me!' he repeated. 'Who says I'm a liar?'

'I do. I say you're a liar,' she retorted. 'You were working until three o'clock this morning, weren't you? You rotten liar, the dance finished at twelve. You mean you were out *yentzing* with some *shiksa*.'

Both babies were now crying. Sadie took them both in her arms and went upstairs. The sound of their wailing drifted down into the shop. And Sadie was coughing.

Morry was still standing there, staring blankly at the stairs, when a breezy voice called out, 'Saying it with flowers, Morry?'

It was his brother, Lou Hyams, looking fresh and rosy after a face massage at the barber's in the Whitechapel Road. He was smoking a cigar. Morry gave a sickly grin.

'Sadie's gone mad,' he said. 'Pots – absolutely pots.'

'We all knew that when she married a dope like you,' replied Lou cheerily. 'What's wrong, anyway?'

'She goes and buys a barrowload of flowers, and when I ask her how much she throws them at me.'

He shook his head sadly as if baffled at the unreasonableness of womankind. He stooped to pick up the blooms from the floor. Lou also picked up a flower. He twirled the stalk between thumb and first finger.

'You know, Morry,' he grinned, 'at Nice, when I went there last year, there was a carnival of flowers on. Everybody was pelting everybody with flowers. You'd look pretty good in that. Why don't you go sometime?'

'Don't be silly,' said Morry, smoothing down his glossy hair.

'Okay, Morry,' said Lou. 'Okay. Don't go losing your girlish laughter on my account. Say, would you like some roller skates?'

Morry stared at his brother. Had *all* the world gone mad?

'Roller skates!' he ejaculated. 'What is this? My wife spends my money on flowers. My brother wants me to buy roller skates. Why should I buy roller skates? Tell me.'

'You sell 'em, don't you? There's a pair in the window.'

Morry shrugged his shoulders.

'I sell a pair once in a while. Well, so what do you want me to do, go into the roller-skate business?'

Lou took the cigar out of his mouth, glanced towards the door and lowered his voice.

'I've got a gross of 'em dirt cheap,' he said. 'You can have the lot for fifteen quid cash-down. That's about two bob a pair. They sell in the shops at twelve-and-six a pair.'

'And what would I be doing with a gross of roller skates?' demanded Morry. 'Play Santa Claus to all the kids in Hessell Street?'

'Okay,' said Lou, putting his cigar back in his mouth. 'Don't get so excited. I was only giving you the chance to make a bit. You're in the trade. I thought you could flog them to some of your friends for a dollar a pair. You'd get thirty-six quid back for your fifteen. But as you don't want 'em – okay.'

Morry looked thoughtful as he pulled the petal of a daffodil.

'I can't afford to take risk,' he said.

'Risk! Aw, go to hell!' said his brother. 'One would think I was asking you to do me a good turn instead of the other way round. I'm not making anything out of the deal.'

Lou walked to the door, chewing his cigar angrily. He stopped at the door, turned and took the cigar from his mouth. The smoke belched forth.

'By the way, what about that two quid you owe me?' he said.

Morry put his head on one side, stretched out his hands, palms upwards and, with an expression of great anguish, pleaded, 'Lou, I give you my word of honour, I haven't got it. My life, I haven't. Sadie's life, the children's life, I haven't.'

'All right, just swear on your own life. That's quite enough,' said Lou. The cigar rolled round in his mouth.

Morry gestured with his hands.

'You know how it is, Lou,' he said. 'Things are bad. When I've got the dough I'll pay you. You know that.'

Slowly, Lou looked him over, from his feet up to his thickly creamed hair. He flicked cigar ash on the shop floor.

'That's just what I don't know,' he said, adding, 'What do you do with all your money?'

Morry laughed. The laugh of a Job. The laugh of a man who does so to stop himself from crying.

'All my money!' he repeated. 'I like that! Ithn't that rich now? All my money! And what do I do with it! Ha, ha! The bithneth is no good. My band asks for more wageth. I'm behind in the rent. My wife buyeth flowerth. And then my brother comes along and thez what do I do with my money? Ha, ha! I only wish I had half yours. I'd be a rich man. My life, I would. Why don't you lend me a pony?'

Lou flicked his cigar angrily, showing an inch of shirt-cuff.

'I go out after my dough,' he retorted. 'Why don't you attend to business instead of playing around with that fool dance-band game. There are hundreds of bands as good as yours and better. Every pound-a-week errand boy is running a dance band in his spare time. You can hire 'em for thirty bob a night – a band of six. Five bob a man. Dance bands! Don't make me laugh.'

'Wait till I get on the air,' said Morry softly, nodding more to himself than to his brother, while his mouth tightened and his eyes narrowed. 'Wait till I get on the air.'

'Nuts!' said Lou, and slammed the door . . .

Swaying slightly as he walked, puffing cigar smoke to left and right, his coat collar turned up, Lou Hyams made his way from Petticoat Lane to The Two Compasses in Marcus Street.

Most of the traders knew him, and with a few he exchanged a brief acknowledgement or a jocular greeting as he went by, a greeting in which there was sometimes a touch of patronage. It wasn't intended perhaps, but it was there. Those whom he did recognise felt flattered, although they would never have acknowledged it. But, anyhow, everybody knew Lou Hyams as a smart boy. He was making plenty of money, and he was still a good boy to his friends and to his old mother, and he was a good sport. Hard as a nail in business, but if one was in real trouble you could go to Lou and say so and so and so and so and so, and Lou would help you out. Unless, of course, you'd let him down in the past or tried to put a stroke over him, and then he'd see you go blind without batting an eyelid. Everybody liked Lou.

He stopped to buy a paper at old Solly Weinbaum's shop,

which was really the front window of a small private house, the counter resting on the windowsill, the customers making their purchases from the pavement, often getting intimate and sometimes embarrassing glimpses of the private life of the Weinbaums on the other side of the counter.

Old man Weinbaum was sitting at the window, a grizzled old man with red-rimmed eyes in a parchment-coloured face. He wore a little black-velvet skullcap askew on the egg-shaped, bald dome of his head.

'Hello, Mr Weinbaum! Got a *Sunday Express*? Okay, don't trouble. I'll help myself.'

Lou took up a paper and threw down two pennies. Mr Weinbaum sniffed the cigar smoke.

'So you're a Lord Lonsdale these days, eh!' he smiled. 'What with your cigars and all the money you make you no longer come to buy my cigarettes, no?'

Lou's laugh was harsh but musical, like a child's rattle.

'You don't sell these cigars, Mr Weinbaum,' he said, 'otherwise I'd buy some from you. They cost half-a-crown each. Here, have one.'

Mr Weinbaum took the cigar which Lou rolled over the counter towards him. The old man crackled it against his ear, sniffed it and then nodded in approval. To think that young Lou Hyams should smoke these cigars which cost half-a-crown each – the little Hyams boy whom only a few years ago he had employed to deliver newspapers at seven shillings a week. It was like one of those bits you read in the papers.

'How's your mother, Lou?' asked Mr Weinbaum.

'Fine, Mr Weinbaum, fine. Going round to see her presently.'

'Good. Give her my regards. And young Fay? Going to be a great musician I hear?'

'I hope so, Mr Weinbaum, I hope so. She's still studying, you know. No use rushing things.'

Mr Weinbaum nodded.

'As you say, no use rushing things, Lou. But she's a lucky girl to have a big brother like you to pay all the fees and things for her. A lucky girl.'

'Oh, that doesn't amount to so much,' said Lou. 'How's your family, Mr Weinbaum?'

The old man chuckled.

'My family? That makes me feel quite young again. They're mostly all grown-up now and married. Did you know little Judie was in America? Ah, yes, of course you did. Bessie is somewhere about. She's the only one who doesn't want to leave her old father.'

He chuckled and called out, 'Bessie! Bessie! Here's an old friend come to see you.'

A young woman of thirty came to the window drying her ears with a fluffy white towel. A plump young Jewess with rosy cheeks and bare shoulders. Bessie, one of Mr Weinbaum's large family of daughters, an attractive girl who seemed a long time getting married.

'Why, Lou! Where have you been all your life?'

She came close to the window, not a bit bashful about her bare shoulders. There was music in her voice and a sparkle in her eyes. Her even white teeth gleamed in a friendly smile. Lou, too, grinned, but felt more embarrassed.

'Aw, you know how it is,' he said a little awkwardly.

'Too busy to come round and see old friends now?' she smiled. 'Or too proud?'

'Me?' ejaculated Lou, pointing his cigar end at himself. 'Me, proud? I like that. What have I got to be proud about?'

'Well, what keeps you away? We're not going to eat you every time you come to see us.'

Lou laughed.

'I know that, Bessie. I know that. I – well, I must be getting along now . . .'

Why do I feel so awkward every time I meet Bessie Weinbaum, he was thinking. It's since – since when? He couldn't remember. Or was it since the day, years ago, when he'd been just a kid working for the Weinbaums, and he'd gone into the kitchen quickly and seen Bessie stepping out of a tin bath?

'Come round to tea some day,' said Bessie. 'I can still bake *strudel* cakes.'

Lou nodded.

'Sure, thanks,' he said. 'That's nice of you. I'll come round one Sunday.'

'That's what you *say*,' said Bessie, digging into her ear with the end of the towel.

'Don't worry, I'll come,' said Lou. 'I haven't had *strudel* cake for years.'

'That's a nice compliment!' mocked Bessie. 'He doesn't come to see us, but he'll come because he hasn't had *strudel* cake for years. You make me smile. I'll believe you're coming when I see you.'

Down the narrow street came the hoarse shout of 'Daffs! Lovely daffs! Tanner a bunch, daffs! Lovely daffs!'

'Just a minute,' said Lou.

He walked over to Bill Higgins' barrow and came back with six large bunches of daffodils, an armful of nodding, golden sunshine. He thrust them into Bessie's bare arms, grinned and walked on his way. Bessie just stared at the flowers.

'Aren't they lovely, father?' she whispered. 'Aren't they lovely?'

Old man Weinbaum nodded. He nodded just as he had nodded in approval over the cigar.

'What a boy,' he said softly. 'What a boy. He comes for a two-penny paper, gives me half-a-crahn cigar and buys you t'ree shilling-worth of flowers. He'll give his heart away next.'

'I wish he would,' Bessie whispered to her heart. 'I wish he would.'

Old man Weinbaum did not hear his daughter's words because they were not spoken aloud. But he looked at her shrewdly.

'Are you still in love with him?' he asked.

Bessie opened her eyes wide. Never before had her father asked her an intimate question like that. It was so unexpected that she blushed a little and then she laughed to cover her embarrassment.

'Well, are you?' her father persisted.

'I've always been fond of Lou,' said Bessie.

'Then the soonest you get fond of somebody else and forget Lou Hyams, the better,' said old man Weinbaum.

'What's wrong with Lou Hyams?' Bessie demanded, a little angrily, but even as she asked the question she knew what her father was going to say. He was going to say the same things about Lou that she herself deplored, and yet she found hot resentment rising within her at her father's words.

'What's wrong with him?' Mr Weinbaum repeated, and added in Yiddish: 'What's right with him? He's a no-good, that boy. I tell you, he's a no-good.'

'You change your opinion pretty quickly, don't you, father?' said Bessie in an even voice. 'One minute you're fawning over the cigar he gives you and saying he's such a generous boy he'd give his heart away, the next minute you call him a no-good.'

'Sure, he's a generous boy,' Mr Weinbaum nodded. 'My life, he's a generous boy, but he's a bad boy, and he's a bad Jew. It's Jews like Lou Hyams that give us all a bad name among the Christians.'

'That's what you think, father,' said Bessie, now thoroughly angry. 'But I happen to know Lou Hyams has got more Christian friends than Jewish friends, so how does the bad name among the Christians come in? I suppose you call yourself a good Jew, but how many Christian friends have you got? Not one.'

Old man Weinbaum shrugged his shoulders.

'He's got friends, certainly he's got friends among the Christians. He's a free-and-easy boy. He makes a laugh and joke and drinks in the pubs. But what kind of friends has he got among the *goyim* – the tramps? He's a bad Jew mixing with bad Englishmen. That's all they have in common – their badness.'

'You seemed happy enough to meet him,' Bessie retorted.

'Sure, I was happy enough to meet him. I've always liked Lou Hyams. His father, God rest his soul, was a good Jew. His mother is a good woman. It's a pity their sons have gone the way they have.'

'We're talking about Lou Hyams, not the whole family.'

'All right, all right, we'll say no more about it,' said Mr Weinbaum, and he smoothed out the stock of Sunday papers on the counter.

'Anyway,' Bessie persisted, 'I couldn't be so two-faced as to take a gift from somebody and then talk about them.'

Old man Weinbaum looked round at her.

'You mean the cigar?'

He took it from his mouth, twirled it in his fingers, thrust it back into his mouth, took a long draw on it and then tossed it across the pavement into the gutter.

'May it choke me if I ever smoke another one of Lou Hyams' cigars,' he said.

Bessie Weinbaum lost her temper. 'All right,' she said. 'I'll ask the *chadchan* to find me a husband, and I'll be a real Yiddisher momma.' Then she went out of the room, digging her ears with a corner of the towel. Old man Weinbaum sat at the window and not a little regretfully watched Lou Hyams' cigar burning itself out in the gutter.

CHAPTER 3

I

The Two Compasses had just opened. It was cosy in the saloon bar, a warm, redolent retreat from the grey, rainwashed streets. A coal-fire shed a cheerful glow across the maple-green linoleum. Dance music, interspersed with eulogistic commentaries on washing powders and laxatives, came not too loudly from the radio set behind the bar. On the counter an array of blue-and-white saucers, imitation Willow pattern, contained gherkins, olives, onions, salted nuts and squares of cheese, free and gratis to all who cared to partake.

Leaning against the bar, drinking light ales and sharing the gherkin saucer between them, were three young men wearing ten-and-elevenpenny imitations of Anthony Eden hats, white silk mufflers, quite smart fifty-shilling suits and patent shoes. They were Alfie Price, Whitey Williams and Dicey Perkins, who was a cripple. A casual observer would never have dreamed that they had been out all night.

The tallest of the trio, Whitey Williams, had once been fancied as a coming lightweight, but being a good-time boy had never seen the fun of punching a bag all day and going to bed early o' nights when other guys were out enjoying themselves. The lobe of one ear was slightly thickened in 'cauliflower' fashion. They called him Whitey because of his skin, which was whiter than any woman's.

Alfie Price, the shortest of the trio, was a dapper little chap with his hat tilted forward so that it shaded his small, bird-like eyes. He wore a thin, Ronald Colman moustache, and had a habit of sucking one of his back teeth when deep in thought. He had a semi-circular scar just below his right cheekbone, souvenir of a Derby-day fracas, when one of the Birmingham boys had tapped a half-pint glass in two and thrust the jagged edge hard into Alfie's face, saying, 'Here's luck, Alfie!'

Perkins, who limped, was called Dicey Perkins by his friends, and Pick Nose Perkins by his enemies. In spite of his lameness, he was still considered to be the best driver of a 'jam-jar' east of Aldgate Pump. The lameness was a legacy from a seventy-mile-an-hour head-on collision when making a getaway from a smash-and-grab job. And he always declared that the hospital authorities had purposely left him crippled on the instructions of the perfidious police. He was a sallow-faced, round-shouldered youth with a slack mouth, decayed teeth and a giggle. When he wasn't shaking dice he was cleansing his nostrils with a spiral movement of his little finger.

When Lou Hyams walked in and joined the trio there were no greetings exchanged. They were obviously expecting him. They had an appointment. To use their own odd idiom, they had 'made a meet'.

'What's the poison, Lou?' Alfie Price put half-a-crown on the counter.

Lou pushed it back. 'It's with me. What are you boys having?'

'Light ales, then,' said Alfie.

'I'm having a Scotch,' said Lou. 'What about a short, eh? Yes, sure. It'll warm you up. Four large Haigs, Edie.'

The soda siphon fizzed three times. Alfie took it neat, and the four men raised their glasses, muttering 'g'luck', and drank. Lou put a packet of cigarettes on the counter and indicated to them to help themselves. As they did so, they all seemed calm enough, but an experienced observer would have sensed an air of expectancy, of tension. There was no small talk, no pleasantries about the weather. They were waiting for Lou to speak.

Alfie sipped his whisky and sucked his back tooth. Whitey Williams bit his thumbnail. Dicey picked his nose. At last Lou put his glass down and said softly, 'No luck.'

'That's buggered it,' said Alfie Price.

'I'm sorry, boys,' Lou continued. 'I thought my young brother would have taken them; but he's too scared or too broke. And it's no use me taking 'em if I've got to go *shlapping* all over London before I can get rid of 'em, is it? After all,' he laughed, 'I'm not in your business, you know.'

Alfie Price sucked his tooth. 'That's properly buggered it.'

Lou's pink face looked at them through a haze of smoke from his own cigar. 'I'd have loved to have helped you, boys. You know that.'

Alfie nodded. 'We thought we'd ask you first, Lou. We didn't want old Bee's Knees to have 'em. He'd probably offer us about a handful. Diabolical old liberty-taker, that he is.'

Lou drew gently on his cigar and the smoke trickled out of his mouth as he spoke. 'That's how it is.' He shrugged a padded shoulder. 'I don't want to preach to you boys; but you're so damned unsystematic. It's your own business how you choose to make a living, but if you must make it this way, why go out and do a job blind? I ask you! Why go and do a job blind, without knowing how much you're going to get or where you're going to get it? Then, because you can't get rid of the stuff you have practically to give it away to an old shark like Beasley. Where d'you keep your brains – in your boots? If I were in your line' – he broke off and laughed – 'if I were in your line, I'd know what I was going to get, and exactly who was going to buy it, and at what price.'

Alfie nodded and pushed his hat back.

'You're right, Lou,' he said. 'Dead right. But actually we went in to do the peter. The bloody thing was empty. There was nothing in the office or the warehouse but this vanload of skates in the yard. So we drove it out as it was and dumped the van later. This is what comes of bloody Whitey's information.'

He looked up at Whitey, his lips curling.

'Eight 'undred quid in the peter, wasn't there?' he said, scornfully. 'Sweet Fanny Adams!'

Whitey Williams looked hurt. He put down his drink and somewhat theatrically folded his arms.

'That's it!' he said. 'That's it. Start rortin' to me, nah. Could I 'elp it if they went and banked all their muckin' dough. Tell me, can I 'elp it?'

''Sh!' said Lou, but unable to resist a smile.

'I suppose you boys are stone cold?' he asked, his fingers groping in his front hip pocket.

'I've got a tosheroon,' said Alfie. 'These two haven't a light.'

Lou was screwing a pound note up into a small pellet. This he pushed into Alfie's waistcoat pocket.

'Pay me when you get rid of the stuff,' he said. 'I've got to blow now. So long, boys!'

'Well, 'ave another one before you go, Lou!' said Alfie, feeling the pleasant crackle of the note in his pocket.

'Yerce!' said Whitey. 'One fer the road.'

'Yerce,' said Dicey, picking his nose. ''Ave another one.'

'No, sorry, boys!' smiled Lou from the door. 'I made a meet with a feller at Aldgate at twelve fifteen. It's that now. So long. G'luck.'

'So long, Lou.'

'All the best, Lou.'

'Thanks, Lou.'

The door closed. Alfie smoothed out the green note on the counter and ordered three light ales. He pushed his hat forward over his eyes and sucked his tooth.

'He's a good boy,' he said.

'Sure, 'e's a good boy,' said Whitey.

Whitey reached for a light ale. 'G'luck.'

'G'luck,' said the other two, raising their glasses.

Whitey reached forward and picked up the cigarettes which Lou had left on the counter.

The light ales being paid for, Alfie handed his companions six and threepence each.

'And don't forget we owe Lou a oncer,' he said. 'I'm tired of paying the debts of this outfit.'

'Yerce,' said Whitey Williams, 'don't forget we owe Lou a nicker.'

The saloon door opened. The trio did not move. But Alfie Price looked into one of the mirrors hanging over the bar. His lips did not move, but he spoke.

'For Christ's sake,' he said softly. 'Here's Fothergill.'

Detective-Sergeant Fothergill, sometimes referred to as 'Farver Gill', ex-middleweight champion of the Metropolitan Police, a perpetually smiling pipe-smoker, the best-hated 'busy' in the East End, walked to the bar and ordered a bitter.

The trio had ignored him. To all intents and purposes they

had not even seen him. They did not know him. A stranger, complete and utter. Alfie had pushed his black hat on one side.

'And then what d'you think 'appened,' he was saying in a loud voice. 'Bryn Jones had the ball in front of an open goal and he goes and boots it over the bar. You oughta 'ave 'eard the crahd!'

'Quite right, Alfie,' said Fothergill. 'It must have been three yards wide. I was there. Worse game I've seen this season. Don't you think so?'

'Yerce,' said Alfie abruptly. 'But I wasn't talking to you.'

'No,' said Whitey Williams. ''E wasn't talking to you.'

Whitey Williams probably detested Fothergill more than any other man in the East End detested him. Added to the natural detestation of a crook for an urbane copper, who smiled and bought you a drink one night and knocked you off the next night, who promised you bail and then went into the box and opposed bail, who advised you to plead guilty and promised to put a good word in for you and then stood up in court and told a string of lies and unblushingly called you 'a pest and a menace to society' . . . added to all this was the one-time professional fighter's contempt for the amateur, a nagging, yearning desire for an opportunity of knocking the life out of him.

'Oh, I'm sorry if I'm intruding,' said Fothergill amiably. 'Have a drink, boys?'

Alfie, always the spokesman for the trio, at first intended to tell Fothergill what to do with his drink, but quickly changed his mind and grinned as he said, 'Yerce, all right, we don't mind if we do.'

Dicey was silent, picking his nostril, gazing at the maple-green linoleum, thinking of the stone floor of a prison workshop.

'Fine,' said Fothergill. 'What'll you have, boys?'

Alfie grinned, tilted his hat forward so that the brim rested on the bridge of his nose.

'Make mine a double Haig,' he said.

'Yerce,' said Whitey, 'make mine a double 'Aig, too. 'Ow 'bout you, Dicey? Double 'Aig?'

Dicey nodded.

'Double Haig,' he said quietly.

'Three large Haigs, please,' said Fothergill. 'You boys are getting expensive tastes.' He glanced at the empty pale-ale glasses. 'What's the matter, beer turned sour?'

Alfie was tempted to say that any self-respecting glass of beer would turn sour when he, Fothergill, was around, but changed his mind and said, 'Well, you know 'ow it is, *Mister* Fothergill, we just couldn't drink common beer with you, could we now?'

And he grinned up at the bland, blue-eyed Fothergill, who stood with a bitter in one hand and a pipe in the other, his rather babyish mouth smiling under a fair moustache.

'No,' said Whitey, 'we couldn't drink common beer wiv you, *Mister* Fothergill. 'Ow could we, you an ex-amatoor middleweight champ an' all. 'Ow could we?'

'I shudder to think what your drinks would cost me if I were a real *professional* champ,' said Fothergill quietly.

Whitey shook his head.

'Ah, that ain't the same fing,' he said. 'Why, everybody knows pros ain't the same as amatoors. Amatoors are in a much 'igher class altogevver. You can drink any ol' muck wiv a pro, but an amatoor – he's a gentleman, ain't 'e?'

'Ah, I see,' the detective nodded over his pipe in appreciation of Whitey Williams' concise summing up of the difference between the status of a professional and that of an amateur fighter. His baby lips pursed into a smile at what Whitey imagined was fine and devastating sarcasm.

Alfie suddenly remembered that even a police officer is entitled to a little courtesy when he buys you a double whisky, and raised his glass, saying, 'All the best, *Mister* Fothergill.'

'All the best, boys,' said Fothergill, then, turning to Perkins, said, 'You're rather quiet, Dicey.'

Dicey rolled a piece of dirt between his thumb and forefinger.

'Least said, soonest mended,' he said succinctly.

'Ah, yes!' Fothergill puffed his pipe. 'A still tongue makes a wise head, eh? Been doing any driving lately, Dicey?'

Of course, there it was, wrapped up among all these common-place pleasantries. Here was the questioning snake raising its head among the grass of small talk. Sooner or later it had to come.

Detective-Sergeant Fothergill didn't buy you double Scotches for the sake of your brown eyes.

Not by the move of a muscle, not by the flicker of an eyelash, the motion of a mouth or by a warning glance, did the trio show any visible sign of being inwardly perturbed by that apparently innocent question directed at Dicey.

Little Dicey sipped his drink and picked his nose.

'Driving? No!' he said. 'Course not. 'Ow can I drive with my gammy leg? It's hard enough to walk with it. I'd like to see you drive with my leg.'

'You've got a driving licence up to date, though, haven't you?' asked Fothergill, and the bluish smoke curled slowly from the stem of his briar pipe.

There it was again. The quiet, innocent question following so logically on the previous question and Dicey's reply. Nothing suggested, mind you. Nothing wrong. Oh, dear, no. Just mild small talk, question and answer, casual discussion over a drink, as innocent as a spider crawling leisurely along the stem of a garden plant. If you don't drive these days, why have a driving licence? Not put in those words exactly; oh, no. This was small talk. Very smooth and silky it was now. It was a tough spot all right. Whitey was thinking, what a beautiful left hook I could plant on Fothergill's chin now! Alfie was sucking a back tooth and hoping that Dicey would use his loaf. Dicey himself was feeling most uncomfortable. Of course, Fothergill had no right to ask these questions. Dicey could have told Fothergill to go, bowl his hoop. Alfie was hoping that Dicey would do no such thing. He didn't.

'Well, you never know,' he said. 'A driving licence is always handy.' 'Yer see,' he added quickly, 'I'm working in the market now, and when yer working in the market yer never know when yer might 'ave ter do a bit of driving, even if it does 'urt yer gammy leg. Yer can't pick and choose yer jobs these days.'

Dicey's excuse for having a driving licence was as lame as his left leg. Dicey knew it. Fothergill knew it. Whitey and Alfie knew it.

'So you're working in the market now, Dicey?' said Fothergill. 'Who are you working for?'

Alfie stroked the bristles of his small moustache. The skin tightened over the knuckles of Whitey's left hand and he looked at Fothergill's chin. Fothergill was smiling blandly. But the last question held no terrors for Dicey.

'My cousin,' he said.

'Oh, I see,' said Fothergill. 'Your cousin. Which one is that?'

'My eldest cousin,' said Dicey.

'Oh, I see! Your eldest cousin,' smiled Fothergill. 'By the way,' he went on in a different tone of voice, apparently changing the conversation, 'somebody did a job at Mackay And Holden's in Great Mansell Street last night. They found the peter empty, but they drove a vanload of kid's skates out of the yard. The van was abandoned near Hackney Marshes.'

There was silence between the little group at the bar for perhaps three seconds. Not Alfie, Whitey nor Dicey made the slightest visible movement, but they all tautened inwardly. Fothergill began to knock his pipe-ash into the ashtray.

Then Alfie put half-a-crown on the counter.

'What's the poison, everybody?' he said. 'Bitter, *Mister* Fothergill? Or would you prefer a short?'

'No more for me, thanks,' said Fothergill, still knocking out his pipe.

''E's in training,' sneered Whitey.

'Three light ales,' said Alfie. 'Sure you won't 'ave one, Mister Fothergill?'

'Sure,' said Fothergill.

He put his pipe in the pocket of his raincoat.

'The van was abandoned near Hackney Marshes,' repeated Fothergill. 'There were fingerprints on the wheel.'

Alfie was passing a light ale across to Dicey. Perhaps the glass was rather full. Some of it spilled on the floor. Dicey took the drink mechanically. He could swear he wore gloves last night. He did take them off to light a cigarette once. But he put them on again immediately. He could swear he didn't touch the wheel with his bare fingers. Or could he? Was this another of Fothergill's tricks? He gulped at his drink.

'G'luck, everybody,' said Alfie amiably. 'What was that you were saying, Mister Fothergill?'

'I said there were fingerprints on the wheel,' said the detective. 'The steering wheel.'

'Well,' Alfie sipped his drink and smiled, 'nothing remarkable about that, is there? There's fingerprints on every steering wheel.'

'Yerce,' said Whitey, 'there's fingerprints on every steering wheel, ain't there?'

Whitey grinned as if the triumph of the deduction had been his own. But Alfie gave him a warning glance to keep his mouth shut. Fothergill nodded several times, smiling as he looked at Alfie Price.

'You're right, Alfie,' he said. 'Dead right. I didn't think of that. By the way, did you know that Tommy Swann's escaped from the Moor?'

Alfie tilted his hat sideways and picked an onion from the saucer with thoughtful selection.

'I don't know no Tommy Swann,' he said, and he sucked his back tooth noisily and spitefully.

II

Outside Aldgate station a street organ was jangling merrily. Men in caps and white mufflers manoeuvred their fruit and flower barrows skilfully around red buses that crawled past, stopped and crawled on again in London's most consistent traffic block. The nearby Lyons' was crowded to suffocation, the windows misted with human breath and steam. A crowd of people sheltered in the station entrance.

Among them was Doris Sandigate. Her blue hat matched the colour of her eyes, and she wore a little spray of violets on the front of her guinea two-piece. She had a new pair of dark-blue shoes on, with quite high heels – five shillings a pair at a Bata sale. Her stockings were a shilling a pair from Marks And Spencer's. The touch of rouge on her face enhanced the natural paleness of her skin. She had curled and waved her yellow hair with an almost professional skill. She looked quite pretty – attractive in a wistful, common way.

She looked up at the clock and then across the road. Then to the right. Then to the left. Through the cheap fabric of her dark-blue gloves she bit her fingernails. She looked at the clock again. It was twelve twenty. John was late.

'Lovely daffs!' came a shout from the kerbway. 'Lovely daffs! Tanner a bunch, daffs!'

It was Bill Higgins with his barrowload of sunshine. She put up her shilling umbrella and ran to the kerb and bought a bunch. She was not in the habit of spending her all too few sixpences on flowers, much as she liked them. But there was a mute, irresistible appeal in the golden glory of that barrow.

Doris was a girl who loved all beautiful things, but they had to be simple in their beauty. It had to be a beauty she could understand before she could appreciate. Sometimes, in passing an art dealer's window, she would pause and be enraptured by a print of a Reynolds portrait or a Constable sunset. But she could not appreciate the beauty of, say, Chippendale furniture or old porcelain or old pewter. She loved Schubert's *Serenade* and the waltzes of Strauss, but Wagner left her cold. At school she had liked poetry, but it had to be the musical seesaws of Tennyson, the rural urbanities of Goldsmith or Gray. Milton was dry stuff. She was something of a dreamer. But she had never been studious. She would be intrigued by word pictures of The Lady Of Shalott, lying robed in snowy-white that loosely flew to left and right.

> *Under tower and balcony,*
> *By garden wall and gallery,*
> *A gleaming shape she floated by,*
> *Dead pale between the houses high,*
> *Silent into Camelot . . .*

That was the kind of jingle that had intrigued her at school, and in that was a key to her mentality. She was no slum intellectual. She was no brilliant child of mean streets. But occasionally she read a good book and liked reading it. Her favourite book was

Thomas Hardy's *Under The Greenwood Tree*. She liked it for the story and not for the rugged grandeur of Hardy's prose. She herself rarely used a sentence with more than six words in it.

As she bought the bunch of daffodils an old blind man came along crying, '*Box o' matches. Spare a copper for a poor blind man.*'

She gave him a penny and walked back to the shelter of Aldgate station. Again she glanced at the clock. It was twelve twenty-five. What had happened to John? She would give him another five minutes. For the next two or three minutes she stood daydreaming, while the crowds and the red buses surged past, the street vendors shouting their wares, the organ jangling merrily.

She came back to earth, almost with a sense of fright. It was like being awakened from a sound sleep. Somebody was whistling 'Little Dolly Daydream' persistently and repeatedly, quite close to her ear. It was Lou Hyams.

'You look like a little bridesmaid,' he smiled.

'Oh, it's you,' she said. 'You gave me quite a fright.'

'Give the cigarettes to the boyfriend?' he asked.

'I'm waiting for him now,' she said.

He clicked his tongue.

'Doesn't he know by now that a gentleman never keeps a lady waiting?'

'Perhaps I'm no lady,' she giggled.

'I think you're a very beautiful young lady,' he said, grinning.

'Go on with you,' she said. 'I'm not beautiful. Not really beautiful.'

'Yes, you are,' he grinned.

'No, I'm not.'

'Yes, you are,' he said. 'How long you been waiting for the boyfriend?'

'Nearly half-'n-hour,' she said, glancing up at the clock again.

'That's bad,' said Lou. 'You want to teach him a lesson. Come into Lyons' for a coffee?'

'Oh, no thanks, really.'

'Have a drink, then, in The Three Nuns?'

'Oh, no thanks, really. It's awfully nice of you. But not now, thanks.'

He shrugged his well-tailored shoulders, puffed on his cigar, fingered the thin gold watch-chain across his waistcoat.

'Some other time, eh?' he smiled.

'Yes, some other time,' she replied.

'I'm meeting a business friend here,' he said. 'But as you're expecting the boyfriend I won't embarrass you by standing with you. The boyfriend might object. G'bye.'

'G'bye,' she smiled.

He sauntered casually into the station entrance and stood by a ticket machine, puffing at his cigar and reading the *Sunday Express*.

Two men came walking unsteadily along the pavement, colliding with passers-by as they walked. Although the public houses had only been open half-an-hour, they were already distinctly under the influence. Perhaps they had been imbibing at some mysterious cellar of a club since early morning. Their coats were creased as if they had both spent the night sleeping on the floor.

One of them collided with Doris. She swayed, nearly fell, regained her balance, then stepped back. The man stopped, looked at her vacantly, raised a dented bowler-hat in mock courtesy, and grinned.

'I'm shorry, miss,' he said.

''Sall right,' said Doris, and took another step backwards.

The drunken man peered closer, nudged his companion, and said, 'Not bad, eh, Ern?'

'Nice bit of stuff, Alf,' Ern agreed.

Alf swayed nearer to the girl, breathing beer into her face as he said, 'D'you hear what my friend shaid? He shaid you're a nice bit of stuff. So you are. Caw blimey, you are. Come 'n have a drink.'

He clutched her arm.

'No – please!' She shrank back. 'I'm waiting for somebody.'

'Come 'n have a drink,' he insisted, still gripping her arm and swaying.

'Please let go my arm,' she gasped. 'You're 'urting.'

'Come 'n have a drink along o' Ern and me,' he insisted drunkenly.

'No! Will you please let go of my arm!'

'Come 'n have . . .'

The rest of the request was stifled this time as a large hand caught the drunken man by the necktie and jerked him away. He looked round stupidly into the eyes of Lou Hyams. The barbershop pinkness had gone out of Lou's face. It was wax-white.

'Let this kid alone,' he said.

The drunken man waved his free hand.

'You shove off,' he said. 'Mind your own bloody business, Jew boy. The lady's gonna have drink wi' me and Ern. Come 'n, beau'ful . . .'

And he again reached out his hand towards Doris, but it did not reach her this time.

Lou's lip quivered and became a taut line. He drew his right elbow back and smashed his fist into the drunk's face.

The drunk rolled over into the kerbway. Ern stared at him stupidly. A bus drew up with a squeal of brakes.

Lou plucked at the girl's sleeve.

'Let's get out of this,' he said.

As if by magic, several hefty young men in trilby hats and scarves appeared on the scene.

'What's the trouble, Lou?' asked one. 'Want any help?'

'No, it's all right, Freddie,' said Lou. 'I didn't want to give him one. He was drunk. But I had to . . .'

'Okay, Lou. You shove off.'

'Oh, and Freddie! I'm expecting Dixie Winters any minute; if you see him, tell him I'm in Lyons', will you?'

'Right, Lou. I'll tell him.'

Lou hurried Doris into Lyons' teashop, and Freddie walked over to the drunken Ern, who was staring down at Alf stretched out in the gutter, a crowd gathering round.

Freddie put a fist under Ern's nose.

'Git your friend aht of 'ere,' he said, 'or we'll kick the chumps off the two of yer. Quick! 'Urry up! Before the coppers come!'

It was crowded in Lyons'. It was two or three minutes before they could find two seats at the same table. Quite a lot of people seemed to know Lou, and greeted him as he walked to a table at the end of the shop. He was still waxy-white about the face when he sat down and pushed the menu card to Doris.

She looked at him over the top of the long yellow card.

'I hope you won't get into trouble on my account,' she said.

'Trouble!' he ejaculated. 'Me get into trouble around here. Huh! I own the joint.'

He laughed, scorning such a preposterous idea.

'Besides,' he said, 'if I hadn't give that geezer one, somebody else would. That's one thing they won't stand for round here. The East End's a rotten dump, but a girl is safe, if she *wants* to be safe.'

He looked up at the waitress and smiled.

'Hello, beautiful! Give me a mixed ice. What'll you have, kid?'

'I'll have a small coffee,' said Doris.

'Like hell you will,' said Lou. 'Have something to eat.'

'No thanks, really. I've just had breakfas', and I'll be having dinner soon.'

'Eat!' Lou invited her. 'Eat! Poached egg on toast. Welsh rarebit. Baked beans on toast. Go on, don't be shy.'

She giggled.

'I'm not shy. Really, I'm not. But I just couldn't eat. Really, I couldn't.'

'Okay. Bring the lady a coffee and some pastries. You can manage a pastry, can't you, kid?'

'Well, yes; I will have a pastry, then.'

'Okay, the lady says a pastry. Oh, hello, Dixie!'

A lean, brown-faced little man wearing a light-grey check suit, a large check cap, a bow tie and black suede shoes, was standing by the table smiling. He was so small that he only came up to the waitress's shoulder.

'Hoxton Freddie told me you were in 'ere,' he said. 'And I said, "Cor blimey, has he gone TT?"'

Lou chuckled.

'No. I'm with a lady,' he said. 'Dixie, this is Miss – er – say, what is your name, kid? Oh, yes, Doris Sandigate. And this is Mr Dixie Winters. The Dixie Winters who knows more about horses than any other man breathing. Sit down, Dixie. What'll you have?'

'Cuppa tea,' said Dixie.

'Eat,' said Lou, waving a hand at the menu. 'Eat.'

'Cuppa tea,' said Dixie stubbornly.

'Okay,' said Lou. 'What's the matter, got to keep your weight down?'

'I got out of the 'abit of eating,' said Dixie.

'You're clever,' remarked Lou. 'I knew a feller who got out of the habit of breathing.'

'No!' said Dixie. 'What 'appened?'

'He died.'

Doris giggled and spluttered as a mouthful of coffee went the wrong way. Lou patted her on the back.

'Choke up, chicken,' he said.

'You *are* funny,' she said, wiping her streaming eyes.

'Thinks he's Max Miller,' said Dixie.

'He's a regular scream,' said Doris.

Dixie had his tea, Doris her coffee and pastry, Lou his mixed ice. Then Lou took out a cigarette case.

'Well, Dixie,' he said in a low voice, 'what do you know? If it does win, I lose a packet.'

Dixie put a lump of sugar in his mouth. He crunched it in his teeth.

'You could give ten, twenty, 'undred to one and be safe,' he said slowly.

'Yes; but what makes you so damned sure?'

Dixie's teeth crunched on the sugar.

'Brinkley's riding it,' he said.

'All the more reason it should win,' said Lou. 'Brinkley's the best jockey over the sticks, bar none.'

'Brinkley won't try.'

'Eh?'

Lou stared at the little brown-faced man complacently chewing sugar.

'You 'eard.'

'Malarkey,' said Lou. 'Brinkley is a straight jockey. It's a straight stable. The owner's straight, and he's riding the best jumper since –'

'Brinkley's gone nuts on a tart,' said Dixie.

Lou's forehead creased into a frown. He pushed the sugar bowl out of Dixie's reach.

'What tart?' he asked.

'Mrs Callaghan.'

'Who the hell is Mrs Callaghan?' asked Lou.

'Mr Callaghan's wife.'

'And who is Mr Callaghan?' asked Lou patiently.

'Callaghan of Callaghan, Wentworth And Askey, commission agents and turf accountants, of Dover Street. If Brinkley's mount loses they clear about a quarter of a million.'

'So?'

Dixie pulled the sugar bowl within his reach.

'I always thought you were a smart boy, Lou,' he said. 'Don't you see? Some men would kill their own grandmuvver for fourpence. Other men would do worse for a bit of skirt. Perticularly a bit of skirt like Mrs Callaghan. She was an American showgirl before she married Callaghan.'

Lou's eyes narrowed.

'Where did you pick up this schmaltz – the pictures?' he asked.

'I never go to the pictures,' said Dixie, complacently. 'Have I ever put you on a stoomer yet? I tell yer it's gospel. It's kosher.'

'All right,' said Lou.

He took a five-pound note from his wallet and folded it carefully, then slid it across to Dixie.

'Ta,' said Dixie.

Lou turned to Doris.

'Finish up the pastries, kid.'

'Oh, I couldn't! Really, I couldn't,' she answered.

Through the window she could see Johnnie Price walking up and down outside, looking to left and right. She was amazed at herself, amazed that she did not go running out to greet him as she would have done at any other time, despite the fact that he was three-quarters of an hour late. She was amazed that she could sit here quite calmly. She did not want to listen to his talk about yesterday's football matches, his motorbike's latest performance, or the possibility of Wooderson breaking his own record. Presently he walked away. She just sat and watched him go.

'That'll teach him to be early next time,' she said.

'Eh?' said Lou.

'That's my boyfriend just gone,' she said.

Lou looked round quickly and saw a large fat man with three chins just passing the cash-desk.

'You don't mean *him*!' he said in mock consternation.

Doris giggled.

'Aren't you a one,' she said. 'No, my boyfriend was outside. He's gone now.'

Then something happened that made Lou jump. The colour flushed back to his face and went again. From outside came the hysterical clanging of an ambulance bell. Then the ambulance itself wisped past the window like a white sheet in the rain. The clanging stopped.

Then the door of the teashop opened. A young man wearing a green trilby hat and a spotted scarf came in quickly. It was Fish-guts Turner. He came straight to the table, walking like a two-footed puma. He whispered in Lou's ear.

'Lou,' he said, 'that drunk hit his head on the kerb when he went down. You'd better beat it.'

Lou nodded and picked up the bill.

III

The atmosphere of the kitchen in the Sandigate home in Coronet Grove resembled that of a hothouse or boiler-room. The Sunday dinner was cooking, and while it was cooking Mrs Sandigate was having a bath.

Mr Sandigate had just gone over to The Two Compasses to drink, play darts and discuss the prospects for the Grand Steeple-chase Stakes and the Cup Final. All the family, except Mrs Sandigate, were out. The small kitchen was clouded with steam from the large tin bath full of hot water in which Mrs Sandigate was performing her ablutions before the fire. Now and again she would stand up in the bath, lean over and adjust one of the taps on the gas stove, or prod the potatoes or the greens with a fork. Then she would relapse into the water again, eventually emerging from the bath the colour of a boiled carrot all over.

Having dried herself and dressed, she opened the kitchen door to let some of the steam out. She was about to close it again when a startled look appeared in her greenish-blue eyes. She looked around her and into the backyard. She saw nothing unusual. She even looked up at the sky. The voice seemed to come from nowhere.

She could have sworn a man's voice had whispered 'Rose'. She looked round the backyard, a square of black, barren earth, boxed in by crumbling walls.

'Rose . . . Rosie . . .'

God! Something was clutching at her heart. He couldn't be here. Not Tommy Swann. No, it couldn't be. It couldn't be. Just couldn't be. He was miles away.

'Rosie.' The whisper was louder.

And then she stifled a scream. There was Tommy Swann's white face staring at her from the door of the old tin shed where they kept the household junk – a bicycle with only one wheel, an old carpet, a rusty bedspring, flowerpots and boxes of nails, things Mr Sandigate hoarded because they might 'come in useful one day'.

For the minute Rose felt as if she was going to faint. Then, giving a frightened glance up at the nearby windows, she walked across the yard to the shed and pretended to take some pegs off the clothes line.

'How did you get here?' she asked, speaking with a peg in her mouth, not daring to look down at Tommy Swann.

'Been 'ere since four o'clock this morning,' he said in a hoarse whisper. 'I climbed over the back wall.'

'Gawd, I nearly died o' fright,' she said. 'You looked like a ghost.'

'I feel worse than that,' he mumbled.

'You shouldn't 'ave done it, Tommy. You shouldn't 'ave done it. They'll only catch you agin. They always do.'

'I'd sooner die than go back, Rose. I 'ad another eight years to do. I jus' couldn't face it, Rose. I jus' couldn't – I . . .'

'You shouldn't 'ave come 'ere, though, Tommy. You shouldn't 'ave. It ain't fair, it ain't.'

'But, Rose, I 'ad to go somewhere. They'll be watching every other place I know. Can yer git me a bit a grub, Rose? It won't 'urt if I stay 'ere a bit. They won't dream of looking fer me 'ere.'

'All right. Better come into the 'ouse. Everybody's out.'

'Nobody looking?'

'No. 'Sall right. Run straight in now and keep yer 'ead dahn. And for Gawd's sake 'urry.'

He scuttled through the rain and into the house like a human rabbit. Rose nearly fainted again as a curtain moved at a window next door.

'P'r'aps it was only the wind,' she muttered. 'Pray Gawd it was only the wind.'

Then she went hot and cold and sick and dizzy all at once. For the same window was suddenly pushed open with a loud squeak of damp, protesting woodwork. But it was only somebody putting out an aspidistra plant to get the benefit of the rain.

Her knees felt weak. She almost staggered into the house. She locked and bolted the back door, and then collapsed into a kitchen chair.

Tommy Swann was crouching by the fire warming his hands, his drenched clothes making a pool on the hearth which Doris had whitened only an hour or two ago. He gazed at Mrs Sandigate from bloodshot eyes.

Rose sat staring at him, her large bosom heaving as her breath came in painful gasps. She could not bring herself to believe that this really was Tommy Swann crouching by her fireplace. It was a strange dream – a nightmare. This wasn't the Tommy Swann of the flash suits, the coloured shirts and the patent shoes, the smart boy who had taken her to West End clubs. No. He looked like his own corpse warming itself into life again, the flames of the kitchen fire causing queer, distorted shadows to flicker over the white face. There was a heavy growth of beard on the chin. His hair was cropped short at the back and sides, leaving a long, thick tuft of hair on the centre of his bullet-shaped head. He looked like one of the characters out of the screen version of *All Quiet On The Western Front*. At last he spoke.

'I didn't know where else to go, Rose,' he was saying. 'Straight, I didn't. They'll be watching every other place I could go. They'll be watching everywhere. They'll be watching. But there ain't no connection between me and this 'ouse. They won't look fer me 'ere. They'll be watching everywhere else. They'll be watching . . .'

He broke off into a fit of coughing. She got to her feet. He was wearing an old mackintosh and a pair of flannel trousers over prison garb.

'The clothes!' she said suddenly. 'They're prison clothes, ain't they?'

He nodded. 'I didn't stop to ask the governor for me suit,' he grinned.

'Take 'em off! Take 'em off!'

'But what can I wear? What else can I wear, Rose?'

'T'ke 'em orf!' she almost shrieked, and began pulling them off with her own hands.

'They're soaking,' she said. 'They're soaking!'

In a few minutes he was standing there with not a stitch on. She gathered the sodden clothes together and took down a beer bottle, full of paraffin, from a shelf.

''Ave a bath in that water,' she said, pointing to the tin bath. 'It's still 'ot. 'Ere's soap and 'ere's a towel. I'm going to burn these under the copper. Then I'll get you something to eat. Oh, fer Christ's sake 'urry up! Don't stand there staring.'

Tommy stepped into the bath and Rose poured the paraffin over the clothes he had discarded. She was stuffing them into the copper grate when there came a *rat-tat-tat* at the front door. It reverberated over the whole house. The very walls seemed to tremble.

The silence in that steam-clouded, kitchen-cum-washhouse was potent. It was broken only by the greens bubbling in the saucepan on the gas range and a clock ticking on the shelf.

Tommy Swann was sitting bolt upright in the bath, a piece of red soap clutched in his hand, soapy water trickling down over his frightened eyes.

Rose was kneeling by the copper, the cleft of her large breasts showing as her pinafore sagged forward. She held a matchbox in one hand, a match in the other – she seemed to be turned into stone in the act of striking the match.

Neither of them spoke. The greens bubbled. The clock ticked. A piece of coal fell from the fire and sizzled on the damp hearth.

Several streets away a Salvation Army band was playing *Rock Of Ages*. Then it came again.

Rat-tat-tat! Bang, bang!

Then Rose did something she had not done for years, although she had been brought up in the Roman Catholic faith. She crossed herself.

''Oly Mary, give me strength,' she muttered.

'Don't let 'em in,' croaked Tommy Swann. 'Fer Christ's sake, Rose, don't answer that door. Don't . . .'

Bang, bang, went the knocker again.

Rose Sandigate walked slowly up the creaking, wooden stairs, Tommy Swann's voice drifting after her, 'Don't open the door, Rose! Don't!'

He had climbed out of the bath and stood with his back to the kitchen door, still holding a piece of soap, the water trickling down his body and dripping on to the floor.

'You ain't opening that door, Rose,' he said.

'Don't be daft,' she said. 'I got to.'

She pushed him aside and went upstairs and opened the street door. A freckle-faced boy in a jersey and cyclist's cape was standing on the step.

'Paper money, ma, please,' he said.

Mrs Sandigate gulped. She leaned a podgy hand against the door to support herself.

'What d'yer mean by banging *rat-tats*?' she demanded weakly, huskily.

The boy stared at her.

'Don't I always *rat-tat*?'

'Do yer? Well, don't *rat-tat* like that any more,' answered Mrs Sandigate, shining with perspiration. 'And fer yer sauce you can wait till next week fer the money.'

And she banged the door in his face. The youth made a wry face, shrugged his shoulders, entered a dash in his small cash-book, and clattered down the steps, scratching his head . . .

IV

Little Mrs Willis, the widow who lived at number 17 Coronet Grove, was the last of the sparse congregation to leave St Saviour's that morning. The vicar, the Rev Philip Black, walked to the door with her.

He was a largish, pink young man, with light-brown hair that fell in a quiff over his forehead, and grey, serious eyes behind rimless spectacles. He spoke in a deep, sonorous voice in which there was occasionally a suggestion of a Durham accent.

'Oh, dear,' he said, looking up at the cloudy sky, 'it's still raining.'

'So it is,' said Mrs Willis. 'I'm glad I brought my umbrella. Do you know, it has rained every Sunday for the last two months!'

'Really, now!' said Mr Black. 'Fancy that. You know, I'm so busy on Sundays that I rarely have time to think about the weather.'

Mrs Willis was putting up her umbrella. She smiled up at the big, pink, grey-eyed young man.

'Yes, Sunday *is* a busy day for you, isn't it?' she remarked. 'Oh, but that was a lovely sermon you preached today, Mr Black!'

'It's very nice of you to say so, Mrs Willis,' said the Rev Philip Black.

The little black umbrella went up with a click, shedding an aroma of mothballs as it did so. Mrs Willis was smiling at the parson.

'You must be awfully clever,' she said, 'to think of such wonderful things to say.'

Her eyes shone as she looked up at him. He smiled gently and shook his head.

'I'm not clever, Mrs Willis,' he said. 'And as for the things I say, I often wish I could put into words the really wonderful things I sometimes feel. Things I feel God wants me to say. Yet . . .'

He broke off and stared up at the overcast sky.

'Summer will be here soon,' he said, so quietly that Mrs Willis did not hear him.

'I must bring my son Vivian to hear you one day,' she said.

'By all means, Mrs Willis. By all means.'

'He's a good boy,' she went on. 'But he just won't go to church, and that worries me so.'

'Don't worry, Mrs Willis,' said the parson. 'There are a lot of good Christian folk who never go to church, although I say it who shouldn't. Your son will come to church when he feels the need. I'm sure he's a good boy.'

'He is, Mr Black. He is that. And my only child, too. Do you know, he went to war when he was only seventeen. Such a slip of a boy he was when he went away in uniform. I was *so* proud of him.'

'I'm sure you were,' said Mr Black. 'I'm sure you still are.'

Mrs Willis was fumbling in her large, old-fashioned handbag. She pulled out a postcard photograph of a white-faced youth in uniform. She thrust it eagerly into the parson's hands.

'That's my Vivian,' she whispered.

The rain pattered on the old lady's umbrella as the vicar looked at the photograph of Vivian Willis. He had seen it, not once, but hundreds of time. He affected to study it carefully before handing it back.

'A fine lad, Mrs Willis,' he said. 'A son to be proud of.'

The old lady looked up at the young clergyman as if he were God Himself.

'Thank you for saying that, Mr Black,' she gulped. 'Thank you.'

She took a few paces into the rain, then turned and smiled.

'I must hurry now to get Vivian's dinner. We've got veal, and Vivian loves veal. Good day, Mr Black.'

'Good day, Mrs Willis. I'll see you next Sunday. Be careful how you go, now.'

And he watched the little old lady as she crossed the square, her cotton-gloved hand brushing back tears of joy from her eyes as she walked, the rain pattering on her umbrella.

Then he walked down the weed-infested, gravel pathway to pick up several pieces of newspaper and an empty cigarette carton. He threw them over the green spearheads of the railings into the gutter beyond.

By the gateway, on a little grass mound, was a grey concrete war memorial. At its base were a few faded flowers in dirty glass jam jars and milk bottles. Beside it was a board on which the words *Roll Of Honour* were inscribed in gilt lettering.

The Rev Philip Black stared at the names, and it seemed as if a ray of sunshine broke through the clouds and picked out one name in shining gold – *Vivian Edward Willis. Killed In Action, 1918.*

Chapter 4

I

Little Bertie Potts, son-and-heir of that JR Potts, who advertised himself to be a chimney-sweep and rat-catcher, was standing in Middlesex Street staring with fascinated eyes into the window of Higham's Music Emporium. Without wishing to be unkind, one might have wondered whether this child really was Mr Potts' son, and not one of those little creatures which it was his profession to catch, a little one which had taken his eye and which he had adopted from childhood, so that it had grown up to resemble a human being. The child's thin, rodent-like face, over a dirty, egg-stained jersey, probably annoyed Morry Higham. It would have annoyed any self-respecting shopkeeper to see that nose pressed against his window. Morry sauntered to the door.

'Now, run along, sonny. Run along.'

'Got any mouth orgins, mister?'

'Thixpence, shilling and two shillings,' said Morry.

The urchin produced a red money-box from beneath the egg-stained jersey. 'There's sixpence in there, mister.'

Morry sighed, took the money-box in the tips of his fingers and walked into the shop, followed by Bertie. The money was emptied on to the counter. 'Ha'penny short,' said Morry.

'Ah, mister, can I owe you ha'penny? I'll pay yer, strite I will.'

Morry shook his head.

'You get another ha'penny, thonny, and you can have a mouth organ.'

Bertie Potts gathered his coppers together and walked disconsolately from the shop. At the door he almost collided with a slim, tallish girl in a green coat and hat. Her make-up was just a shade too vivid. She smiled a fixed smile.

'Well, well!' said Morry. 'This is a thurprise.'

Vi giggled a little self-consciously. He was holding her hands, standing close and smiling into her eyes. Yes, the girl was beautiful. She leaned forward and whispered in his ear. She was heavily perfumed, but Morry didn't mind that.

'What did you do with my street-door key?' she whispered. 'I can't find it anywhere.'

'I put it in my pocket when I helped you up the stairs,' he smiled. 'Wait here; I'll get it for you.'

He ran up the stairs and she looked round the shop.

'Nice shop you got 'ere,' she remarked when he came back with the key.

'Not bad,' he conceded. 'Would you like to hear some records? I promised you some, I believe.'

'No 'urry,' she smiled. 'No 'urry.'

She knew it wasn't ladylike to appear too eager.

'Better take your choice now,' he said. 'Because the shop will be getting bithy prethently. Take your choice, my dear, anything you like.'

He waved his hand in the direction of the racks of gramophone records. Upstairs Sadie was coughing and a baby was crying. Vi looked towards the stairs beyond the door at the back of the shop. She nodded in that direction and whispered.

'Your wife. Can she 'ear us?'

Morry shook his head.

'Now, what record would you like to hear?'

'Have you got "Change Partners"?'

'Ah! Irving Berlin fan, eh?'

She nodded vigorously. Her eyes rolled and sparkled.

'Oh, I love 'is stuff! I just adore 'im! Don't you?'

'He's not bad,' conceded Morry. 'Tell you what I'll do,' he went on. 'I'll give you a whole set of his records. All the *Alexander's Ragtime Band* tunes and as many more as I can find. Remember "How Deep Is The Ocean?"'

'Do I remember it!' said Vi. 'It's my fav'rite.'

And, swaying slightly, she began to croon softly:

'Ow much do I love you?
I'll tell yer no lie.
'Ow deep is the ocean?
'Ow 'igh is the sky? . . .'

'Say, you've got a nice voice,' he said.

'Gaw on,' she said. 'You don't mean that re-eally?'

Her blue eyes lit up with pleasure.

'You wouldn't kid me, Morry, would yer?' she asked coyly. 'Do you really think I've got a nice voice?'

'Well, you know, it isn't too bad,' he said. 'Not at all bad, in fact.'

'O-oh, I'd love to sing with a dance band. I've always wanted to be a crooner like the Boswell Sisters or Vera Lynn.'

Morry nodded and seemed deep in thought.

'You never know,' he said. 'I've got an eye for talent.'

Her eyes sparkled anew, and she squeezed his hand. To Morry her cheap perfume was delicious.

'Do you think I could ever be good enough to sing with a band? Really and truly?' she asked.

'Well,' he said, pursing his lips, 'the voice is there, and the personality is there, but it's untutored. It lacks the professional touch. And we'd have to improve the diction.'

'What's diction?' she asked.

He stared at her. Could the girl really be so ignorant?

'I'll show you sometime,' he said. 'Would you like to hear some records?'

At the end of the shop was a little sound-proof cubicle containing a radiogram. Morry turned off the wireless amplifier in the shop and they went into the cubicle and shut the door. The place was scarcely larger than a telephone booth. Morry put a record on, released the switch and closed the lid. The place vibrated with music.

He looked at Vi. They were standing face-to-face, bodies touching. He could see every sweet-smelling, minute grain of cheap face powder on her skin and the carefully smeared-in rouge, the too-perfectly shaped crimson mouth parted over small white teeth.

The jazz record whirled on. They were not listening. He put his arms round her and kissed her.

Sadie, standing at the foot of the stairs, watched them. Then she turned and retraced her footsteps up the stairs. The baby was crying. A babble of voices drifted from the marketplace . . .

II

Little Alfie Sandigate walked along Coronet Grove to number 13 to meet his friend Bertie Potts, who was two years his senior. He found Bertie sitting on the top step, a handkerchief knotted round his head as a protection against the rain; a red money-box in one hand and some coppers in the other.

'Mum!' he was calling out.

A window opened and Mrs Potts, a sharp-featured woman with a beak of a nose and untidy hair, thrust her head out.

'What y'want?' she shouted. 'Come in orf those wet steps.'

'Gimme a penny,' wailed Bertie.

'No,' said Mrs Potts. 'Come in outta the rain. You'll catch yer deafa cold.'

Bertie Potts' voice rose to a higher pitch.

'Da-ad, gimme a penny!' he yelled.

'Yer farver's out and yer can't 'ave a penny,' announced Mrs Potts, with resolute finality.

Bertie Potts screamed out a really obscene word, and repeated his request with renewed vigour.

'Gimme ha'penny, then!' he yelled. 'I want ha'penny.'

'If I come aht there I'll tan yer arse for yer,' said Mrs Potts, and closed the window.

The card in the window announcing *J Potts* to be a *Chimney Sweep And Rat Catcher* had been disturbed by the movements of Mrs Potts and swung to and fro.

Alfie Sandigate walked up the steps and sat down beside his friend.

''Ullo,' he said.

''Ullo,' said Bertie.

'What you want a penny for?' asked Alfie. 'You got some money.'

'Gimme ha'penny, Mum!' yelled Bertie.

The window opened again and Mrs Potts threw out a half-penny. It jingled as it bounced down the steps to the pavement.

'Nah, git orf those steps, the two of yer!' she yelled.

Bertie bounded down the steps to pick up the coin, followed at a more leisured pace by Alfie. Grazing his knuckles as he picked up the halfpenny, Bertie commenced to run.

'Come 'n, Alfie,' he panted. 'I'm gonna git a mouth orgin.'

Alfie trotted after him.

'What you want a mouth orgin for?' he panted as they sped across Coronet Square.

'Cos I want one,' Bertie jerked out.

Dodging round the stalls of Petticoat Lane, colliding with shoppers, treading on toes, followed by curses and dire threats, they crashed through the black-and-silver door of Higham's Music Emporium, and came to an abrupt, panting standstill.

Vi and Morry Higham were just coming out of the cubicle. Vi was buttoning up her blouse. She stared, open-mouthed at the two urchins.

Alfie Sandigate was grinning. He pointed at Morry.

'O-oh,' he said, 'I know.'

'Now, what do you two want?' asked Morry brusquely.

'O-oh, you were kissing my sister,' said Alfie.

'Shut up, you brat,' said Vi.

Morry stared at her.

'Is *this* your brother?'

'Yes. This is my 'alf-brother.'

She turned on Alfie, who was still grinning, the gap in his front teeth showing where he had had an extraction a week ago.

'I'll tell yer mother you're round here,' she said. 'You know she told yer not to go away from the Grove.'

'Yeah!' sneered Alfie, sticking out his tongue. 'And I'll tell 'er about you kissing that man.'

And he pointed again.

'Don't tell lies, you little sod,' she swore, and then lost her temper.

She hit him across the face and began shaking him. He howled and kicked her in the shin. She hit him again across the ear. He punched her in the stomach and bit her wrist. She gasped with pain and hit him across the ear with such force that he fell against the counter. His small face was purple with juvenile rage. Tears made white lines down his grubby cheeks.

'Now I will tell 'er,' he screamed. 'And I'll tell 'er what you called me.'

Vi caught hold of him again.

'Will yer, will yer!' she said, shaking him until his teeth rattled.

'Go easy,' said Morry. 'My wife'll hear.'

He turned to Bertie Potts.

'Aren't you the little boy who wanted a mouth organ?' he asked.

Bertie nodded.

'Well, suppose I give you and your friend a new mouth organ each, for nothing? Will you both be good boys?'

Bertie nodded.

'I will, mister,' he said, and turned eager eyes to Alfie, hoping that he would not be recalcitrant enough to spoil this wonderful peace offering.

Morry turned to Alfie.

'And what do you say, young man?' he asked.

Vi had now relaxed her hold and Alfie was standing by the counter, scowling and rubbing his bruised ear.

'Will you be a good boy if I give you a mouth organ?' asked Morry.

Alfie nodded, and Morry went behind the counter and came back with two sixpenny mouth organs in oblong red boxes. He gave the boys one each.

'Now promise to be a good boy,' he said to Alfie. 'Kiss your sister and be friends.'

'Ugh!' said Vi.

'I don't wanna kiss 'er,' said Alfie sullenly.

'All right, but be a good boy now, won't you?' said Morry.

Alfie nodded, and the two urchins went out of the shop, blowing and sucking vigorously on their unexpected gifts, producing the most ear-splitting noises imaginable.

'Do you think he'll say anything?' Morry asked Vi.

'I'll kill 'im if 'e does,' said Vi.

Just then a customer came in to buy a bicycle lamp. Upstairs, Sadie was coughing and the baby was crying . . .

III

Mrs Hyams was white-haired at fifty. She lived alone with her daughter Fay in a little house in Bellington Street. Fay, who was sixteen, was studying at the Guildhall School Of Music, the fees being paid by brother Lou.

Tall for her age, she looked becoming in her short school tunic, her legs shapely in dark stockings. She wore her auburn hair in two long plaits over her shoulders.

When Fay was practising, Mrs Hyams always sat and listened. No matter whether it was the monotonous repetition of scales or a Bach fugue, she would sit there quiet as a mouse, watching her daughter's long, white fingers twinkling over the keys, and listening.

Mrs Hyams knew nothing about music. Beethoven, Bach, Handel, Wagner, Chopin, were mere names to her. She was incapable of criticism. Everything Fay played was beautiful to her ears. It was her one joy.

The big, black piano which Lou had bought several years ago looked incongruous in that little front room, with its cheap wallpaper, lace curtains, antimacassars, ornaments and the myriad framed photographs on the walls.

Mrs Hyams polished the piano with zealous care every night and morning until it shone like black marble. Mrs Hyams never went to the pictures. She never went to a theatre. She could speak English with a slight accent, but she had never learnt to read it.

'It is enough that I can speak the language,' she used to say in her soft, gentle voice. 'Why should I bother my poor head about learning to read it? So that I should read the newspapers? And what should I read in the newspapers but of wars and killing and persecutions – no? My mind gets quite sad enough at times with the sadness of people near me, the sadness of things people

94

tell me, without reading even more of terrible things that happen.'

Her husband, Reuben, had been a cabinet-maker, but a very studious cabinet-maker; a cabinet-maker who dreamed of other things.

'But, Hetty,' he would protest, 'would you not like to read the wonderful books that are written? Would you not like to read the thoughts of great men and stories of human endeavour?'

At which she would chuckle softly, and her eyes wrinkle up.

'My own thoughts are enough,' she would say. 'And as for stories, are there not enough real stories on our very doorstep, Reuben? Poor Rebecca Rosenberg is dying of consumption, and the thought of it is driving her husband out of his mind. Sarah Kadisch has had another baby – another girl. They wanted a boy, but they say she will never have another baby, boy or girl. The doctors had to cut her open – what do they call it, a Caesarian? There was a fire at Mrs Fineberg's and all her daughter's wedding presents were burned. Little Benny Kersh has won a scholarship. He is going to a big college at Oxford. Stories, you say, Reuben? Did I ever tell you the story of the night I was born, when my mother's home was being burned down about her ears . . . and my father outside, shot dead in the snow? Stories . . .'

She would shake her head and sigh as she darned a sock.

'If it pleases you, dear Reuben,' she would say, 'you can read to me out of the nice books you get from the library. Not the sad ones, the happy ones.'

And in the evenings Reuben would read to her, while she sat and stroked his hand and looked at his curly hair and fine lips moving as he read. She listened because it was Reuben reading, and she loved Reuben.

Now that her beloved Reuben could read to her no more, she would sit and listen to Fay playing, listening and looking at this daughter who was so beautiful and gifted.

Dear Reuben! His books were still there in the bookcase he had made himself. The books he bought with a few coppers, week by week, from the secondhand stalls in the Whitechapel Road. Nobody read them now, but at nights, when there was nobody to witness her display of sentiment, she would take them down and put her lips to the pages he had thumbed so often. And she would hear his voice again.

Mrs Hyams was in the kitchen, and Fay was playing the piano, when Lou walked in. 'Hello, Ma! Hello, Fay!'

Mrs Hyams' eyes wrinkled in a smile of real pleasure. Lou looked so big and strong in this tiny house where he had grown up from a sickly childhood. It grieved her that he no longer lived at home, but for business reasons, he said, kept a bachelor flat over the amusement arcade in the Whitechapel Road. She looked forward to his visits and wished he would come more often.

Fay, on the other hand, was always glad to see Lou, but she wouldn't have pined her heart out if he had stayed away for weeks, even months. The trouble with Lou was that he was too much of a go-getter, and he expected everybody else to be the same. He had some peculiar idea that she was a musical wonder, and that if she worked hard she would end up as a famous concert artist, but she knew in her own heart that she would never be anything of the kind. She didn't want to be. She had neither the necessary talent nor inclination. At best, she knew she would never even be a passably good pianist. In fact, her teacher had told her so. 'Sometimes I think you are the worst pupil I have ever had the misfortune to teach,' he told her.

And she had replied, 'Yes, Mr Frobell. I think you are quite right, Mr Frobell.' Everything William Frobell said met with Fay's approval. In fact, everything about him met with her approval. With his silver hair and his perfect profile, she thought him the most distinguished-looking man she had ever met. He was the Perfect Man. She was madly in love with him. Nobody knew about it, of course, least of all Mr Frobell. Indeed, if he had suspected it he would have been profoundly shocked and not a little disturbed. He regarded his pupil as a child, incapable of thoughts like that. That's what everybody thought. Only Fay knew what was within her. Only Fay knew that although she was a child in years, all the emotions of womanhood were surging within her. And after all, she thought, am I such a child? I'm getting on for seventeen. Wasn't mother married at seventeen? Didn't lots of girls have babies at seventeen, even sixteen? I could have a baby, couldn't I? A baby with Mr Frobell's perfect nose and light-grey eyes. She turned to greet Lou. 'Oh, hullo!'

'Don't stop playing,' said Lou. 'I've come to hear you play.'

'Oh, I'm tired! I've been playing all the morning.'

'Ma!' Lou called out. 'Has Fay been playing all the morning?'

Mrs Hyams came in from the kitchen.

'Well, I wouldn't say *all* the morning.'

Fay sighed and played a few desultory bars, lackadaisically, without spirit. It's a good thing, she thought, that neither of them know the first thing about music. If they did they'd realise what a lousy pianist I am. I am. I am. I know it. And if it wasn't for Mr Frobell I'd have told Lou the truth and left the school long ago. But if I leave the school I will never see Mr Frobell again, and I would die if I thought I would never see him again. Why doesn't he realise I love him? Why doesn't he realise that's why I always edge up so close to him at the piano? And when he says irritably, 'Miss Hyams, will you *please* look at the music,' why doesn't he realise that I'd sooner sit and look at his profile? Am I wicked to allow Lou to go on paying fees? No, I don't think I am. It's Lou's own fault, anyway. He shouldn't be such a big show-off. He buys a grand piano cheap at an auction sale – and it isn't as grand as it looks, anyway – and just because of that he thinks I'm going to become a female Paderewski. He shouldn't be so cocksure about everything. If he's making so much money out of his silly pin-tables that he can afford to chuck it away right and left, just to satisfy his vanity, I can't help it. And I can't help it that I love Mr Frobell. I love his hair. I love his eyes. I love his hands. If only he would put his hands on me sometimes. Even when he touches me by accident it sends a thrill, an exquisite thrill, right through my body. I'm older than most girls of my age. I must be . . .

'Don't stop playing, Fay. I'm listening.'

'I hadn't stopped. I was turning over the page.'

Puffing on his cigar, hands in pockets, Lou strolled over to the bookcase as he listened to Fay's playing. What a queer assortment of books the old man had collected! Collected from secondhand bookstalls with a purchasing power limited to coppers – shillings when he felt extravagant. There was Haeckel's *Riddle Of The Universe*, Spencer's *First Principles*, Fitzgerald's *Omar Khayyám*, the *Works Of Shakespeare*, novels by Sholem Asch, *War And Peace* by Tolstoy, *David Copperfield* and *Practical Woodwork*. A queer assortment.

'You know,' said Lou, 'one of these days I'm gonna be in the real big money, and d'you know what I'm gonna do? I'm going to buy good books, and . . .'

'Who's going to read them?' Fay asked over her shoulder.

Lou ignored the jibe. He sat down again, jingled the change in his pockets, surveyed the pinkish-grey ash of his cigar, rested his right ankle on his left knee, and admired the delicate stripe in his sock. And Fay, sitting at the piano, watched him in the mirror and almost hated him. She hated him for his self-assurance and his prosperity and his unconscious air of patronising everybody with whom he came in contact.

Who is he, this brother of mine? This man so virile, so complete in himself, so sleek and so well tailored. What was he? A proprietor of pin-table saloons, a bookmaker and gambler, a frequenter of boxing arenas and dog tracks. A man whose ambition was to become a big-time sports promoter. A man without culture or even the remotest pretence to it. Yet he didn't need culture. He would always be at ease anywhere. He was never abashed.

'You know what, Fay?' he was saying.

'What?'

'If you plugged away at that piano playing . . .'

'Oh, Lou!' She stopped playing and swung round to look at him, hands folded in her lap. 'Don't start that pep talk again,' she pleaded.

He pointed his cigar at her. 'You're going to be a famous pianist. You'll give two or three concerts a year, and people will flock to them.'

'I know,' she said calmly. 'I know.'

'You'd better know,' said Lou.

'Don't worry,' answered Fay. 'Your little *protégée* won't disappoint you.'

'And don't go and get married,' said Lou. 'That would spoil everything.'

'Married!' Mrs Hyams broke in. 'Why, the girl isn't seventeen yet.'

'She mustn't get married for another ten years,' said Lou.

'My God,' said Fay. 'It seems as if I'm condemned to a life of crowded concert halls and barren spinsterhood.'

She gave a tragic, theatrical sigh over her box of chocolates.

'One day,' said the white-haired lady by the window, 'she'll fall in love.'

'Great artists mustn't fall in love,' said Lou. 'Except with their work.'

At this Fay laughed out loud.

'Have you been reading a book, Lou?' she asked. 'Or perhaps you've been to the pictures?'

'Neither,' snapped Lou. 'I know what I'm talking about.'

He puffed on his cigar and fingered his watch-chain.

'Who's that boy you've been writing to?' he asked.

Fay picked up her chocolates and walked to the piano. She sat down.

'Oh, just a boy,' she said, beginning to play. She thought: how can I say they're to Mr Frobell; but I never post them? . . .

'There's wine in the cabinet, Louis,' said Mrs Hyams. 'The dry kind you like.'

Lou walked to the cabinet and there was a tinkle of glasses.

'You'll have some yourself, Ma?' he asked.

'A small glass, please, Louis.'

'Is this child allowed to drink?' he asked, nodding at Fay.

Fay stopped playing; her fingers stretched wide on a chord. She inclined her head.

'Yes, and fill it up – a large glass,' she said, then went on playing.

Lou chuckled.

'Got a drunkard in the family now, eh?'

'God forbid,' said Mrs Hyams.

'Only my joke, Ma,' said Lou, tugging at the cork.

The girl at the piano swung her auburn plaits.

'Was that a joke?' she asked.

Lou, with an exasperated grin, put the bottle down, walked over and flicked her on the nape of her white neck with his finger and thumb.

'You carry on with your practice,' he said.

Oh, what a fool my brother is, she thought. Oh, what a fool! The auburn plaits swung again.

'If you knew anything about it,' she said over her shoulder, 'you'd know this isn't practice. It's relaxation.'

'So that's what they call it!'

Lou went back to the table, grinning. He poured out the drinks.

'Don't put Fay's on the piano, Louis,' said Mrs Hyams. 'It stains.'

'No, put it in my mitt,' said Fay, swinging round and stretching out her hand.

She raised her glass.

'*Mazel tov!*' she said.

Mrs Hyams and Lou smiled and raised their glasses.

'You'll stay to lunch, yes?' Mrs Hyams asked her son.

'Well, you see, Ma . . .'

'I've got curried chicken,' she went on.

'Of course he'll stay to lunch,' said Fay over her shoulder. 'The only time he eats is when he comes home.'

Lou jerked his thumb.

'Listen to your daughter,' he said. 'Yes, Ma, I'll stay to lunch. Good music always gives me an appetite.'

'For what?' asked Fay.

'That's something you'd know nothing about,' he replied.

'That's what you think,' said Fay.

'Fay!' protested Mrs Hyams. 'Come and help me lay the table.'

Mother and daughter went into the kitchen. Lou sauntered to the window chewing on his cigar, hands in pockets, rattling his change.

Two urchins went past the window (which was on the street level) blowing lustily on mouth organs. They had knotted their handkerchiefs over their heads as protection against the teeming rain, but in odd and perverse contrast to this apparent desire to keep their heads dry they were getting their feet very wet by splashing ankle deep in a puddle which had formed in the gutter, owing to one of the drains being blocked. Drains in Bellington Street were always getting blocked.

Lou pushed up the window and put his head out.

'Hey!' he shouted. 'Come out of that puddle. Walk on the pavement.'

The two urchins looked round, snub-nosed and defiant.

'Garn,' said one, sticking out his tongue.

And the other made a rude noise with his lips.

IV

Rose Sandigate poured some whisky into a glass of hot milk.

'Drink that,' she said.

Tommy Swann was sitting at the kitchen table, wearing a suit of Mr Sandigate's flannel pyjamas, and one of his old working jackets. He had just eaten a hot meal prepared by Mrs Sandigate, and he had just shaved with Mr Sandigate's shaving set. He already looked fatter in the face. He sipped the whisky and milk.

'Then you'd better go upstairs into the bedroom and 'ave a sleep,' said Rose.

'What!' Tommy Swann stared at her.

'You'll be all right there,' she reassured him. 'Nobody'll know you're up there if yer don't snore. I'll lock the door and keep the key in my pinafore.'

'But suppose yer old man wants to 'ave a nap this afternoon?'

''E'll nap on the sofa in the front room. 'E never goes up ter the bedroom, I tell yer, except at night. Tonight, when 'e goes out to the pub you can come down agin.'

'And then what?'

'Gawd knows.' Mrs Sandigate shrugged her plump shoulders. 'You should 'ave thought of that when you did a bunk. Although I dessay I can put a few blankets in the shed for yer, and I'll find yer a few clothes. But tomorrer you'll 'ave to 'op it.'

He swallowed the last drains of the milk and whisky and followed her up the stairs to the bedroom. She pulled back the bedclothes and he relaxed on the soft mattress with a luxurious sigh. He closed his eyes.

'I fergit the last time I slept on a bed like this,' he said.

She sat on the side of the bed. She, too, sighed, but not with the softness of the bed. She was used to that. She sighed because this scarecrow of a man was Tommy Swann – her hero. This was the smart young fellow who had ordered drinks all round the bar in West End clubs. The tough young blade with shampooed hair and a diamond prop in his striped tie. The swaggering gallant with his thumbs in his waistcoat armholes. The smart boy. The wide guy. The feller who ate policemen between two slices of toast. Fugitive from justice skulking in her backyard.

'What a fool you are, Tommy,' she said softly.

He looked up at her from the pillow.

'What d'you mean?'

'You know what I mean. When I first met you I thought you were such a smart feller. And what 'ave you bin doing since? Spending 'alf your life in prison.'

He took her hand.

'Do yer really care, then, Rose?'

'Course I care, Tommy. You know that. Otherwise you wouldn't 'a' come 'ere, would yer?'

He nodded.

'I suppose that's so,' he said. 'D'you love me, Rose?'

'I've always loved yer, Tommy.'

'Gawd, Rose.'

He put both his arms round her and pulled her bulky weight down towards himself.

'Rose,' he said hoarsely. 'I bin in the Moor since the Christmas before last.'

She pulled herself free and straightened her pinafore.

'Tommy, I got the dinner to cook.'

She went out, locking the door, dropping the key into the pocket of her pinafore. She went slowly down the stairs, breathing huskily, her face flushed.

As she reached the passageway the street door opened and Doris came in, holding a bunch of daffodils.

'You're back early,' said Rose, suspiciously.

'Yes, I missed John, and as it's still raining I came home.'

'Where d'you git the flowers?'

'Off a stall. Where would you like them? In the front room?'

'Gaw on, don't pretend yer bought 'em for me. Put 'em where yer like.'

Doris pouted. Her gift had not been received with any noticeable enthusiasm. Unwrapping the white tissue paper, she decided the flowers would look best in the front room. She went to look for a vase. None of those available appealed to her. Daffodils, to look their best, should be put in a nice, slinky sort of vase. Then she remembered the long, green and amber glass one upstairs in her parents' bedroom.

She ran quickly up the stairs, still holding the flowers. The bedroom door was locked. She rattled the handle to and fro, a puzzled frown on her face.

'Mum!' she called over the banisters.

''Ullo,' answered her stepmother from the depths of the kitchen.

'Your bedroom door's locked.'

'What abaht it? Can't I lock me own bedroom door if I want to?' Rose's angry voice floated huskily up the stairs.

'Nosey little bitch,' she was adding under her breath. 'She would go sticking 'er nose in where it's not wanted.'

'But I wanted to get the green vase!' pleaded Doris.

''Tain't in there.'

'Yes, it is.'

'No, it ain't.'

'It is. I noticed it this morning when I brought the tea in. You've got some artificial flowers in it.'

'Well, let 'em stay there. And you come dahn 'ere and find another vase. Come on, come dahn this minute.'

Slowly, Doris came down the stairs. She found another vase and went into the kitchen to fill it with water. Her face had a puzzled frown as she looked at her stepmother. Mrs Sandigate did not look at her stepdaughter. She was bending down, her face hidden in the half-open oven door, from which wafted the fatty smell of roasting beef.

Upstairs, Tommy Swann was trying to make himself flatter than a pancake, the bedclothes pulled up over his head, his pulse racing, perspiration trickling down his nose.

Half-an-hour later Vi came in, with her eyes full of smiles and her arms full of gramophone records in brown paper carriers. She went straight into the front room and pulled out the old portable gramophone from beneath the sofa. Mr Sandigate had obtained it some years ago by smoking Kensitas cigarettes. Nowadays it was rarely used. Vi dusted it off, and in a few seconds the whole house was filled with the sound of moaning saxophones, bleating crooners and the sweet shrills of violins.

Vi sat down on the sofa to listen. She was happy. She was enjoying herself to the utmost. The saccharine music and the love-sick rhymes stirred her pleasure-loving senses profoundly. As she listened she chewed sweets, and between chewing sweets she smoked a cigarette. She listened with her eyes half-closed and a smile on her pouting lips. Now and again she would get up to put on another record, then relax back on to the sofa, her shapely legs curled and her skirt slipping up, so that her suspender clips were visible on the tops of her stockings and above that an inch of bare leg.

Doris came in.

'Where d'you get the records?'

'Boyfriend,' said Vi casually, her jaws clamping on a caramel.

'Same one who brought you home last night?'

'That's my business.'

'All right, snappy. It doesn't matter to me, anyway.'

'Why ask, then?'

'I won't ask again, don't worry.'

'I shouldn't. Anyway, I don't do wiv crooks.'

'What do you mean – crooks?'

'That Johnny Price you go wiv.'

'He's not a crook. How dare you say that!'

'His brother Alfie's a crook. Everybody knows that.'

'What his brother does is nothing to do with John. He can't help it. You might as well say I get drunk just because you come 'ome at four o'clock in the morning blind drunk.'

'Why, you rotten little bitch! That's it, shout! Shout, so that Rose can 'ear.'

'I wasn't shouting. You don't like the truth, do you?'

'Oh, shut up! You're only jealous.'

'*Wa'ercress!*' shouted a man in the street. '*Lovely wa'ercress. Shrimps. Winkles.*'

'Do-ris!' Mrs Sandigate shouted from the kitchen. 'Go and git some watercress and a pint of winkles.'

'*How deep is the ocean?*' sobbed a voice from the soundbox of the gramophone. '*How high is the sky?*'

'An' tell 'im there was worms in the watercress last week,' shouted Mrs Sandigate.

Doris went to the street door and relayed the order to the man with the barrow. Then there came a clatter of feet up the steps, into the passage, down the stairs and into the kitchen, accompanied by a ceaseless stream of shrill, unconnected and unmusical notes from a mouth organ. Alfie was home.

His rain-soaked handkerchief knotted over his head, his socks down round his ankles, his boots squelching water, he stood on the kitchen mat, blowing and sucking with all the gestures and eye-rollings of a Larry Adler, but with less pleasing results.

'Where you bin?' Mrs Sandigate asked her darling child. 'Tike those boots orf! Go and dry yer 'ead. Where d'you git that mouth orgin?'

Vi, in the front room, had been in the act of changing a record. She went quickly into the kitchen. She stood at the door scratching the back of her leg, her eyes fixed on Alfie.

'Where d'you git it?' Mrs Sandigate was asking again.

'A man gave it to me,' replied Alfie, and blew another terrific note.

'What man?'

Mrs Sandigate had her hands on her vast hips. Vi was staring at Alfie as if trying to hypnotise him.

'What man?' repeated Mrs Sandigate.

'Shall I lay the table?' Vi asked quickly.

Mrs Sandigate stared at her.

'Gawd!' she ejaculated. ''Er Ladyship Hoity-Toity wants ter do some work. Wonders'll never cease.'

To Vi's great relief, Alfie seized the opportunity to dash through the kitchen door into his beloved playground, the backyard, where he began to march round and round, still puffing and sucking on his new toy, producing a veritable inferno of noise.

'Come in out of the rain!' scolded Mrs Sandigate.

'It's stopped,' replied Alfie.

'The grahnd's still soaking. Come in.'

Alfie continued playing and marching round and round to such an extent that any sensitive person might have been forgiven for screaming at the agony of noise this small child inflicted. But presently he stopped. There was a sudden hush. Then he spoke.

'O-oh, Mum,' he said.

'Now what yer want?'

'There's footmarks all over the garden, Mum.'

Mrs Sandigate dropped a plate. It shivered to fragments on a corner of the gas stove.

Doris, who had just come into the kitchen with the winkles and watercress, looked down at the smashed plate and then at her stepmother. Alfie came running in.

'Footmarks all the way up from the garden shed, Mum!' he said, breathless at his discovery.

'Oh, shut up, will yer!' Mrs Sandigate bawled at her only child with surprising ferocity. 'Course there's footmarks. I bin aht there to git the pegs in.'

'But these ain't your footmarks, Mum. They're like a man's.'

'Well, yer father's bin out there.'

'No, he ain't Mum. Not today he ain't.'

'Oh, shut up, will yer!' yelled Mrs Sandigate in a fury. 'Take those boots off, will yer! And dry yer 'ead before I knock it orf.'

Alfie began unknotting the handkerchief round his head.

'Wonder if it was a burglar, Mum,' he speculated.

'Shut up!' screamed Rose.

Doris was staring down at the patch of faded green lino between the doormat and the kitchen table. On the lino was the wet, muddy print of a man's boot.

Just then Mr Sandigate came in flushed with beer and darts victories. He had a bottle of Guinness in one hand and a quart bottle of ale in the other hand. The yellow paper flights of his darts protruded from the breast pocket of his blue Sunday suit. He put the bottles on the kitchen table.

'There's yer Guinness, Rose,' he said. 'You know a funny thing 'appened. I left all me money in me old trousers this morning. Don't know what made me do it. 'Ad to borrow a dollar orf the guv'nor at The Compasses. One of you kids go upstairs and bring dahn my old trousers.'

Mrs Sandigate had put a dish down quickly and was already at the door, wiping her hands on the hem of her pinafore.

'I'll go,' she said.

'No, let one of the kids go,' protested Mr Sandigate. 'You know the stairs puff you out.'

But Rose Sandigate was already halfway up the stairs.

'You kids are a lot of use!' growled Mr Sandigate, unscrewing the top of one of the beer bottles.

Doris had picked up a house flannel from under the sink and was swishing it over the floor in quick, nervous circles.

'I scrubbed this floor once this morning,' she grumbled. 'I wish some of you people would wipe your feet when you come in.'

Her knees on the kitchen floor, she heard a lock click upstairs. She strained her ears. She thought she heard a mumble of voices, but couldn't be sure. The lock clicked again. Mrs Sandigate came down, her husband's trousers dangling over her arm.

'Thanks, Rose,' said Mr Sandigate. 'You look 'ot. 'Ave a swig of this.'

'In a minute. I've got the greens to do.'

In the street a man was singing 'Mother Machree', sure sign that the public houses had just closed. Water poured from blocked gullies and gurgled in the drains. The grey roof slates shone like glass. Smoke belched from the squat red chimneys. Wireless aerials swayed gently in the breeze.

In the Sandigate kitchen, Doris threw the house flannel back under the sink where it fell with a splosh. Mr Sandigate took his jacket off and draped it over the back of a Windsor chair. Vi was sorting out knives and forks. Rose Sandigate was straining the vegetables.

'Dad,' said Alfie, 'there's a man's footmarks in the backyard. D'you fink it was a burglar?'

'Did you tell the man abaht the worms in the watercress, Doris?' Mrs Sandigate asked in an unnecessarily loud voice.

V

The law required that the street traders in Petticoat Lane ceased business at two o'clock on Sunday afternoon, but it took all the efforts of six hawk-eyed policemen, constantly patrolling to and fro, to see that the traders were all packed up by half-past two. There was far keener competition to take the last shilling than to take the first shilling. At stalls where two men were grafting, one would continue selling and inveigling the crowd while his colleague was packing the goods. The most surprising aspect was that packing up the goods and putting them on the barrow or in the suitcase, preparatory to departure, always took longer – considerably longer – than unpacking them and displaying them on the stall, preparatory to commencing the day's trading.

Morry Higham had enjoyed quite a rush of business, and most of the kerbside traders had already departed before he was able to close the shop door and go upstairs to lunch, first pocketing the contents of the till.

Perspiring freely, his collar and tie slackened, jacket over his arm, he combed his hair back with his fingers.

'Whew!' he said. 'Ith warm work.'

He sat down at the dining-table. He was rather surprised that there was no meal ready for him. Sadie was sitting at the window, her back towards him. The children were playing by the fireguard.

'Sadie,' he said.

She did not answer him. She continued to stare out at the falling rain, chin cupped in her hands, elbows resting on the window frame.

'Sadie!'

She turned her head and regarded him dispassionately from her sad, dark eyes over the small curved nose and full lips.

'What's for lunch, Sadie?'

'Nothing,' she said, and gazed out of the window again.

Morry stood up, his brow wrinkled.

'Sadie! What is the matter with you?'

A policeman's voice drifted up from the street telling a trader to clear up his rubbish before he departed. A motorcar back-fired.

'Sadie! What do you mean – nothing? There's food in the house.'

The clock at the Houndsditch Warehouse Company struck a quarter to three.

'Sadie!'

Morry was shouting now, in a thin, cracked voice. His face was suffused crab-pink. He banged his fist on the table and kicked a chair over. A baby began to cry. Sadie turned her head again.

'The children have had their lunch,' she said. 'If you want to eat, ask that *shiksa* to cook it for you.'

And she stared out of the window again. The veins stood out on Morry's forehead.

'Sadie!' he screamed.

'Don't you shout at me,' she spoke quietly, without looking at him.

He walked to the window and stood over her, his narrow chest heaving under the coloured poplin shirt. His fingers clenched and unclenched.

'You'll be sorry if I lose my temper.'

'Go ahead – lose it!'

She got up and walked past him to attend to the crying baby. Then she walked out of the room holding a soiled napkin.

'You'll be sorry for this!' he shouted after her. 'You'll be sorry for this.'

Muttering to himself, he went to the Easiwork in the kitchen and got out a loaf of bread and some cold meat. He put them on the dining-table and began to cut the bread. The knife slipped, and with a howl he jerked his hand away, the top of his thumb gushing blood.

In mingled pain and fury he hurled the knife across the room. It knocked off the head of a little green plaster Aphrodite and then fell into the fireplace a few inches from where the children were playing.

Morry's face had taken on a sickly hue, like that of a man forced to watch an amputation of one of his own limbs. Clasping his monogrammed handkerchief round his thumb he called out weakly, 'Sadie, Sadie, I've cut myself.'

Sadie reached for the iodine and a roll of bandage.

VI

The freckle-faced boy who collected the paper money clattered down the steps at number 17 Coronet Grove. This brought him on a level with the basement window and the door of the coal cellar. Old Mrs Willis always insisted on him calling this way instead of at the front door. Otherwise his muddy feet dirtied the front steps which, rain or shine, were always snowy white.

He rapped on the window. There was no reply. He rapped again. There was still no reply.

He peered into the window. The fire was alight in the room, and there was a white cloth on the table, which was laid for two people. He could see the food steaming on the plates.

There were two chairs at the table, one of them empty. In the other sat Mrs Willis, a knife in one hand, a fork in the other.

Something about her attitude attracted the boy's attention. She slumped forward – motionless. The steam from the plate was wreathing about her head. He tapped on the window.

'Mrs Willis!' he called.

There was no response.

'*Mrs Willis!*'

Now this paper boy, like most freckle-faced boys, was an enthusiastic Boy Scout, and having plenty of juvenile initiative as well as a mind prepared – in fact, looking for emergencies – he climbed through the window.

'Mrs Willis,' he said.

The fire crackled in the grate. A little Dutch clock ticked on the mantelpiece. Above the clock was a large coloured photograph of a youth in khaki in a gilt oval frame. On the mantelpiece were several smaller photographs of the same youth, depicted at various ages. There was a musty, old-lavender-mixed-with-mothball smell about the room.

'Mrs Willis, are you all right?'

No, obviously she isn't all right, this intelligent boy thought to himself. A fainting fit, perhaps. Mentally, he began to repeat to himself the textbook instructions regarding *Shock, Fainting (Syncope), Collapse, Symptoms And Treatment Of.*

Putting a hand on the old lady's forehead he raised her head and looked into her face. He was surprised to find her eyes open.

'Mrs Willis, are you all right?'

Her eyes just stared at him. Not a blink. Not a quiver of a lash. Funny. They were like the eyes of a doll – glassy, unseeing.

Then the realisation dawned upon him. His self-control fled. He released his hold, and the body of Mrs Willis slipped sideways and fell to the floor.

The freckle-faced boy ran into the street, shouting.

'Mrs Willis is dead,' he babbled. 'Mrs Willis is dead.'

'Wa'ercress!' shouted a man with a barrow. *'Shrimps! Winkles! Wa'ercress!'*

And a man in a bowler hat and a white muffler stopped singing 'Mother Machree' to be sick in a drain. A dog sniffed a lamp-post. From within the houses came the chink of cutlery and the rattle of plates. Coronet Grove was having its Sunday dinner. The freckle-faced boy ran to look for a policeman.

CHAPTER 5

I

Between the hours of two and five on Sunday afternoon a vast peace descends upon the streets of London. Nearly seven million sets of teeth, a high percentage of which provide a remarkable demonstration of the efficiency of the modern dental workshop, are busily masticating, or, having masticated, the corresponding seven million stomachs which are biologically natural, no satisfactory stomach having so far been evolved in a laboratory or workshop, are somewhat less efficiently digesting the most formidable meal of the week. The few people seen in the streets are mere stragglers, flotsam and jetsam without homes, youths hanging round snack bars and billiards saloons, with here and there decrepit old men teetering down suburban roads, singing hymns to blank-windowed houses, sometimes to the accompaniment of a squeaking harmonium, while bored policemen stand in shop doorways or walk in seemingly endless circles.

Peace had descended to Coronet Grove. And the peace that comes with deep slumber had taken Tommy Swann. He slept the sound sleep of a physically exhausted man. In the same house George Sandigate was also sleeping. His mouth was open and he snored with perfect rhythm, blissfully unconscious that his home was sheltering a fugitive from justice.

Mr Sandigate was sleeping on the sofa. Opposite him, Mrs Sandigate was curled up in a wickerwork armchair. She was reading, or making a pretence of reading, a *True Love Romance*. Doris Sandigate was in the back kitchen having a bath. Vi was up in the girls' bedroom making up her face. She was meeting Morry Higham at five o'clock at Gardiner's Corner. He was driving down to Brighton on business, and thrillingly she had agreed to accompany him.

As she shaped her lips and surveyed her face she felt pleased with life. A warm glow of physical anticipation surged within her body. She knew what would happen on that car ride. At last she was beginning to live. She was now a woman of the world. Tonight, when most girls she knew would be lining up for the pictures, parading the Whitechapel Road, jostling boys in amusement arcades, or flirting in dark doorways, afraid to go too far in case a policeman's torch was flashed on you suddenly. No more of that furtive doorway stuff for Vi Sandigate. Tonight she would be in a band-leader's car, flashing along the Brighton road, his arm round her waist. Going to Brighton on a Sunday night just as if it were no more than a penny tram-ride along Commercial Street. It was marvellous.

Presently Doris came into the room. She was wearing a Marks And Spencer's dressing-gown in black and pink. She held a towel in one hand and her underclothes in the other. Her pale face and body were flushed from the hot bath, and the pores of her skin were glistening. She sat on the side of the bed, shook her yellow hair down over her eyes and began to dry it.

'By the way, what's diction?' Vi asked suddenly.

Doris stared at her. It seemed an odd question.

'Well, it's the way you talk,' said Doris.

'What yer mean, the way you talk?'

'Well, aitches and things like that. You know, talking nicely, like the announcers on the wireless. Why?'

'Oh, nothing. I jus' wondered.'

And she went on shaping her mouth. So that was it! That was what Morry meant by improving her diction. She was totally unaware that her own voice carried a twang and whining drawl that would have been abhorrent to sensitive ears. She was occasionally aware that she had failed to sound an aspirate, and for the next minute or two would endeavour to talk with a sort of mincing delicacy that was even worse. She was also aware that Doris had a much nicer manner of speech (although hers was far from perfect), and this annoyed her not a little. She was convinced that Doris 'put on' her talk. It was all swank. If Doris could do it, so could she.

'Going out?' Doris asked.

'Course I'm going out,' said Vi, scorning the very idea that she would be without a socially important engagement on a Sunday evening.

She had intended to keep her rendezvous a thrilling secret, but her inordinate vanity, always paramount, was too strong. She must tell somebody.

'I'm going to Brighton,' she said.

'Brighton!'

'Yes, Brighton. I told you, Brighton.'

'What you going to Brighton for?'

'Just for a run. My boyfriend's got some business there. I'm going in 'is car.'

'Oh!'

Vi's announcement seemed to have received a flat reception. She was annoyed, and jabbed at her mouth with the lipstick.

'Do-ris!'

Mrs Sandigate's voice drifted up the stairs.

'Hullo!'

'Yer father wants a cuppa tea.'

'Oh, all right.'

'Damn.' Vi had smudged the shaping of her lips. 'I can't see properly in this glass.'

She crossed the landing to her stepmother's bedroom, intending to use the dressing-table mirror in that room, as it was provided with a better light. She turned the handle. The door did not budge.

'What the –' she muttered, and then called out, 'Mum, your bedroom door's locked.'

From the depths of the house Rose Sandigate swore with exasperation. She was glad Mr Sandigate was still snoring and had not heard Vi's shout. Panting, cursing, Rose Sandigate climbed the stairs. Vi was still rattling the handle of the bedroom door.

'Your bedroom door's locked,' she repeated.

Rose Sandigate came to the top of the stairs and stood, framed for a second against the fading light from the landing window, an untidy curl of copper hair over her shoulders, a fat white hand resting for support against the banisters, her large bosom heaving beneath the coloured pinafore, her lips parted.

'Whassit to do wiv you if me door's locked?' she demanded.

'I want to use the mirror,' said Vi.

'Use yer own bleeding mirror,' replied Rose. 'Come on, get aht of it.'

Vi stood there, uncomprehending. With all her faults, Rose had never acted in this way before. Vi was baffled, and she had never been a girl to accept complacently a decision she could not understand. She uttered a whining protest.

'But why can't I use your mirror?'

'Come aht of it, I said,' and Rose Sandigate reached forward and caught Vi by the neck of her dress and pulled her away from the door. There was a sharp rending sound as the cheap fabric split down almost to the waist.

Vi looked down in mingled astonishment and rage at her ruined dress. As the elder of the two sisters, she had been more or less immune in the past from Rose's frequent outbursts of temper, which were usually directed at the more tractable Doris.

'My dress!' wailed Vi. 'Look 't my best dress. Look 't it!'

She pointed at the gaping aperture, the fabric hanging loose revealing her young breasts socketed in a pink brassiere. Tears of temper brimming to her eyes, she lifted the torn cloth and then, realising the futility of it ever being restored to its original shop-window modishness, stamped her foot and grasping the torn edges of the dress completed the damage which her stepmother had started. Vi tore her dress into two pieces, screwed one piece into her hands and threw it into the face of Rose Sandigate.

'You've torn it, you can 'ave it!' she wailed. 'You rotten fat cow!'

'What did you call me?' shrieked Rose Sandigate. 'What did you call me?'

'You 'eard. You 'eard. You rotten fat cow, you!'

Rose Sandigate, her face darkened with anger, dug her podgy fingers into her stepdaughter's fair hair and pulled her closer. Then she smashed the back of her hand across the girl's face. Vi staggered, lost her balance and fell backwards down the stairs. Her head cracked against the banister rail as she went down.

'I'll show yer,' panted Rose, standing at the top of the stairs, her bosom heaving, long wisps of Vi's yellow hair clinging to her podgy fingers.

'I'll show yer. I'll show yer, me lady. Call me a fat cow, would yer? I'll skin yer. I'll show yer.'

Vi was halfway down the stairs, kneeling. There was a bruise on her forehead, and her carefully painted lip was already beginning to swell. She looked up at Rose Sandigate standing on the top stair, and a paroxysm of humiliated rage seized her. With both hands she began to tear at the worn green linoleum on the staircase. Then she stood up, her mouth set, one half of her body clad in the remains of her best Sunday frock, the other naked except for pink brassiere and brief pink knickers. In her hand she held a brass stair-rod. She ran up the stairs.

'Vi!' screamed Doris. 'Don't!'

She rushed forward into the fray, her hands outstretched to pull the stair-rod from her sister's grasp. In the dim light of the landing the thin strip of brass whirled to and fro, round and round, up and down, like a flash of lightning imprisoned in that dingy house.

Behind the wardrobe door crouched Tommy Swann, clad in a suit of Mr Sandigate's flannel pyjamas. Downstairs, Mr Sandigate opened his eyes, listened with a puzzled frown to the confusion of sounds and feminine screams from upstairs, then got off the sofa and walked to the kitchen door.

'What's all the bloody row abaht?' he shouted up the stairs.

'Vi! Vi!' Doris was screaming. 'Let go of it!'

'I'll kill 'er!' Vi screamed back.

'Yer would, would yer, yer little bitch!' Rose Sandigate's scream was louder than the other two. 'I'll show yer. I'll put paid ter you, me lady. I'll skin yer before I'm done with yer.'

With a sigh, Mr Sandigate began to climb the stairs. Downstairs, the kettle was on the boil and the watercress, green and fresh, was spread out in a blue-and-white bowl. The black cat purred before the fire. Ten thousand East End kettles were on the boil. Watercress, winkles and shrimps – tea-table triumvirate of green, black and pink spread out on best Sunday tablecloths. Spoons were digging into jars of Sunday jam. With renewed vigour, smoke belched from myriad chimneys. Rain dripped from the grey-blue roof slates. A tinkling bell sounded through dismal streets as the muffin man went his round, tray wobbling, but never falling from his grey head. *Ting-a-ling. Ting-a-ling. 'Muff'ns. Fresh muff'ns.' Ting-a-ling.* A corner of the coloured poster on the advertisement hoarding at the end of Coronet Grove flapped in the wind. It was Sunday teatime.

At the top of the stairs Mr Sandigate was startled to see the three womenfolk of his household struggling for the possession of a brass stair-rod.

They were all screaming hysterically. Vi's clothes were torn down to her waist.

Being a practical man, his first step was to get possession of the stair-rod. He did this by hitting both his daughters over the ear in quick succession, so that they fell against the wall. He then pushed his wife so that she sat down abruptly. He then picked up the stair-rod.

'What's it all about? You all gone bloody mad, or what?'

'Look what she did to my dress!'

'Lying little bitch; she did it herself.'

'She knocked me down the stairs.'

'Yerce, and I'll knock yer down again. I'll teach yer.'

'You just try!'

'I'll teach yer to call me a rotten fat cow.'

The shrill reproachments and recriminations were hurled to and fro by Mrs Sandigate and her stepdaughter, Vi Sandigate.

Doris said nothing. She got up and leaned against the banister, nearly weeping.

Mr Sandigate looked at Vi, realising for the first time, perhaps, that his daughters were grown up.

'You'd better get some clothes on.'

'I ain't got no clothes now,' Vi wailed. 'She tore my best dress.'

'Go and get some bloody clothes on, before I lam yer!' he bellowed.

Vi went sulkily into the bedroom. Doris followed her. Mrs Sandigate was still sitting where her husband had pushed her.

'Come on, get up, Rose.' He extended a hand to assist her to her feet.

Rose Sandigate suddenly recollected that it was her own

husband who had pushed her over. Once again her voice shrilled through the little house.

'Keep away from me, George Sandigate! Take yer hands away from me.'

'Now, come on, Rose.'

'I'll 'ave you in court tomorrer for assault, that's what I'll do!' she screamed.

Behind the locked door of the Sandigates' bedroom Tommy Swann was hastily dressing in one of Mr Sandigate's old suits. As far as he was concerned, the situation was fraught with extreme danger. Any minute now Mr Sandigate might demand to know the reason why the bedroom door was locked.

In preparation, Tommy Swann picked up a long brass poker from the fireplace. If the old fool came blundering in, Tommy wouldn't waste any time in arguing. He put the poker in a convenient spot and proceeded to lace up a pair of Mr Sandigate's heavy boots.

From outside he heard Mr Sandigate's voice, 'What was all the shemozzle about, any'ow?'

Rose's powerful voice again filled the house.

'I told you, ain't I? She called me a rotten fat cow, and you stand for it, don't yer? Course, I know yer bloody kids always came before me. I'm just the bleeding char. D'you 'ear me?'

Her voice rose to a shrieking pitch.

Mr Sandigate sighed and went into the girls' bedroom. Vi was putting on her second-best frock. Doris was sitting on the bed, looking very white.

'What was the trouble about, Doris?' he asked.

Doris looked up and shook her head dumbly. Vi, standing by the lopsided mirror of the wardrobe, pulled down her skirt and swung round.

'I wanted ter use 'er mirror but the door was locked, and when I asked 'er why, she grabbed 'old of me dress and tore it.'

'Well?'

Tears crept into Vi's voice.

'Ain't that enough? It was me best dress.'

'Then what happened?'

'She knocked me down the stairs.'

'And what did you do?'

Vi hesitated and turned to pout at her own reflection in the mirror, behind which she could see her father's reflection – a red-faced, stocky apparition, with shirt-sleeves rolled up over hairy forearms, a strip of brass in his right hand.

'Well, what did yer do?' he persisted.

Vi pouted again. Her voice welled up with tears of self-pity.

'She shouldn't 'ave torn me best frock.'

Mr Sandigate moved nearer to his daughter. Vi edged away.

'I don't care what she shouldn't 'ave done. What did *you* do?'

Vi made no reply. She stood in front of the lopsided wardrobe mirror, fastening the catch at the neck of her frock.

'Yer going ter tell me or not?' he asked.

'I didn't do nothin',' Vi wailed.

Mr Sandigate grabbed his daughter by the shoulder and spun her round so that she faced him. He held up the brass stair-rod.

''Ow did this get in yer 'and?' he asked.

Vi gulped.

'She – she was goin' ter 'it me with it – and I tried to stop 'er.'

At this the bedroom door was flung open and Rose Sandigate came in, her face flushed, fury in her eyes, her copper hair dishevelled, one lock of it hanging down over her shoulder, one hand rubbing her tender buttocks.

Without speaking, she moved slowly round the room to where Vi was standing. Mr Sandigate's arm barred her further progress.

Rose Sandigate turned on him.

'That's it! Protect yer darling daughter.'

'Shut up!'

'I won't shut up. Did you 'ear what she just said, the lying little cow. She'd swear away yer life. So I was gonna 'it yer wiv the stair-rod, was I – was I? And I suppose you believe the little bitch, eh?'

Her voice rose to a shrill crescendo. She pushed her red, flaming face to within an inch of her husband's. Shining globules of moisture clung to her open mouth as she repeated the question.

'And I suppose you believe the little cow?'

It was now Mr Sandigate's turn to shout.

'Did I say I believed her?'

'No, you wouldn't. You wouldn't commit yerself; but wait till I get yer in court tomorrer morning.'

'Now you're being silly,' said Mr Sandigate. 'Plain, bloody silly.'

'That's it, swear at me now!'

'Will you shut up screaming, or do you want all the neighbours to 'ear?'

Her voice rose again.

'I don't care who 'ears me. I'll tell 'em what sort of an 'usband I've got. Driving me to me grave, that's what you're doing.'

'Shut your mouth, or I'll shut it for you.' Mr Sandigate was now thoroughly angry.

Rose Sandigate was opening her mouth to scream again when the back of her husband's hand swept across her face, sending her spinning. There was a protesting squeak from the mattress as her vast weight collapsed on to the bed. There she gave a howl of grief, and, face downwards on the bed, she began to sob, her shoulders heaving.

George Sandigate, his face drained of colour, looked at his two daughters – the sulky Vi and the white-faced Doris. He nodded towards the door.

'Get out – the two of yer!'

'But this is our room,' Vi protested.

'Oh, come on, Vi,' Doris pleaded from the door.

'I don't see why we should 'ave to clear out of our own room,' Vi protested.

Mr Sandigate suddenly raised his arm. The brass stair-rod flashed, and Vi screamed as it cut her across the fleshy part of her thigh.

'Now get out!' shouted Mr Sandigate. 'Get out!'

They went out – Doris without speaking a word; Vi howling and with one hand clasped round her thigh.

Mr Sandigate sat on the bed beside his wife, whose sobbing convulsions caused the mattress to provide a creaking theme song as a background for the lachrymose scene in that dim, dingy room. While pictures of film stars looked down from the faded wallpaper.

He placed his hand gently on her shoulder.

'Rose.'

She sobbed all the louder and sniffed. 'Don't Rose me.'

II

Peace had even descended, like one of its own grey blankets, on Spry's Hotel. The paying guests had departed for the day, all except Henry, the big negro, who, being a privileged person, was still in the kitchen, humming 'Ol' Man River' as he lathered his black face.

'Ned!' It was Maria Spry calling. She was reclining in bed in her own room, a room dingy enough, but a luxurious boudoir when compared with the other rooms. The lace curtains had been washed within the last three months, at any rate. There was a carpet on the floor. Perhaps it hadn't been brushed for a long time, but it was still a carpet. There were pictures on the walls – *Brighton Aquarium In 1890, The Little Soldier, HMS Repulse, Rounding The Horn, A Good Catch* and *Beefeaters At The Tower*. It is true the pictures were festooned with cobwebs, and it would have been necessary to make a close inspection to decide which lines belonged to the pictures and which belonged to the cobwebs. However, some maintain that there is an old-world charm about cobwebs.

Maria Spry's hair might have been a profusion of cobwebs, hanging as it did down her neck and over her eyes. Those eyes were bleary with gin. She had been drinking the stuff all the morning, and as Ned Spry came in she was pouring out the last dregs of the bottle.

''Ullo,' he said.

He stood by the door, pail in hand, surveying her sullenly. The bitch was drunk again, he thought.

She poured the last of the gin into her slack mouth and threw the empty glass at him. It missed him by a yard and splintered against the wall.

'Don't stand there scowling at me,' she screamed.

'What d'you want?'

'Git some 'ot water ter soak me feet. Me corns 'urt.'

Ned Spry went out of the room and returned some minutes later with a bowl of hot water. Maria Spry sat on the side of the bed, pulled her nightdress up around her thighs, and put her large feet into the water. She sat thus for ten minutes soaking her feet. On Sundays even the great unwashed sometimes wash.

'Now cut me toenails.'

Ned Spry got a pair of scissors and cut her toenails. It was entirely Maria's fault that she moved one of her feet and the sharp scissors dug into the soft flesh of her little toe.

With a howl of pain and fury she pulled her foot back and then shot out her huge leg and kicked her dwarf-like husband full in the face.

He went over backwards, turning a complete somersault like a music-hall acrobat, the bowl of hot water going with him. He struck his head on the corner of the wardrobe, and for some minutes sat on the floor, dazed. Blood poured from his nose. He sat there, wiping it with his sleeve and the tip of his tongue.

Maria Spry sat on the side of the bed, her right foot curled up in her lap as she nursed her sore toe.

'Wicked little bastard,' she murmured to herself. 'Did it for the purpose 'e did. I might'a'known. Wicked little bastard . . .'

Then she looked at him, sitting on the floor by the wardrobe, drenched with water, a bump on his head, blood flowing from his nose. She forgot all about her own pain. She began to laugh, jeering and pointing at him.

'Serves yer right, yer little bleeder. Dig scissors in me, would yer? I'll show yer.'

Then Ned Spry got to his feet. His small eyes narrowed in his ugly head. He walked to the bed and picked up the empty gin bottle. He brandished it in the air and leered at Maria. She shrank back.

'You'll show me, will yer, you big fat cow? For twenty bloody years you've treated me like a dog in me own 'ouse. Ned, do this, and Ned, do that. Jus' now you kicked me like a dog, didn't yer? Now I'm gonna show you something, see. I'll take you apart, you great, big, fat whore.'

He moved nearer, breathing heavily, brandishing the gin bottle over his head. She held up her hands to cover her face.

'Ned!' she pleaded. 'Ned, darling.'

He laughed.

'So it's Ned, darling, now, is it? I'll give yer Ned, darling. You've 'ad this coming for a long time.'

She cowered back against the wall on the far side of the bed. She watched him coming nearer, the gin bottle swinging over his head. He grasped the counterpane of the bed, and for a brief second seemed to hesitate. In that second she regained her self-control.

'You dare touch me, Ned Spry! You dare! And I'll tell 'em! Yerce, I'll tell 'em! You can't kill me like yer killed Manchester Taffy. People'd miss me. Nobody missed pore old Manchester Taffy. Killed 'im fer his money yer did. Kep' me mouf shut all these years I 'ave, but I ain't keeping it shut any longer. *Murderer!*'

She was now screaming to the fullest extent of her powerful lungs, pressing both her hands into her balloon-like breasts, above which her veins stood out like blue whipcord.

'Murderer! You'll swing yet! It won't take much of a drop fer a bleeding little dwarf. But you'll swing all right. I'll see to that.'

The effect on Ned Spry was one of complete transformation. He lowered his arm and dropped the bottle to the floor. The rage had departed from his small, pig-like eyes. He returned to the role he had suffered for over twenty years. A despised lackey in his own dosshouse. A grunting, sullen monstrosity. A performer of menial tasks; kicked, ridiculed and bullied. Fear gleamed in his eyes. The fear of The Thing that Maria had held over his ugly, dwarf's head for nearly a quarter of a century.

'Maria!' he pleaded. 'Maria! Be quiet, please, before somebody 'ears you. Maria, please, they'll 'ear you. Oh, Maria! I didn't mean it. 'Onest, I didn't. Maria, please, I'll do anything. But don't tell 'em. Maria, they'll 'ang me!'

She stopped screaming to burst into a fit of drunken laughter.

'Yerce, they'll 'ang you all right. Don't worry abaht that. They'll 'ang you, little man.'

'Oh, Maria! Maria!'

Tears brimmed into his eyes.

'Ha, ha, ha! Look at 'im! Going to take me apart, was you, eh?'

'Maria!'

'Go and git me a cuppa tea.'

'Certainly, Maria. Certainly.'

He turned to do her bidding with eagerness. She relaxed on the bed again, smiling to herself. She groped under the pillow for a packet of cigarettes.

Ned came back with the tea. He put the tray on a bedside table.

'Call 'Enry,' she said.

Ned Spry went to the door and called down the stairs. Henry, the negro, came up grinning.

'What's going on here?'

He stood by the door, six foot tall, wide-shouldered and narrow-hipped, in a blue jersey and dirty grey flannels.

'Nothing,' said Maria. 'Come in and 'ave a cuppa tea.'

'I sure will,' he nodded, coming into the room, rubbing his hands, his teeth showing in an expansive grin.

Maria turned to Ned Spry.

'And you get out!' she shouted.

'Yeah, little man, you get out,' said Henry, and with the back of his hand knocked him spinning through the doorway.

Then he shut the door. Ned Spry went slowly down the creaking stairs. Henry went and sat on the side of the bed. It creaked with his weight. Maria Spry was pouring out the tea.

III

Alfie Price, Whitey Williams and Dicey Perkins stood on the top step of a house in Coronet Square. It was rather a large house. In fact, it was two houses knocked together to combine both the domestic and business life of Mr Caleb Beasley, the honorary organist at St Saviour's and zealous church worker.

Across the entire frontage of the upper half of the two houses was a large, cream-painted board, upon which bright-red lettering announced *CF Beasley* to be a *Painter, Decorator And Sanitary Engineer.* It also told the world that the said CF Beasley undertook house renovations of all descriptions, and that estimates were free.

Messrs Price, Williams and Perkins, however, had not called to discuss house renovations with Mr Caleb Beasley. The paint-work of their respective abodes might be blistered, but that did not worry them. They were quite satisfied with the sanitary arrangements of the houses in which they lived. Neither had they called to take an interest in Mr Beasley's ardent church work, which had earned him his due meed of praise in the neighbour-hood, as well as a goodly number of contracts from the pious people connected with the church. No, none of these things interested Messrs Price, Williams and Perkins. Neither was it a social call.

When the front doorbell jangled in the hallway, Mr Beasley had just finished his Sunday dinner. (He was still sufficient of a plebeian to call it dinner and not lunch.) Sunday dinner in the Beasley home was a most solemn affair. First he lowered his head and said grace with a sonorous intonation that was quite a good imitation of the Rev Black's best pulpit style, joined in a respectful murmuring chorus by Mrs Beasley and the three Beasley daughters – Agnes, Edith and Emily.

Then he would tuck a serviette into his collar, pick up knife and fork and, with much grunting and clicking and squelching of his false teeth, would proceed to prove for the next half-hour that there is nothing like voluntary church work for giving a keen edge to the appetite.

So few visitors called at the Beasley abode on the Sabbath, that the ringing of the bell caused quite a flutter among the womenfolk. (Although the Beasley girls and their mother were so sedate that perhaps I ought not to call them 'womenfolk'. 'The ladies' would be more appropriate.) They were just collecting the dirty crockery when the bell rang, for although Mr Beasley could have afforded to employ a maid, he did not see why he should do so when he had three lanky daughters cluttering up the house. Incidentally, Caleb Beasley had a secret grievance against God about this matter. He felt that He might at least have given him one son whom he could have put into the business and saved the wages of a foreman, instead of three useless daughters.

'Why, I do believe that was the bell,' said Edith, who was twenty and had a perpetual sty on her eye and wore heavy beads that clattered as she walked.

'I'm sure it was the bell,' said Agnes, the eldest, who was twenty-nine, looked forty-nine, had red hands and was what the Americans call a sourpuss.

'It *was* the bell,' announced Mr Beasley, crushing this futile feminine speculation with his magnificent masculine certainty.

'Emily, go and see who it is,' he added.

'Yes, father,' said Emily, eighteen years old, the youngest of the trio and the most human of the family, but still a mouse-like creature, with her colourless hair parted in the middle and coiled over each ear.

She straightened the white lace collar on her dark-blue frock and went up the stairs. On the step were three young men in black trilby hats and white scarves. Quite rough-looking young men.

'Afternoon,' said Alfie. 'Mr Beasley in?'

'Yes, he is. But –'

'Tell 'im I'd like a word with 'im, please. Mr Price. Alf Price. He'll know.'

'Can you tell me what you wish to see him about, please?'

Alfie Price pushed his hat back and frowned, sucking his back tooth. Dicey Perkins fingered his nostril.

'Er – tell 'im it's about the drains in Great Mansell Street,' said Alfie.

'I'm sorry, but Mr Beasley never sees anybody about business on Sundays. You'll have to come to the office tomorrow morning.'

Alfie pushed his hat forward. His frown deepened.

'But this is perticularly important, see? It's imperative I see 'im s'afternoon, see?'

'Yerce,' said Whitey. 'Tell 'im it's im-per-ative. Special business. You tell 'im that.'

Alfie gave Whitey a look of annoyance.

'All right, Whitey. Can't you see I'm talking to the lady?' he said, and then addressed himself to Miss Beasley again.

'I'm sure Mr Beasley will see me if you tell 'im it's me, miss. Mr Price – Alf Price.'

'All right,' said Miss Beasley doubtfully. 'I'll see. Will you step into the passage and wait, please?'

'Thank you, miss,' said Alfie, accepting her invitation, Dicey and Whitey following.

Then Alfie took his hat off. Dicey and Whitey also took their hats off. Miss Beasley went to see if her father would care to disturb his Sabbath rest by according an interview to Mr Price – Alf Price.

There was a muttering of voices from the trio as she went down the stairs. Alfie Price was telling Whitey Williams not to interfere so much and to keep his ugly nose out of things in future. He, Alfie Price, was the mouthpiece of the trio, and intended to remain so.

'All right,' Whitey was muttering in the dim passage. ''Ave it yer own way. But there ain't no need to jump down a feller's throat. Rorting at me like that in front of that tart. Made me look a fair chump, you did.'

'Yer mother did that,' said Alfie contemptuously. 'Or yer father. I ain't sure which.'

Dicey picked his nose – giggled.

Just then Caleb Beasley came up the stairs. Mr Beasley's clothes, like his first name, belonged to a past age. He was invariably clad in a black cutaway coat and narrow black trousers. He wore a grey waistcoat with black pinstripes and pearl buttons, decorated with a heavy gold watch-chain, to which were attached a number of medallions, gold and silver coins and various insignia. He wore a high white collar, starched shirt-front and cuffs. When in the street he wore a black, chimney-pot hat, something a little more than a bowler and not quite a top hat. He was not, of course, wearing this now, and it was possible to see that his hair, although greying at the sides, was jet black in the centre. It was combed straight down to his forehead, and there was no suggestion of a parting. But the most ridiculous detail of his complete appearance was the black tie he wore knotted round his high collar. It was no wider than a shoelace.

He motioned the three men into the front parlour and closed

the door. If Messrs Price, Williams and Perkins had been in any doubt regarding the welcome they were about to receive, the doubt was short-lived.

Caleb Beasley's black eyes gleamed at them furiously from his thin, parchment-coloured face. His false teeth clicked as he spoke.

'What does this mean? How many times have I told you never to come to my 'ouse on a Sunday! If you want to see me you can see me at the office next door, weekdays. Or you can telephone to make an appointment to see me elsewhere; but to come to my 'ouse in broad daylight, Sunday afternoon . . . Do you think I want my 'ouse known as a rendezvous of gaol birds? Do you . . .'

Alfie held up his hand.

'Just a minute, Bee's Knees. Just a minute. Not so much of the gaol-bird stuff. You've been pleased enough to see us plenty of times in the past. All right, you don't want to see us any more. That's okay with us, and we'll take our business elsewhere. You ain't the only buyer in London.'

He thrust his hat on the back of his head and walked to the door, followed slowly by Whitey and Dicey. The other two could not help feeling that Alfie was taking too many liberties. After all, they needed Beasley's dough, and they needed it bad, and when you want a feller's dough you can't talk to him just as you please, no matter how sore you feel.

Caleb Beasley's prominent Adam's apple, crisscrossed with little red veins, bulged between the cleft of his collar. He put a yellow, claw-like hand on Alfie's sleeve.

'All right, boys,' he said. 'I'm sorry. I lost my temper. I can't afford to take risks, you know.'

'No, but we can, can't we?' sneered Alfie. 'That don't matter, do it?'

'All right, boys. We don't want to fall out over a few 'asty words, do we? As you're here, let me see what you've got.'

Alfie flicked his hat back, stroked his little moustache. Then he nodded to Dicey.

'Okay, Dicey. Show 'im.'

Dicey stopped fingering his nostril to take a somewhat bulky package from beneath his jacket. He unwrapped it, revealing a pair of boy's skates.

'We've got a gross of 'em. They sell at twelve-and-six a pair.'

Caleb Beasley was turning them over in his yellow hands. He went to the window and stood by the lace curtain, examining them in the serrated light.

'Very nice,' he said softly. 'Very nice indeed.' He shrugged his shoulders and handed them back to Dicey. He shook his head like a yellow-faced, black-polled parrot. 'My skating days are over. Don't waste my time. I can't use stuff like that.'

'You got rid of the toy pistols we sold you last Christmas,' said Alfie.

'Last Christmas, yes. That was different. There's a demand for almost anything at Christmas-time. Even so, I had them on my 'ands for ten days, and I can't afford to have anything on my 'ands.'

'But Mr Beasley, there's bound to be somebody who'll buy them. Kids are always buying roller skates, aren't they? If there wasn't a demand for them, nobody would make 'em.'

'Well, there it is. I'm sorry, but they're no use to me. Pleased to see you any time you've got something more interesting. Stones, old gold, furs, silk or even 'andbags – anything like that. Only too pleased.'

He ushered them towards the door. Dicey was wrapping up the skates.

'But, Mr Beasley, be fair. Christ, take the rough with the smooth occasionally. We 'ad to risk our liberty getting them. We can't pick and choose. You know we always give yer the first offer on anything we get. We're screwing a gaff at Chingford on Toosday night. It's a five-thousand-pahnd job. We only want something to tide us over.'

Caleb Beasley hesitated. He pursed his lips and tapped his fingernails thoughtfully against his white cuff.

'I really don't see what I can do,' he said slowly and softly, as if speaking to himself. 'I really don't. But if you boys are hard-pressed, I don't mind helping you out.'

'Ah, thanks, Mr Beasley.'

'What were you thinking of asking for these skates?'

'Well, we thought a couple of handfuls.'

'What did you say?'

Mr Beasley looked at them as if somebody had asked him to play 'Flat-Foot Floogie' on the church organ.

'Well, ten pahnd ain't much to ask for a gross, is it, Mr Beasley? They sell at twelve-and-a-kick a pair, and . . .'

'Yes, yes. You've told me all that. But, unfortunately, I haven't got a toy shop. I said I was prepared to help you boys out, from sheer good nature. And then you spoil yourselves by asking for fantastic sums. Really, I'm not a millionaire, you know.'

'Well, Mr Beasley, what would yer think of paying? We ain't unreasonable.'

'I couldn't possibly think of giving you more than three pounds at the most. Even then I'm not sure I ought to do that. I shall probably have the stuff left on my hands.'

Three pounds! Alfie looked at Dicey, and Dicey looked at Whitey. Three lousy oncers! Alfie sucked his tooth – a long, shivering suck. Whitey looked at the white knuckles on his hand.

There was a silence in the front parlour of the Beasley home. A shocked, stunned silence in that dim, airless room, with its cream lace curtains, its aspidistra plants in brass bowls, the Chinese lacquerwork screen in the fireplace, the green cushions on the black horsehair sofa, the harmonium in the corner and the religious texts on the walls.

'Well?' said Caleb Beasley.

The brim of Alfie's black hat tilted forward as he scratched the back of his head.

'Okay,' he said quietly. 'Three nicker it is.'

IV

In the CID office of Stepney police station, Detective-Sergeants Fothergill, Leech and Nicolson were drinking tea and smoking.

Smiling little Leech poured a liberal quantity of sugar from a blue Tate And Lyle packet into his lukewarm tea. It was his fourth cup.

'You know,' he said, 'I haven't had a Sunday off for six weeks.'

Detective-Sergeant Fothergill was writing a report.

'Indispensable, old man,' he said. 'Indispensable.'

'I had arranged to take the missis and the kids to Whipsnade today, too,' Leech continued. 'We went to bed early last night so as to be up early this morning, and I'm just taking my pants off when the telephone rings. It's the Old Man.'

'To say "nighty-night, God bless you",' put in Fothergill.

'"Leech," he says, "you'll have to come in tomorrow." "Why?" I asks. "There's a gentleman named Swann escaped from Dartmoor," he says. Did you ever hear anything so bloody silly?'

Fothergill blotted a page of his report and looked up, smiling over his fair moustache and babyish mouth.

'On the contrary, Leech, it strikes me as being bloody logical. Dangerous criminal escapes from Dartmoor. Hawk-eyed Leech, who has had dealings with said dangerous criminal in past, having derived exquisite pleasure from getting the bastard more than one lagging, and knowing every detail of his ugly clock, is ordered to report for Sunday duty. Mrs Leech and all the little Leeches may howl disapproval at being deprived of Whipsnade treat, but old man Leech must do his duty and join in Big Man Hunt.'

'Blimey, this tea's cold,' said Leech.

'Considering it's your fourth cup, old boy,' said Fothergill, 'you can't grumble. Give me a match, will you?'

Leech tossed over a box of Vestas.

'If he's in London,' said Leech, 'which I very much doubt, he would scarcely be fool enough to venture near the East End, where every flattie knows his face better than his own grandmother. I'll lay five-to-four-on that he makes for the Leeds district.'

'You never know,' said Fothergill, tossing back the matches. 'By the way, did you ever feel Alfie Price's collar?'

'The little feller with the Ronald Colman moustache? Sucks his teeth as he talks to you?'

'That's him. He works with Dicey Perkins and Whitey Williams. Alfie and Dicey aren't bad kids, although Alfie's a bit vain. But if anybody gets my goat it's that third-rate pug Whitey Williams. I'd love to smack him on the snoot.' He sucked his pipe. 'I will one day, too,' he added.

'What have they been up to?'

'I'm damned sure they did that job in Great Mansell Street last night, but I haven't got a damn thing to work on. There isn't a sniff of a print anywhere. The three of them were out all night, I know. But if I asked 'em what they were doing, they'd swear they were playing cards all night, or hanging round a coffee stall. They'd probably prove it, too.'

'Wasn't much of a job, was it?' asked Nicolson, a plump, sandy-haired young man who had his feet up on a desk and was reading an American magazine called *Ace Detective Yarns*.

'No, a load of roller skates. But the trouble is, the same gaff was screwed last Christmas, when a load of toy pistols went, and the stamps in the peter.'

'Roller skates,' murmured Leech. 'My eldest kid has been whining for a pair for his birthday.'

'If anybody offers you a pair cheap, let me know,' said Fothergill.

'I will not,' said Leech cheerfully. 'Ready, Freddy?'

Detective-Sergeant Nicolson took his feet off the desk and pushed the magazine into the drawer. He looked out of the window. It was still raining.

'Bloody fine weather for a manhunt,' he said.

V

Morry Higham, sitting in his car parked at the end of Leman Street, opposite Gardiner's Corner, glanced at the clock on the dashboard and then compared it with his wristwatch. Then he looked at the clock over Gardiner's Corner. There was a few minutes' discrepancy between each of these three timepieces, but the general result was that Vi Sandigate was more than half-an-hour late.

Morry was more than a little peeved. He had been looking forward to this trip. He knew just the right spot to stop the car when it got dark, a leafy alcove near the Brighton Old Road. Tempting as this prospect was, however, Morry wasn't waiting for more than half-an-hour for any woman, let alone a kid who couldn't speak King's English.

He switched on the engine and then cut it off again as he heard Vi Sandigate's voice.

'Sorry I'm late,' she said, slipping in beside him. 'Can I put this on the back seat?'

She twisted round and dropped a cheap fibre attaché case on to the back seat. He stared at the bag.

'Hey,' he said. 'We're not staying for the weekend.'

'I know.'

'Then what's the bag for?'

'I've left 'ome.'

'You've what?'

'Left 'ome.'

Morry looked at her and saw that her face was swollen, and that she had been crying. He had a sudden premonition of trouble ahead.

'What's wrong?' he asked.

'Oh, Morry!'

She turned to face him. The tears welled up in her eyes as she did so, and then, with a sob, she buried her face against his shoulder.

Much as Morry enjoyed her physical proximity, he wasn't so keen on it in these circumstances. But he found himself in duty bound to display a little sympathy. He put his arm round her.

'Vi'let, darling, what's wrong? Tell me.'

'O-oh, Morry, you will 'elp me, won't you?' she sobbed.

A startled look came into Morry's dark eyes.

'Why, yes, my dear, of course. But what is it all about?'

Vi moved her head so that she could look up into his eyes while she told him the lie. Violet Sandigate was no feeble sort of liar. Her lies sounded all the more convincing when she looked you in the eyes.

'They found out about last night,' she whispered.

'You mean – about us?'

She nodded. Her pretty face was wistfully puffy, and a tear trickled down the Tokalon face-powder.

Morry's face was tense.

'What did they find out exactly?'

'About me going wiv you.'

Morry pushed his hat back, dug his fingers into his wavy hair. This was too much. It was outrageous.

'But who told them?'

'My kid brother, the little sod, told them about seeing us in the shop today.'

'But that wouldn't prove anything about last night,' Morry protested.

'No, but it started my father off asking questions about where I'd been all night,' she lied.

'And you mean to thay you told him?'

Morry was astounded, appalled, but more than that, he was conscious of the chilling prospect of more unpleasant things to come.

'I don't see why you had to tell him,' he went on.

'But, Morry, he made me tell him!'

'Don't talk nonsense,' said Morry irritably. 'How could he *make* you tell him?'

Vi gave another gulp as another inspired lie came into her mind.

'He – he beat me with a stair-rod until I told him the truth.'

'I don't believe it.'

By way of answer, Vi pulled up her skirt, pulled down one leg of her knickers, and twisted round to show him an angry, blue-red weal across the white flesh.

'There! See! I've got marks like that all over me.'

Morry was appalled.

'But he mustn't do things like that. It's criminal. He'd get six months in gaol for that. You must go to the police at once.'

'Fat lot of good that'll do me,' said Vi. 'They'd probably say it served me right.'

Morry was suddenly struck by the thought of opening his shop one morning to be confronted by this demoniac Mr Sandigate brandishing a stair-rod. It was not a pleasant thought. When Morry spoke again, his voice was dry, painfully dry.

'Does he know where I live?'

Vi nodded.

Morry groaned.

'I'm ruined,' he said. 'Ruined!'

Vi adjusted her knickers and smoothed down her skirt. Then she turned on him.

'*You're* ruined,' she said. 'I *like* that. If you're ruined, what am I? And 'ow d'yer know I might not be going to 'ave a baby?'

'Now, listen,' said Morry. 'Don't meet trouble halfway. Don't invent trouble.'

'I ain't inventing nothing. Did I invent last night? And I'm not meeting trouble 'alfway,' Vi wailed. 'I've got it now. They've thrown me out, and they've torn me clothes up. What am I going ter do?'

'And what am I going to do when your old man comes round to my shop kicking up a row?' Morry demanded.

'Don't worry. He won't.'

'Eh?'

A lightness came into Morry's heart. Could it be that there would be no trouble from Mr Sandigate after all – no unpleasant scenes, no scandal? In the circumstances it seemed too optimistic, but the girl seemed sure of herself.

'He won't trouble you,' Vi repeated. 'He says it was probably my fault for throwing myself at every man I meet.'

'Oh, he said that, did he?'

'Yes, so you needn't be afraid.'

'I'm not afraid, but one must be circumspect.'

'Must be what?'

'Never mind. What are you going to do now?'

'Morry . . .'

Her voice was soft, coaxing.

'Well?'

'You've got to find me a room.'

'A room!'

Something in his tone exasperated her. She bit down on her mouth in suppressed rage, smudging the cheap lipstick.

'Yes, a room. One of those things people live in. Don't yer know?'

'But, my dear, why should I have to find you a room?'

Morry's tone was genuinely puzzled, not to say peeved. He failed to see under what obligation he was to find – and, what was more to the point, probably have to pay for – living accommodation for this girl whom he had not known twenty-four hours. Yet, even as his voice gave vent to the protestation within him, he felt his mood changing. Perhaps it wasn't such a bad idea, after all. A cheap furnished room somewhere, and the freedom to drop in to see her just when he felt that way inclined. It wasn't such a bad idea after all.

'Of course I'll get you a room, darling,' he said softly.

Instantly she relaxed. She was softer, more pliant. She had achieved her purpose. She moved into his arms. He felt the warmth of her body through the cheap fabric of her second-best frock.

'Will you really, Morry, darling?' she asked as softly and huskily as she knew how.

'Certainly I will.'

'You didn't seem too pleased about it just now.' Her voice was a soft, pouting reproach.

'I only thought it would be better for you to choose your own room,' said Morry. 'Women are much better than men at that sort of thing. I'd pay the rent, anyway. Don't worry, darling, I'll find you a room.'

'A nice room?'

'I'll do my best.'

'With a divan, 'lectric light, a bathroom and a gas stove? Perhaps even a kitchenette, eh?'

Morry nodded. He hoped this furnished room wasn't going to develop into a furnished flat. These girls who came from mean streets often had the most expensive imaginations.

'It's a pity you've got ter go to Brighton tonight,' Vi was saying.

'Why? I thought you wanted to come.'

'Yes; but if you didn't 'ave ter go, we could fix up a room somewhere right away, couldn't we?'

'Sunday night,' said Morry, 'is a funny night to go looking for furnished rooms.'

'I don't see 'ow Sunday night's any different to other nights,' said Vi, getting less compliant.

Morry switched on the engine again.

'All right, we'll find you a room tonight.'

Vi sighed contentedly as she leaned her fair head against his shoulder.

'Got a cigarette, Morry?'

'In my hip pocket.'

The rain splashed on the windscreen and the cracked windows as the little car hummed along the Whitechapel Road. Violet Sandigate was elated, content. She was saying farewell to Coronet Grove.

Chapter 6

I

And to this East End ferment on this rainy evening came a young man in a mackintosh, a shapeless trilby hat crushed down over his untidy, string-coloured hair, a cigarette drooping from his drooping lips. A young man with pale, codfish eyes. A young man who spoke with a tired, refined accent, but nevertheless chewed his fingernails and picked his teeth with the sharpened end of a matchstick. A young man with a perpetual sneer and a *blasé* outlook. Known to his colleagues as Slopey Collins.

He was nicknamed Slopey because he sloped forward from the hips as he went about his daily tasks. He was not, as this nickname might suggest, a gangster. He was not even a sneak-thief, except when it came to a question of news, and then he would steal the shirt off your back if he thought it was worth a paragraph. Slopey Collins was a newspaper reporter, and that is the only reason why he comes into this chronicle of events in mean streets.

Just about the same time that Mr Sandigate was climbing the stairs of his household to ascertain what all the hullaballoo was about, Slopey Collins was warming himself by sitting on the radiator that stood between the tape machines and the telephone booths in the reporters' room of the London *Daily Mercury*, which, as you all know, has a certified daily net sale of 1,725,356 copies.

Slopey had not the least idea that he was destined to play so momentous a part in the lives of an East End family that evening. True, he had glanced at the astrology feature, 'Let The Stars Guide You', in that day's issue of the *Sunday Mercury*, and had noted that 'a journey to the East will be discussed', but had not been greatly impressed. After all, he knew some of the guys who wrote these astrology features.

Slopey Collins had already turned in a couple of stories, and saw no reason why he shouldn't go home. On the other hand, he was wondering whether it would be worthwhile telephoning a girlfriend, who was a chorus girl and lived in Brixton. Deciding it was worthwhile, he went into the telephone kiosk and spun the dial for the number which he knew by heart.

'Hullo, Margie.'

A sugary voice gurgled in his ear.

''S'at you, Slopey?'

'Yes. What are you doing, beautiful?'

'Eating chocolates.'

'Tch, tch. Who gave you chocolates?'

'You guess.'

'Some filthy old man, I suppose.'

'No, a clean, young man.'

'What's his name?'

The sugary voice giggled.

'I don't know. I can't pronounce it.'

'A foreigner, eh?'

'Not exactly, darling.'

'What d'you mean – not exactly?'

'I think he's a Hindu prince or a Rajah, or something.'

'Oh, you do, do you!'

'Yes, darling, and he's awfully rich.'

'Oh, he is, is he? And I suppose he's with you now?'

'Of course not, darling.'

'Then you're going out to meet him?'

The sugary voice protested.

'Of course I'm not. I'm in bed – resting.'

'In bed, eh! All right, stay there. I'm coming over.'

The girl giggled and Slopey put down the telephone. As he came out of the kiosk he saw that Banks, the news editor, had come into the reporters' room and was standing by Slopey's desk.

It was an annoying habit Banks had, suddenly bursting into the room and bawling a man out, instead of sending for a man as every decent news editor should.

Mr Banks didn't seem to feel the cold. His jacket was off, his shirt-sleeves rolled up to the elbow, and his tie was slackened.

'Want me, Mr Banks?' Slopey asked.

'Who were you yapping to in that kiosk? I've been standing here ten minutes.'

'Sorry, Mr Banks, but I was talking to the Countess of – er –' The news editor glared at him.

'The Countess of who?' he demanded.

'The Countess of Sludgewater. I got a tip she was goin' to marry her chauffeur.'

The news editor's voice was silky.

'And is she?'

'No, Chief. I guess it was a phoney tip.'

'Pity,' said Banks. 'That would have been a great story, Collins.' Slopey looked at the news editor uncertainly.

'Yes, it would have been a great story,' Slopey agreed.

'An even better story would be the news that Mr Collins, news-paper reporter, was in the habit of keeping bed dates with the Countess of Sludgewater. The next time you use the office phone calling up your society friends, make sure the door's shut. Here, take this!'

Banks thrust a scrap of paper into Slopey's hand, a leaf torn from a memo pad. Slopey was half-afraid that it was a month's notice, but it wasn't, much to his relief. It was an address, written in Banks' own familiar scrawl: *Coronet Grove, Coronet Square, E1.*

'Book to Whitechapel or Aldgate station,' said Banks. 'I'm not quite sure which. Or, maybe, it's Bow Road.'

Nice, concise instructions, Slopey thought bitterly.

'What's the story?' he asked.

'An old woman's been found dead with her face in the Sunday joint. That's the address.'

Slopey stuffed the memo slip into his waistcoat pocket. He sighed, thinking regretfully of Margie in bed with half a pyjama suit on.

'What is it?' he asked. 'Murder?'

'No, the old girl just died – heart failure. She lived entirely alone, but every mealtime – breakfast, dinner, tea – the table was always laid for two – herself and her son.'

'Where's the son?'

'He was killed in 1918.'

'That doesn't make sense.'

'No, of course it doesn't. But it makes a damn good story. She's been buying him a packet of cigarettes every weekend for twenty years.'

'Who smoked 'em?'

'Nobody. There's cigarettes in every room, so I hear.'

'She must have been crazy.'

'Crazy, maybe, but it makes a nice human story,' said Banks. 'Get the rest of the dope from her neighbours.'

Slopey Collins watched Banks stride out of the room, and cursed him for handing out such a lousy assignment on a wet Sunday night. News editors had peculiar ideas as to what constituted human stories.

And Margie was in bed wearing half a pyjama suit. Blast!

He put his mackintosh on, pulled the trilby over his untidy hair and then telephoned down to the commissionaire to get a taxi. He was damned if he was going to mess about on Underground trains on a night like this. He'd take a taxi both ways and put it on expenses. To hell with Banks.

Slopey Collins would have been a good reporter but for one failing. A story had to interest him before he showed any enthusiasm, and this story about the old lady of Coronet Grove didn't interest him in the least.

He was sitting in the taxi-cab flashing along Queen Victoria Street when he suddenly leaned forward and spoke to the driver.

'Turn round. I want you to go to Acre Mansions, Brixton.'

'Make up yer mind,' growled the taxi-man.

'I have,' said Slopey.

He'd go to Brixton, spend a pleasant half-hour with Margie and then go on to Coronet Grove. There was no great hurry about the story. It was essentially a London-interest story, and the London editions didn't go to press until long after midnight.

Slopey stayed rather longer at Brixton than he had intended. Consequently, he did not arrive in the East End until twenty past eight. Even then he did not go straight to Coronet Grove. Having drunk three cupfuls of cheap port at Margie's, he was feeling thirsty. So he stopped for a drink. The pub at which he stopped was The Two Compasses. He called for a pint of bitter.

'Nasty night,' commented Edie, the barmaid.

'Um,' said Slopey. 'Do you happen to know Coronet Grove?'

The girl put two raw, red elbows on the shiny counter.

'Oh, yes, sir. Quite well.' She jerked a thick-jointed thumb. 'It's just round the corner. Back of the church.'

'You've got churches down here!'

Edie failed to appreciate Slopey's mordant humour.

'Oh, yes. We've got lots of churches 'ere. It ain't all pubs and pawnshops, you know.'

'No, I suppose not. I suppose you don't happen to know a Mrs Willis, who lived in Coronet Grove?'

'Mrs Williams. You don't mean the tram-conductor's wife – she wears an artificial boot thing?'

'No,' said Slopey. 'Mrs Willis.'

'Oh, Mrs Willis. Now, lemme see. No, I can't say as 'ow I do. Tell you what, though. I know a Mrs Sandigate.'

Slopey sipped his beer.

'Would she know Mrs Willis?'

'Bound to. She knows everybody in the Grove. You just tell 'er Edie sent you. Rose – that's Mrs Sandigate – used to work 'ere.'

'She did, eh!'

Slopey was not greatly interested. He took another gulp at his beer and stared moodily at the froth patterned on the inside of the glass. But the barmaid was of the garrulous type. She leaned forward confidentially.

'And I tell you something else,' she said. 'She used to go out with Tommy Swann.'

Slopey looked up. Tommy Swann! Wasn't that the fellow who . . .

'You know. 'Im what was in the papers this morning.'

A light shone in Slopey's pale eyes. His voice became curious, confidential.

'You mean the same Tommy Swann that escaped from Dartmoor?'

'That's 'im, sir. 'E used to use this 'ouse – when Rose worked 'ere, that is.'

'You're quite sure it's the same Tommy Swann?'

Edie's bosom rose with thrilling impatience that anyone should doubt this thrilling titbit of scandal.

'I saw 'is picture in the *News Of The World*. Of course, it's 'im all right. I'd like as many pounds as pints I've served 'im.'

'Have a drink,' said Slopey.

'Oh, thank you, ever so much, sir. I'll 'ave a white port. Or shall I 'ave a Guinness?'

'Have both. Take the port in the Guinness.'

'O-oh, d'you think I really ought to?'

'Go on, do you good.'

Slopey flicked half-a-crown on to the counter. The barmaid poured the port into the beer, smacked her lips and widened her eyes.

'Cheerio, sir. All the best.'

'Cheerio.'

Globules of froth were clinging to the barmaid's red lips. She removed them with the tip of her tongue.

Arms on the counter, she leaned closer to Slopey. The neck of her frock sagged downwards.

'Nice drink that. Just what the doctor ordered.'

'Good,' said Slopey. 'So Rose used to go out with this fellow Swann, did she?'

'I'll say she did. She was a one, Rose was.'

'Where did he usually take her?'

'O-oh, up the other end. You know, West End clubs, and sort of 'ot places where girls danced naked.'

'And what did her husband say about that?'

'Mr Sandigate, yer mean? Oh, she wasn't married then.'

'Oh, she wasn't.'

'No; she only married Mr Sandigate after Tommy Swann went in the nick.'

'Oh, I see,' said Slopey. 'When was that?'

'O-oh, mus' be nine or ten years ago now. I remember they got married the Sat'dy after my nineteenth birthday, the year my sister Betty chopped her little finger off in the biscuit fact'ry, and I'm twenty-nine now, so it must be ten years, mustn't it?'

'I suppose it must be.' Slopey swilled the dregs of the pint round the glass. 'Give me a whisky, will you?'

'Certainly, sir. White 'Orse, Black 'n' White, Johnny or . . .'

'Make it a Haig,' said Slopey.

'And don't be vague!' said the barmaid, giggling at what she imagined was wit.

She sipped her own drink and then turned to get a spirit glass. Slopey gazed idly at the contour of her buttocks beneath the tight skirt. She looked over her shoulder, smiled and came back with his John Haig.

He rolled the liquor over his tongue.

'Have another one yourself,' he said.

'Oh, no, sir. I wouldn't do that. It's very nice of you, but I wouldn't take advantage.'

'You're more than welcome. Tell me about this Tommy Swann.'

'O-oh, 'e's a regular bleeder, if you'll pardon the language. Bin in and out of prison ever since Rosie got married.'

Slopey nodded. He gave the barmaid a sly grin.

'But I bet Rose kept in touch with him, eh?' he said quietly.

Edie considered the question as she scratched her leg somewhere in the region of the suspender clip before she renewed the conversation.

'Well, I always did 'ear that Rose was a straight girl. But you never know, do yer?'

'No,' Slopey agreed, 'you never know.'

'But Rose is bound to know that Mrs Willis you was asking after. Bound to.'

'Thanks,' said Slopey.

He wasn't really interested in Mrs Willis now. He was sensing a story bigger than a couple of paragraphs about an old woman who should have died in a mental home instead of her own home.

Tommy Swann was still at large. Tommy Swann was still news. Tommy Swann was still the big story. He wondered whether the cops were wise to this Rose Sandigate woman. Of course, it was only a hunch. Maybe there was nothing in it. On the other hand . . .

'What number does Mrs Sandigate live at?' he asked.

'Twenty-six,' said Edie.

She scratched her leg again. She heard the door in the public bar close. She looked across, and then at Slopey again.

'Excuse me, sir,' she whispered, 'that's Rose's 'usband just come in the public bar.'

Slopey looked through the glass panels into the public bar, saw a red-and-blue dartboard pitted with holes, a slate covered in chalked figures, several men grouped round the hockey line, some older men playing dominoes at a long, well-scrubbed table, some fattish women sitting in an alcove by a door conveniently marked *Ladies* and a thickset, red-faced man in a blue-serge suit, in the breast pocket of which three yellow dart flights were visible.

Edie nodded in his direction.

'That's 'im.'

'Doesn't look very pleased with himself,' commented Slopey.

'You're right. Looks as if he'd lorst a pound and found a tanner.'

'His wife isn't with him?'

'Can't see 'er. Funny, now you mention it.'

'Why funny?'

'They usually come in tergether Sunday evenings. Reg'lar as clockwork, they do.'

Slopey put down his empty glass. The barmaid mopped the counter.

'Per'aps they've 'ad a row,' she commented. 'Did you want another drink, sir?'

But Slopey had gone.

II

Doris Sandigate had never felt more miserable at any time in her life. Not even when her mother died had she felt as depressed as she felt now, as she walked across Coronet Square, not knowing where she was going or how she would spend the evening. The rain pattered on her umbrella and seeped through the thin soles of her shoes.

Violent quarrels always affected her this way, but never had a quarrel made her as sick in mind and body as she felt tonight. Why did people have to quarrel? She was of the type that would sooner suffer an injustice than complain about it.

As she crossed the square, the door of the Beasley household opened and Emily, the youngest of the three Beasley daughters, came down the steps. She was also carrying an umbrella. Neither of the girls would have noticed each other but for the fact that they nearly collided at the Beasley gate.

'Why, Doris!' said Emily, so obviously pleased to see her.

'Oh, hullo, Emily!'

Doris Sandigate and Emily Beasley had been at the same council school together. Emily was about a year older than Doris, but as they had both been in the school basketball team they met quite frequently and became friends. It was not one of those 'until death do us part' friendships which schoolgirls often feel for each other, and when they left school they drifted apart, meeting only on these rare occasions of a chance encounter.

'You do look nice,' said Emily, genuinely admiring the other girl's cheap blue hat, with its spray of violets, the guinea two-piece with a skirt short enough to show the shapeliness of the legs below, and the dark-blue shoes with the slim high heels.

'You look nice, too,' said Doris.

Emily was dressed in a rusty-brown costume trimmed with imitation Persian lamb, and she didn't look at all nice. Her shoes were stout-and-sturdy brown brogues, with low-cut, flat heels. Mr Beasley would not have approved of anything more *chic*.

'But you look really lovely,' said Emily. 'Blue suits you a treat.'

Doris was genuinely pleased with the compliment, but being unable truthfully to pay any further compliments to Emily in a similar strain, attempted to belittle her own appearance.

'Oh, go on with you,' Doris protested.

'No, I mean it,' said Emily. 'I wish I could look as nice as you.'

'I bet your clothes are much better than mine,' said Doris.

'They don't look as nice,' said Emily.

'Going to the pictures?' Doris asked, and then realised what a silly question it was.

'No,' said Emily, 'church.'

The Beasley family went to church twice every Sunday – morning and evening. Doris looked up at the church clock.

'You're early for the evening service, aren't you?'

'Well, you see, I'm in the choir, and . . .'

Emily's sentence trailed away, incomplete. She smiled diffidently and looked down at her awkwardly placed, brogue-covered feet. Good heavens, what big feet I've got! she thought.

'I bet you sing nice now,' said Doris, eager to pay the dowdy Emily a compliment. 'You always did 'ave a lovely voice, even at school.'

Emily simpered, happy at the tribute, but anxious in her modesty to refute it.

'Oh, no, not a *really* lovely voice.'

'But you have got a lovely voice,' Doris insisted. 'Miss Llewellyn always said you 'ad.'

'What did Miss Llewellyn know about voices?' asked Emily in somewhat disparaging reference to the music mistress of their old council school.

'She was our music teacher, wasn't she?'

'Not a real music teacher. Real music teachers teach only music. Miss Llewellyn only taught it when she wasn't teaching geography or 'istory or arithmetic.'

'But she was Welsh, wasn't she?' Doris insisted. 'And Welsh people know all about good voices, don't they?'

'She wasn't really Welsh. She only 'ad a Welsh name.'

'Anyway,' said Doris, 'I still bet you sing really nice. Not like them crooners on the wireless, but nice and sweet.'

Such unstinted praise made Emily blush with pleasure.

So restricted, so dull, so drab was her day-to-day existence that her schoolfriend's halting tribute came to her more intoxicating than the champagne she had never tasted. Her eyes shone with happiness, and her nose shone with perspiration.

'Doris,' she began, and then hesitated.

'Yes?'

'Well, you won't think I'm silly, will you?'

'Course not.'

'An' if you're not doing anything special tonight . . .'

Again Emily hesitated.

'No, I'm not doing anything special,' said Doris.

'I was wondering if you'd like to come to church tonight and hear me sing in the choir. I never really enjoy singing to those dull ol' people in there. They cough and sneeze and shuffle their feet all the time. But I'd enjoy it if you were there. Besides, I'm singing a solo tonight, and – well, if you're not doing anything special . . .'

Emily broke off, breathless after such a long speech. She looked at Doris with the unmistakable hope in her eyes, the hope that she would say 'yes'.

In all probability Doris would have said 'yes'. She would have accepted the invitation, not because she wanted to go to church, but because she knew that in doing so she would make Emily Beasley very happy. She would have gone even if it had been an ordeal for herself. She *would* have gone had not it been for the distressing and somewhat embarrassing distraction that occurred at that moment.

She had allowed her gaze to wander in the direction of the church itself. Some small boys had climbed through a break in the railings and were playing in the drab, grass-starved church-yard. Among those boys was her young half-brother, Alfie.

Alfie at that precise moment was not playing with the other boys. He had broken off to attend to more urgent business. Facing the roadway, with the sublime indifference of a young dog at a lamp-post, he was competing with the rain that fell from above.

Doris, realising that Emily had also witnessed this disgrace, blushed hotly. So confused was Doris that she did not even say 'goodbye' to Emily. She ran across the road to the church railings.

'Alfie, you dirty little beast!'

Alfie looked up, but did not appear unduly embarrassed.

'What's the matter?' he asked.

'Do your buttons up this minute and go home.'

'Shan't!' said Alfie, still unbuttoned.

Eventually, Doris forcibly performed this adjustment herself and then, white with humiliation, she took Alfie by the wrist and dragged him protesting, kicking, screaming, sliding and swearing, back in the direction of Coronet Grove and home, followed by the jeers and whoops of his amused playmates.

She was still white with humiliation when she finally dragged Alfie indoors. She gave him his supper and put him to bed. Mrs Sandigate did not appear, and Doris presumed that she was either in her bedroom or at The Two Compasses. Rose Sandigate was, in fact, sitting alone in the front parlour, waiting for a suitable opportunity to go up to the bedroom and get Tommy Swann out of the house as quickly as possible.

Having put the shameless Alfie to bed, Doris went out again. For the second time that evening she crossed Coronet Square, head down and umbrella up to protect her new blue ensemble. As she crossed the square, she heard the strains of St Saviour's organ and the voices of the choir singing 'There Is A Green Hill Far Away'. The church lights twinkled prettily through the macabre scenes depicted on the stained-glass windows. Doris thought of Emily in there, looking, for all her outdoor dowdiness, rather appealing in a white surplice, her colourless hair parted in the middle and coiled chastely over each ear, lips parted and eyes shining sad.

For a minute, Doris was tempted to go into the church, not because she liked church services – she didn't – but because she knew her presence would have given pleasure to Emily. She decided against the impulse, however. Firstly, because she was still feeling somewhat embarrassed at Alfie's indelicate demonstration. Secondly, to go in now would mean walking in during the middle of a service, and all eyes would have been turned upon her.

So she went past St Saviour's church, and the sweet, mournful moan of the organ soon gave place to more cheerful sounds as she made her way towards Whitechapel High Street. Tramcars clanged along Commercial Street. Music blared from amplifiers in pin-table saloons. A Salvation Army band, red-jerseyed and sallow-faced, played a hymn as if it were a Sousa march. A little old woman, with a face like a shrivelled nutmeg, stood over a basket and shouted her wares like a Bren gun spitting bullets, *'Peanuts! Peanuts! Penny a bag, peanuts! Chocolate, chocolate! Cadbury's! Rowntree's, Cadbury's! Tuppence a bar, tuppence a bar!'* Chatter of crockery from cafés, coffee stalls and delicatessen shops.

Restaurants, *Strictly Kosher Under The Beth Din*, and all-night snack bars, strictly tough and under the watchful eyes of the police. Thump of beer pumps and voices, both raucous and shrill, from the ubiquitous public houses. Boys and girls in their best Sunday clothes swaying along, arm-in-arm, caring naught for the rain and shouting pleasantries to any friends they happened to pass, sometimes singing snatches of the latest song hits. A group of young men in tight-fitting overcoats whistling shrilly and jeering at an old man who walked the gutters between sandwich-boards on which in red letters were inscribed the words *Jesus Loves Me*, while he himself added to this silent boast by shouting *'Repent, ye sinners, repent!'* Rolling clouds of steam drifting from the open doors of Sunday-night fried-fish shops. Crowds round the jellied-eel stalls. Fun and laughter and five-hundred shop windows ablaze with light and decorated with neon.

That was the Whitechapel Doris Sandigate walked through on that wet Sunday night during the spring before the Second German War came upon the world, with its blackouts and its sirens. As she walked along, she could not help feeling a little pang of loneliness. Everybody seemed happy – laughing, chattering, full of vitality. That was it, vitality. *Vitality* and eagerness for life and new experience, confident and optimistic. Every girl seemed to be clinging to a boy's arm. They gathered outside Boris, the photographer's, where the wedding groups, coloured and sepia-tinted, were floodlit, and all the brides looked beautiful. They stood outside the jewellery shops in Black Lion Lane, where a thousand rings sparked and glittered and dazzled the eye from a hundred heart-shaped pads.

Doris lingered here, lingered there. She looked at the wedding groups, beautifully gowned brides and silk-hatted grooms under the *chuppah*. She looked at the stocking shop. She looked at the hat shop, with its cute models ranging in price from five shillings to a guinea, many of them exact imitations of those to be seen in the more rarefied atmosphere of Bond Street. She looked at the gown shop, the dresses looking so attractive on those lifelike wax models with the slanting eyes.

She was indeed lonely. She could have called for Johnny Price, but he would probably be on his motorcycle; the wet weather didn't deter him. In fact, he liked the roads to be wet so that he could get a thrill out of skidding round the corners. In any case, if she did meet him, she knew there would be a quarrel because she had not waited for him that morning. Added to which, he would probably want to talk about the football match he saw at Highbury yesterday. Or he might talk about his voluntary work with the newly formed AFS, and how, if war and air raids came, he would be automatically mobilised, and he'd be a motorcyclist messenger riding breathlessly and thrillingly through the fires and the explosions and the shrapnel. It all sounded very thrilling, but thrilling in a *cinematic* way. Doris was no student of politics or international affairs, but she didn't believe war would ever come to England again. Not for another five years, at any rate. That was what she had heard her father say, and he should know. He read the articles in the papers. She herself had several times read an astrologer's prediction that there would be no war, either this year, next year or the year after. And hadn't Mr Chamberlain come back from Munich last September waving a piece of paper and declaring that it was 'peace in our time'? She had seen that with her own eyes on the newsreel, and she had noticed how happy Mr Chamberlain had looked, almost hugging himself with joy and pride at his achievement. And Mr Chamberlain should know what he was talking about, because he had been face-to-face with Hitler. He had even had tea with him. She couldn't quite visualise Hitler doing a nice, peaceful thing like having tea, but she had seen that on the newsreels, too.

Thoughts like these occupied her mind as she walked along Whitechapel High Street. Her association of ideas was simple. There was no difficulty in tracing her mental processes. Other girls had boyfriends. She had no boyfriend, except John, and he bored her. John was in the AFS. The AFS. War.

It was this trend of thought which reminded her of her own ARP activities. She had started attending first-aid classes at the Toynbee Hall. She went to them not because she believed that the knowledge thus gained would ever be useful for attending to air-raid victims. She could not conceive that there would ever be any air-raid victims to attend to. She believed, however, that the knowledge would be useful for everyday life and everyday accidents. Although secretly she was afraid that if she ever did encounter a serious accident, accompanied by bloodshed, she would be more distressed than the patient.

Nevertheless, she thought there was something fine about devoting oneself to the relief of human suffering. How fine! How noble! At times she had visualised herself as a nurse in starched, spotless white with a red cross on her bosom. A sort of Florence Nightingale of Aldgate East. She sighed.

At the first-aid classes she had met Bessie Weinbaum. Bessie, of course, was considerably older than Doris, and she already held one first-aid certificate.

Bessie Weinbaum was a research secretary to a trade-union organisation. Doris liked her, and had been awed to learn that she was a Bachelor of Arts of London University. Miss Weinbaum, in fact, was well-liked by everybody. She had such a pleasant personality. Her voice, too, was pleasant. She was always quite smartly dressed, although never ostentatiously so. Usually she wore a tailor-made two-piece, with a simple blouse or jumper.

Doris had felt attracted towards the elder girl. It could not be said that they had a great deal in common. They had little or nothing in common. But there was a magnetic quality about Bessie Weinbaum's *niceness*. That was the only word you could use to describe it. *Niceness*.

Even so, Doris sought her friendship but diffidently. Besides, she was somewhat overawed by that BA. It seemed to place Bessie in a different category, even more than the fact she belonged to a different race and a different creed.

'It's nothing,' Bessie had once told her. 'Lots of people have BAs, but that doesn't prevent them being BFs as well!'

Doris had giggled a little at the remark. It was the nearest she ever heard Bessie Weinbaum come to swearing. At first Doris had wondered why Bessie was content to live in a mean street of little houses amid a labyrinth of similar mean streets, many of which were also marketplaces as well as residential thoroughfares. Somehow, it didn't seem to fit her position.

Doris would never have asked her about it, but it was Bessie herself who gave the answer without being questioned.

'I love the East End,' she said one night as they were walking home from first-aid classes. 'I love its colour, its variety, its virility, its simplicity and its cunning; and – yes, I love its crudeness. I was born in the East End, and I hope I shall always live here.'

Bessie Weinbaum was scornful of the people who made their money in the East End and then went to live elsewhere, who were ashamed of their origin, and pretended they had never heard of Brick Lane or Osborne Street, or Stoney Lane or Hessell Street, or Old Montague Street.

'What's wrong with the East End, anyway?' she demanded as they walked along. 'Some people say it smells. Sure it smells. It smells of public houses and marketplaces and fried-fish shops. I love the smell of fried-fish shops, don't you? Come and have some chips.'

'You talk like somebody out of a book,' said Doris.

'Not a school book, I hope?'

'No, you're very int'resting.'

Bessie Weinbaum had laughed.

'Come round and see us some evening. Any evening you like.'

Doris had not taken advantage of the invitation. In fact, she had not treated it very seriously, but on this wet Sunday night, walking down the Whitechapel High Street, with nobody to talk to and nothing to do, she was feeling an aching need for companionship. She suddenly made up her mind to call on Bessie Weinbaum.

Bessie herself opened the door, and at first failed to recognise the visitor.

'I 'ope it's no inconvenience,' said Doris, with a stiff, smiling primness.

'Why, it's Doris! How nice of you to call! Come in!'

'Who is it, Bessie?' Old Man Weinbaum called out.

'It's Doris Sandigate, father. We met at ARP classes.'

'Ah, ha!' exclaimed Mr Weinbaum. 'Are you preparing for the war, too?'

'Well, I 'ope there won't be no war,' said Doris awkwardly. 'I mean I 'ope there won't be a war.'

'But you're going to be all prepared if it does come, eh?' he chuckled. 'Let me take your coat and umbrella.'

He fingered the cloth with unconscious deprecation as he helped her off with her coat. Bessie corked the red-ink bottle.

'I was beginning to think you'd never call to see us.'

Although the Weinbaums were such obviously nice people, and there was a sincere friendliness in their welcome, Doris was wishing that she had not called. She did not feel at ease. These people were being pleasant to her, but she suspected that they were wondering why she had called. After all, they had nothing in common. True, Bessie Weinbaum had invited her, but even so, she found herself anxious to give them a reason for this unexpected visit.

'I tell you one reason why I called. I – I – was wonderin' if you'd lend me your first-aid book.'

'Why, certainly,' said Bessie. 'But sit down first. You're not in a hurry, are you?'

'No, I – I'm not in a 'urry.' And she sat down on the edge of a chair and looked round the room. It was Bessie's own room.

'This is ever such a nice room.'

'Like it?' said Bessie.

'Ever so much. I like the bookshelves, and – o-oh, aren't those daffodils lovely. That's a nice picture on the wall. You wouldn't think it could be so cosy in 'ere, judgin' from the . . .' She broke off. What an awful thing I've nearly said! she was thinking.

'You mean the inside of the house is an improvement on the outside?' said Bessie.

'Well, I didn't mean that exactly.'

'Well, I think it is. At least, I hope so. The outside of the house is the landlord's responsibility; but I don't think he's realised it yet. Landlords never do.'

'There she goes! There she goes!' Mr Weinbaum waved his hand. 'Waving the red flag again.'

'My dad's always 'aving rows with the landlord,' said Doris, and then relapsed into silence, thinking, What a poor conversationalist I am! What a dull thing to say! 'My dad's always 'aving rows with the landlord. My dad's always 'aving rows with the landlord . . .'

'Would you like some coffee?' said Bessie.

'Er – er – no thanks, really. Thanks, all the same, though.'

'Don't you like coffee?'

'Oh, yes. I like it, but . . .'

'Coffee in two minutes,' said Mr Weinbaum, and went out of the room.

Doris looked round the room again.

'You got a nice lot of books, 'aven't you?'

'Are you fond of reading?' Bessie asked.

'Yes, I love readin',' said Doris. 'When I'm in the mood.'

She got up and walked to the bookshelves. She felt easier standing up. She picked out a thin, blue volume.

'Thomas 'Ardy,' she commented. 'I like 'im, don't you? I mean, I like his books.'

'Yes, I like him,' said Bessie. 'He's rather gloomy at times, though, don't you think?'

'Mm. But I like sad books.'

She looked up at the next shelf.

'You've got a lot of poetry, too,' said Doris.

'Yes, at one time I was poetry crazy, but nowadays I don't seem to have the patience for it.'

'Have you got any of Tennyson's poetry?' Doris asked, anxious to prove that she did know something about the subject.

'No, I'm afraid I haven't.'

Doris was surprised at this admission. She had learned Tennyson's poems at school, and she thought every well-read person lucky enough to possess a library would have his works occupying an honoured place on the shelves. Besides, Tennyson had not only been a poet. He had been a lord, too.

'Don't you like Tennyson's poetry?' she asked.

'Not very much,' Bessie admitted. 'Seen any good films lately?'

'I haven't been this week.'

'I thought you usually went to the Troxy on Sundays with your boyfriend – you know, the one with the motorcycle.'

'Sometimes. I was s'posed to 'ave met him this morning, but he was late.'

'And you didn't wait for him?'

'Well,' said Doris, 'it was funny what 'appened. Although it wasn't really funny at the time. I was scared, I can tell you.'

Doris recounted the morning's episode, her encounter with the two drunken men, and the appearance of Lou Hyams on the scene.

'I don't know what I should have done if Lou hadn't come up suddenly,' she was saying, when Bessie took a more lively interest in her story.

'If *who* hadn't appeared?' she said.

'His name's Lou. He runs the pin-table machines and things. I met him on Sat'day, and he wanted to run me 'ome in his car – such a swanky car, too – and this morning, when I met him again, he told me I looked like a bridesmaid, and he asked me to have a drink with him, an' . . . he's ever so nice.'

She was quite garrulous on the subject of Lou Hyams until Mr Weinbaum came in with the coffee. He had just put it on the table when they heard a ring at the front door.

'I'll go,' said Mr Weinbaum. 'You pour the coffee out, Bessie. I expect it's Mr Zimmerman. The old fool always thinks he's entitled to buy his cigarettes after closing time. One of these days I shall tell him a thing or two, my life I will.'

And he went out grumbling.

'Actually, old Zimmerman is father's best friend,' said Bessie, as she poured out the coffee. 'Although you wouldn't think it from the arguments they have. He comes for a packet of Goldflake and stays half the night playing chess. Have a sandwich? Yes, please do.'

But the caller was not the argumentative, chess-playing Mr Zimmerman. They heard Mr Weinbaum's voice as the door opened.

'You've got another visitor, Bessie!'

And then came Lou Hyams' cheery, somewhat too noisy voice.

'I've come for some of that *strudel* cake, Bessie!'

III

It was half past eight that evening before Rose Sandigate dared to unlock her bedroom door. Tommy Swann had been waiting in an agony of suspense for some hours. As the key turned in the lock he slipped into a recess not more than a few inches wide between the wall and the washstand. The poker was clasped in his hand. He was ready to make a dash for it.

In the darkened room he heard a creak as the door opened. A faint tremor of light crept in from the landing. He scarcely dared to breathe. Then he heard Rose's voice, 'Tommy!'

'Is it all right, Rose?' he whispered back.

'Yes, where are you?'

She came in and shut the door, locking it again from the inside. He went to her.

'What 'appened, Rose? What 'appened?'

In the darkness he was standing close to her, and as she sighed he felt her breath hot on his face.

'What's 'appened?' she repeated. 'What ain't 'appened!'

'What was it?' he persisted anxiously. 'Sounded as if it was a regular bleedin' rort on. Proper rough 'ouse.'

'It was a rough 'ouse,' said Rose. 'All over you.'

He looked startled.

'You don't mean to say they come a tumble?'

'As near as makes no odds. But you must 'ave 'eard. It was right outside the door.'

'I woke up in the middle of it. Fair give me a start at first, I can tell you, when I 'eard everybody shouting and rortin' at once.'

'Give *you* a start!' said Rose. 'My 'eart's so bad, I don't think I'll ever git over it, never. Tommy, you got ter git out of 'ere right away.'

He gave a laugh that sounded more like a bronchial cough.

'You're tellin' me.'

'Got any money?' she asked.

'Not a coal.'

'You'll 'ave ter 'ave some, won't yer? The most I can let yer 'ave is a couple of quid, if it's any 'elp.'

'I'll never ferget yer for it, Rose.'

Once again her breath was hot on his cheek.

'Look, Tommy,' she said, 'you'll be doing me a favour if yer did fergit me.'

'Don't talk like that, Rose. I'll be in the money again some day, and . . .'

'Tommy, you'll never be in the money again. Fer the rest of yer life yer goin' ter be on the run – that's even if they don't catch yer before you turn the corner.'

Tommy Swann stuck out his chin.

'All right, we'll see. I got out of that bastard hole, and I'm gonna stay out. One thing's certain, they won't take me back alive. Where's the two quid?'

'It's downstairs. I'll get it for yer. 'Ave yer got a hat?'

'None of yer old man's cadies fit me. They're all too big.'

'You'll 'ave to 'ave a hat. 'Ow you goin' to 'ide yer face if you ain't got nothing on yer 'ead? Wait a minute, there's one of the old man's caps in the wardrobe that got shrunk in the rain. I'll put the light on.'

She took a box of Brymay's from her pinafore pocket and went over and lit the gas. The mantle popped and spluttered. She turned the gas off for a second to get the air out of the jet, then lit it again.

As the pale lemon glow of gaslight spread over the bedroom, illuminating the light-oak suite set out on the green carpet and the ruffled green-and-gold eiderdown on the bed, Mrs Sandigate suddenly remembered that the blinds were not drawn. Quickly she crossed the room and jerked the cord. The first blind fell into position.

The other blind was caught up in the curtain rod. It refused to budge, in spite of several energetic tugs at the cord.

''Urry up, Rose,' said Tommy nervously.

'All right, all right.'

She stood somewhat precariously on a small basketwork chair and pulled the blind down into place.

''Ope nobody saw the light,' she said, stepping down so heavily that she nearly capsized.

Slopey Collins, coming across the street, had seen the light go on and off. Then he saw it go on again. Then, against the lemon rectangle of illuminated window, he saw the pinafore-clad, many-curved outline of Rose Sandigate as she stood on a chair, reaching up to the blind.

And in that second, before the blind fell, screening the bedroom from the rainswept street, he saw another figure. The figure of a man standing by the chair. He was looking up, and one hand was supporting Mrs Sandigate as she wrestled with the recalcitrant blind.

He did not know for certain that the man he saw was Tommy Swann. Neither did he know that the woman he saw drawing the blind was Mrs Rose Sandigate.

He did know, however, that this was number 26, and the barmaid at The Two Compasses had told him that Rose Sandigate lived at 26 Coronet Grove. And he did know that Mr George Sandigate was round the corner in the public bar drinking a pint of old and mild.

There was not much doubt about the large woman being Mrs Sandigate. And if the man wasn't Tommy Swann, who was he? A lodger? A relation? A secret lover? . . .

Slopey Collins lit a cigarette, took one deep draw, and let the smoke out slowly through his nostrils. Then he pushed open the gate of number 26 Coronet Grove and walked up the well-worn, whitened doorsteps.

He lifted the cast-iron knocker and brought it down with a brisk double knock.

The sound reverberated right through the little house. Then there was silence again, the creaking silence of old houses.

Slopey took another deep draw on his cigarette. Then smoke wreathed patterns around his battered, rain-soaked trilby. Water gurgled in a blocked gully.

He waited two minutes and then he knocked again, louder this time.

CHAPTER 7

I

Just after Slopey Collins had left The Two Compasses, three young men entered. Three young men, all wearing black, ten-and-elevenpenny imitations of Anthony Eden hats and white mufflers. Three young men with cigarettes jutting from their mouths and aggression manifest in their jutting chins. Young men with tight-waisted overcoats and padded shoulders – Alfie Price, Whitey Williams and Dicey Perkins.

Edie, the tight-skirted barmaid, swayed her hips as she moved forward to serve them.

'Good evening, gentlemen,' she smirked. 'Can I serve you?'

Whitey Williams raised his eyebrows and folded his arms somewhat theatrically.

'D'you 'ear that, boys? My Gawd, ain't she gettin' perlite!'

'Shut up!' said Alfie Price. 'Three light ales, please, miss.'

He flicked half-a-crown on to the counter.

Whitey Williams gazed admiringly at the barmaid's tight-skirted buttocks as she bent to the light-ale crate and then dexterously jabbed the necks of the bottles into the cap-remover.

The amber liquid frothed up and oozed into the three glasses, all of which she held in her left hand. She then slid the drinks over to the thirsty trio.

'She knows 'er stuff, our Edie does,' said Whitey.

'Shut up!' said Alfie Price.

Whitey shrugged his shoulders and reached for one of the drinks.

The cash register rang. Alfie Price picked up his change. He sucked his back tooth noisily as he dropped each coin singly into his side pocket.

'Nearly skint again,' he muttered.

'Yeah,' said Whitey. 'Nearly skint again.'

'It's a bugger, ain't it?' said Dicey Perkins, reaching for a drink. 'G'luck, anyway.'

'G'luck,' said Whitey.

'G'luck,' said Alfie Price. 'How much you got, Whitey?'

Whitey Williams did not reply immediately. He was taking a long, deep gulp of beer. When the glass was half-empty he put it down and then spread a handful of small change on the counter. Counting, he separated coppers from silver.

'Four and tuppence. That's me lot.'

''Ow much you got, Dicey?'

'Four 'n' seven,' said Dicey, without counting.

'Um,' said Alfie.

Whitey Williams emptied his glass.

'Beasley's a thieving bastard. Three light ales, Edie.'

'All the same, we cut up three quid between us today,' Alfie ruminated.

Dicey Perkins picked his nose and studied the result.

'What do we do wiv all our money?' he asked.

'Money!' said Whitey Williams scornfully, folding and unfolding his arms. 'Yer mean what ol' Beasley paid us fer them skates? Yer call that money?'

'That's it,' said Alfie. 'Tell the world. Why don't yer get up on the counter and shaht!'

'Still, it ain't money,' Whitey went on in a quieter tone. 'It's chicken feed. It's peanuts. That's what it is. An' I still say ol' Bees Knees is a thieving ol' bastard. G'luck.'

'G'luck,' said Alfie.

'G'luck,' said Dicey.

'You know what?' said Whitey, putting his glass down.

'What?' said Alfie, spitting on the floor and rubbing it in with his foot.

Whitey leaned forward and lowered his voice to a confidential tone.

'I'm gonna do him.'

Alfie curled his lip contemptuously.

'Ur, shut up.'

'I tell yer, Alfie, I'm gonna do him.'

Dicey Perkins wiped his finger on his coat lapel.

'Fat lot of good that'll be to yer,' he commented.

'Dicey's right,' said Alfie. 'Okay, yer do 'im. Yer kick the daylight out of 'im. But that still leaves yer with the change of four an' tuppence by the time you've paid fer these light ales.'

Whitey Williams swivelled round to pay for the light ales and then turned to renew the absorbing topic of whether or not Mr C Beasley should be 'done'. Once again he folded and unfolded his arms.

'When I say I'm gonna do 'im, I mean I'm gonna do 'im good and proper. Yer don't think I'm gonna do 'im just fer the sake of kickin' 'is guts in, do yer?'

'I'd sooner do her,' said Alfie, nodding towards the barmaid. 'Good and proper.'

Dicey Perkins giggled.

'So would I. Not 'arf.'

'Look,' said Whitey. 'I ain't only goin' ter do 'im fer the satisfaction of kickin' 'is guts in. Don't fergit ol' Beasley always carries a century in 'is sky.'

'That's clever,' said Alfie. 'Bloody clever. Yer know what that is?'

'Robbery wiv vi'lence,' said Dicey Perkins.

'That's right, Dicey. Robbery with violence. And d'yer know what yer can get fer that?'

'The cat,' said Dicey.

Whitey Williams emptied his glass.

'I'm still gonna do 'im. I'm gonna do 'im good and proper. I'm gonna . . .'

'For Christ's sake shut up!' said Alfie, between his teeth. 'Here's Fothergill.'

Whitey Williams swung round on his elbow.

'I'm gonna do 'im, too.'

'You're drunk,' said Alfie.

'Who's drunk?'

'Three light ales,' said Dicey.

Detective-Sergeant Fothergill – Fothergill The Patient, as some of his colleagues called him – was smiling blandly as he came into the saloon bar. Rain dripped from his mackintosh on to the green cork linoleum. Tobacco smoke wreathed about his smiling, baby-blue eyes.

'You boys like this pub,' he said cheerily.

'We did,' said Whitey, 'until a minute ago.'

'I'll buy it,' said Fothergill. 'What happened a minute ago?'

'You came in,' said Whitey. 'Huh, huh, huh!'

Fothergill smiled mildly, and Alfie Price gave Whitey a vicious warning kick on his instep, an action which the detective pretended not to notice. Whitey winced and scowled at Alfie.

'Well, don't let me spoil your fun, boys,' said Fothergill, and he passed down to the far end of the bar.

When the CID man was out of earshot, Whitey turned to Alfie. His indignation bubbled over.

'Watcha wanna kick me ankle for?'

'Just ter make you button yer mouth up.'

'What for? What for? You ain't afraid of 'im, are yer?'

Whitey jerked a not very clean thumb in the direction of Fothergill, who was now standing by the glass partition that divided the saloon bar from the public bar.

'Aw, use yer loaf,' said Alfie irritably. 'There's nothing clever in trying to get tough with Ds. Because if you do, they can get just as tough with you, see?'

In reply to which Whitey pursed his lips and gave vent to a vulgar sound.

Alfie glanced furtively at Fothergill, but he seemed engrossed in his half-pint of bitter. Then Alfie edged nearer to Whitey and caught him by the second button of his waistcoat.

'Listen, you mug. Fothergill might 'ave thought you meant that fer 'im.'

'So what?' said Whitey, reaching for his glass. 'I did mean it for 'im.'

'And you did, eh? And s'pose he'd a run you in for it?'

Whitey pushed his hat back over a perplexed brow.

'Run me in? What for?'

'Givin' 'im the raspberry.'

At which Whitey Williams laughed out aloud. He raised his newly replenished glass.

'G'luck,' he said.

'What would yer do with 'im, Dicey? What would yer do with 'im? Tell 'im, am I right or wrong?'

Dicey stopped picking his nose.

'You're right. Dead right. Fothergill could 'ave run yer in, Whitey.'

Whitey laughed again.

'Oh, yeah! And what would the charge be, Mr Bloody Clever Dick Sir Norman 'Astings Birkett?'

'Insulting be'aviour,' said Dicey.

'That's right,' said Alfie. 'Insulting behaviour.'

'That's right,' said Detective-Sergeant Fothergill, passing them on the way to the door. 'Insulting behaviour.'

The trio swung round, thinking it really was a pinch, but Fothergill hadn't stopped. He opened the door and went out, a rich aroma of Bondman tobacco trailing in his wake. There was a moment's silence. The black-hatted, white-scarved trio seemed to be swallowing something. Then Alfie spoke very softly.

'That was a quick drink, wasn't it?'

'Too damned quick,' said Whitey.

Dicey shook his head.

'I don't like this. I betcha 'e's gonna do us fer that job last night.'

'Aw, shurrup,' said Whitey irritably, not so cocksure as he had been a few minutes ago. 'I wonder where 'e's gorn?'

Alfie tilted his hat forward, then pushed it back, raised an eyebrow, then sucked a back tooth long and thoughtfully. His next action was to swallow his beer with all possible speed.

'Let's get out of 'ere,' he said.

So they went, leaving behind them a cloud of cigarette smoke and three froth-patterned, empty glasses.

Outside, the trio turned up their coat collars. Then they looked right and left along the rain-drenched street, the light from the public-house windows reflected in the gurgling puddles.

Opposite them a street lamp was reflected three times in pinpoint miniature in the three brass balls hanging over the pawnbroker's. Outside the sweetshop a tin sign advertising Rowntree's Clear Gums creaked in the wind. From a wireless set in an upstairs room above the fried-fish shop Big Ben could be heard striking nine o'clock. Alfie chewed the damp end of a Woodbine.

'Which way did 'e go?' Whitey asked.

''Ow should I know?' retorted Alfie.

At that moment the wooden door of the men's urinal next to the public house swung open and Fothergill came out. The door closed with a bang.

The CID man walked slowly towards them. Alfie swallowed a piece of tobacco. Whitey clenched his fists and felt dry in the throat.

'What did I tell yer!' said Dicey, but so softly that neither Whitey nor Alfie heard him.

'Use yer loaf,' Alfie was whispering. 'Use yer loaf.'

But there was no cause for alarm. Detective-Sergeant Fothergill walked right past them and back into The Two Compasses.

'I'm going 'ome,' said Dicey.

'So am I,' said Alfie.

'I feel like another drink,' said Whitey.

'What yer gonna use fer money?'

'Look, Alfie . . .'

'No,' said Alfie flatly.

Whitey stared at him.

'What d'yer mean – no? Yer don't know what I was gonna say.'

'All right, say it.'

'Well, yer see, I was finking . . .'

'Yeah?'

'Yer still got the nicker to pay back Lou Hyams, ain't yer?'

'I 'ave, and it's going back to Lou Hyams.'

'Yeah, I know that, Alfie. But look, Lou don't need it straight away, so if we cut it up between us – well, it would be six 'og each, wouldn't it?'

Alfie didn't reply for a minute. He took his hat off and shook a brimful of raindrops into Whitey's face.

''Ere, 'ere!' protested Whitey. 'Nark it, nah.'

'I told yer "no", and I mean "no",' said Alfie. 'I told Lou we'd pay him back when we sold the skates.'

'I know that, Alfie,' Whitey persisted. 'But we expected more than three nicker, didn't we?'

'Doesn't matter 'ow much we expected,' said Alfie. 'We told Lou we'd work it back to 'im, and he's gonna get it back.'

'Who's sayin' 'e ain't gonna get it back?' Whitey's voice became almost high-pitched. 'Lou won't mind; 'e ain't in no 'urry for a day or two.'

'No,' said Alfie. 'No! No! No!'

'I'm goin' 'ome,' said Dicey. 'See yer at the coffee stall tomorrer morning. Goo' night.'

Hunching his shoulders, the diminutive Dicey limped away, head on one side, his small finger digging into his nostril.

'Goo' night, Dicey,' said Alfie.

'Goo' night,' said Whitey, and then turned to Alfie again.

'Come on, Alfie,' he coaxed. 'Give us 'alf a bar.'

'I should say,' said Alfie, and walked away.

Whitey Williams stared after him.

'You're telling me!' he shouted back.

Alfie made no reply. He walked on and vanished into the night.

Left alone, Whitey began to count his money under the lamp-light to ascertain whether he had sufficient to buy himself a double whisky and a large Woodbine. He swayed slightly as he counted his money. Yes, he had just enough for a large whisky and a packet of Woodbines. And after that, what? Ah, after that he had a little bit of business to do. He'd show Alfie and Dicey he wasn't such a mug. He was going to do ol' Caleb Beasley. He was going to do him good and proper. Why, you never know, the old villain, the diabolical liberty-taker might have as much as fifty nicker on him! And then wouldn't Alfie and Dicey look sick? They'd come crawling round him asking for a loan of a fiver apiece. He'd tell 'em a thing or two then.

His fingers groped in his waistcoat pocket for a cigarette end. He jabbed it into his mouth. The stub was so short that when he lit it the flames of the match scorched the tip of his nose. Never mind, after he'd done old Beasley he'd be smoking cigars. Yes, he was gonna do ol' Beasley – do him good and proper. But first he must go and get himself some more fags and a double whisky – a good, strong whisky that puts fire into your guts. Ah! He pushed open the door of The Two Compasses and then hesitated.

Detective-Sergeant Fothergill was still there. He let the brass-bound door swing back and stepped out into the street again. He'd have his drink at The Duke Of Teck, farther along the street. Then he'd go and do ol' Beasley, do him good and proper. Kick his guts in, take his wallet, take his lot. But first, he must have a drink. A good, strong whisky.

II

Violet Sandigate looked round the room which Morry had found for her on the third floor above a café in Lisle Street, just behind Leicester Square.

She had never heard of Lisle Street. True, she had heard of Leicester Square. It was the place soldiers of the last war had shouted farewell to when they sang 'Tipperary'. Dotted around that frowsty patch of green, with its brave, rail-enclosed trees, its pigeon-splashed seats and its bust to Will Shakespeare, were no fewer than five cinemas.

Violet, of course, knew nothing of the memorial to our greatest poet, but she had once been to the Empire to see a film première, and she had talked about it for weeks afterwards. In fact, she still talked about it, if only to show that she was *au fait* with what was then the world of bright lights. Actually, her knowledge of the West End of London was less than scanty. She knew you got there by taking a 25 or a 15 omnibus, and she had once bought a pair of so-called 'Film Star Shoes' at a shop in Oxford Street. On two occasions she had had tea at the Coventry Street Corner House, and once, when she had been to a Nippies dance at Covent Garden, she had several drinks at a public house in the Strand. Beyond that, she knew nothing of the West End.

When Morry's car had stopped outside the café in Lisle Street, Vi couldn't help thinking it a dingy sort of thoroughfare, even judged by Stepney standards.

Morry had gone into the café and fixed about the room there and then. To do him justice, he hadn't thought about the temptations life in Lisle Street held for a girl of Violet Sandigate's promiscuous propensities. She had asked him to find her a room and he had found her a room.

The landlord, who was also the café proprietor, was a Saffron-Hill-born Italian, whose son had played the guitar in Morry's band. It was the only address Morry could think of off-hand. At any rate, nobody would ask questions here.

So it was that Vi Sandigate became installed in her new home on this wet Sunday night. East was meeting West. A factory girl in a room three floors above a café in Lisle Street, within sound of the drone of the Wurlitzer organ in the Empire, and the traffic blaring in Leicester Square.

There was one small window in the room. It would have provided a picturesque view of the whirling electric signs above the Square and Piccadilly Circus, but the view was intercepted by a blank brick wall.

To Vi, however, the room itself compensated for any exterior gloom. In her eyes, it was decidedly cosy. There was a thick, cream-coloured rug in front of the glowing gas-fire (operated by a shilling in the slot meter), and there was an old Pye radio set near the green-covered divan. There was a dressing-table with a full-length oval mirror (in which she could examine in detail the puffy bruise on her face as well as the weal on her thigh). There was a highly polished wardrobe (inside which was an old pair of stockings and a crumpled pair of red garters belonging to the previous tenant). There were some framed art plates from *London Life* and *La Vie Parisienne* adorning the walls, and in one corner of the room was a pile of cheap novels, American crime magazines and an illustrated volume entitled *The Sex Life Of Savages*. (She found this quite absorbing.) There was a gas stove on the landing outside, and the lavatory and bathroom combined was on the next floor, down a flight of uncarpeted stairs. There were several bugs exploring the sepia-tinted wallpaper, but as yet Vi had not noticed them.

Morry had left nearly two hours ago, anxious to get down to Brighton on urgent business. He told her it was about fixing his band for the summer season at one of the dance halls there. He had persuaded her against going to Brighton with him. She was tired and upset, he told her, and he wanted to take her with him when she was looking and feeling at her best. Vi could never resist an appeal to her vanity, and so she agreed.

Morry had promised to call in to see her tomorrow evening. Meanwhile, she could order any meals or cigarettes she wanted at the café downstairs, Morry having arranged to pay for these extras later in the week.

She had already taken advantage of this most convenient arrangement to the extent of having two fried eggs, bacon and chips, bread and butter, two cups of tea and a pastry, followed by a packet of twenty Players and a box of matches.

Sitting in front of the gas fire in her room, she had already smoked four of the cigarettes, had spent a most intriguing hour over *The Sex Life Of Savages*, looked at all the pictures in the crime magazines and was now beginning to feel decidedly drowsy. So, for lack of something better to do, she had started to repaint her lips when there came a knock at the door and a woman of indefinite age walked in.

''Ullo, dearie,' she said.

''Ullo,' said Vi, somewhat puzzled.

''Ope you don't mind me coming in, duckie, but 'ave you got such a thing as a shilling for two sixpences?'

'I'll 'ave a look in me bag,' said Vi.

The visitor had a shining mop of untidy platinum hair, with a dark, greenish-bronze line running down the parting. Her eyes were hazel and had quite a mellow prettiness about them, but the lashes had been so heavily blacked that many of them were sticking together in untidy clusters, and the colour had run down on to her lids, giving her the appearance of having been standing in a cloud of coal dust. She seemed to be wearing nothing but a faded-blue dressing-gown and a pair of stockings. She was not yet fat, but she was getting on that way, and her flesh was of the flabby, inert kind. As she talked, she opened the front of her dressing-gown to scratch her stomach, a stomach which Vi noticed was streaked with salmon-pink marks left by overnight corsetry.

Vi held out a shilling.

'Thanks, dearie.' The visitor dropped two sixpences into Vi's hand. 'I'm Lulu Blair. I'm next door to you.'

Her voice still retained a faint northern burr.

'My name's Sandigate,' said Vi. 'Vi'let Sandigate.'

'You're new on the game, aren't you?' the woman asked.

Vi was far from being an innocent child, unversed in the ways of the world, but even so, she did not comprehend the woman's question.

'I – oh yes. This is my first night 'ere.'

'Going out tonight?'

'I 'ad thought of it.'

'Not much doing, kid. The rain drives 'em 'ome. Anyway, good luck.'

The woman scratched herself again and padded, shoeless, to the door, a shapeless big toe sticking up out of a hole in her stocking.

'Mustn't keep the mug waitin' too long,' she said, smiling. 'Oh, by the way, if you want any letters, I can get 'em cheap.'

She closed the door and was gone. Two sixpences in one hand, a lipstick in the other hand, lips parted, Violet Sandigate stared at the closed door.

Outside the rain streamed on the rooftops. The buses thundered down Piccadilly and up Shaftesbury Avenue. A band played in the amber, saccharine warmth of the Coventry Street Corner House. Painted women stood in doorways or beneath their chubby umbrellas, looking up to say, 'Hullo, darling!' to men they had never seen before and would never see again, or to walk on quickly if a policeman's helmet came into view. And an old blind beggar, who had walked all the way from the East End, stood in the rain-pitted gutter and cajoled a cinema queue with his whining cry, *'Box o' matches! Box o' matches!'* . . .

III

When Slopey Collins knocked at the door of number 26 Coronet Grove that night, Tommy Swann was just trying on one of Mr Sandigate's caps. The result was so odd, so grotesque, that Mrs Sandigate was actually laughing.

'It's like a pimple on an 'aystack,' she said.

The cap was of a thick, grey, worsted material, and although the peak remained its normal size, the crown had shrunk considerably, so that it covered only a very small portion of Tommy Swann's bullet-shaped skull; but the peak came down almost to the bridge of his nose and looked like a tennis player's eyeshade.

'You look jes' like Burglar Bill,' she said, as if Tommy Swann were anything but a burglar.

He looked at himself in the mirror and did not feel so amused. Rose's laughter irritated him. He did not realise that her laughter was as much the laughter of hysteria as anything else. Outwardly, she laughed. Inwardly, she was taut with fear.

'I don't see what there is ter laugh abaht,' said Tommy.

'Oh, but, Tommy, yer don't 'arf look a sight!'

Tommy Swann certainly did look a sight. Mr Sandigate's old suit fitted him in no place at all. He was a taller man than the stocky George Sandigate, but considerably slimmer, so that while the rear of the trousers hung down in a sort of pouch, the turn-ups dangled forlornly several inches above his ankles. He was wearing one of Mr Sandigate's old blue shirts, the neckband of which was several sizes too large.

Tommy Swann knew he looked ludicrous. In a cheap way, he had always been clothes conscious. Out of prison, he had loved to strut around the billiards halls dressed up to the nines, trousers pressed to a razor edge, small-brimmed hat at a jaunty angle, a boldly striped tie and a coloured shirt, a tight-fitting jacket showing plenty of cuff, wide lapels and flapless pockets.

That was Tommy Swann in his heyday. The Tommy Swann remembered by Rose Sandigate. The Tommy Swann who had taken her up West. The smart boy who had pulled a roll of notes out of his hip pocket to pay for drinks. The wide boy who went racing while mugs went to work. The chain-smoking dandy who loved to have his nails manicured, and made appointments to have his hair cut in Jermyn Street, and took a taxi-cab to keep the appointment. It was just swank, because everybody knew that nowhere in town could you get a better haircut than at Charles', next to Aldgate station.

Now he was a fugitive in baggy trousers and brown boots. A

scarecrow in a frayed blue shirt and shapeless grey cap. Eyebrows meeting over his nose like a dab of soot, ears sticking out like a pair of yellow fins on a ridiculous fish.

'Ha, ha, ha! Oh, Tommy, you don't 'arf look a sight for sore eyes.'

'Fer Gawd's sake, Rose, 'urry up and let me clear aht of this. Where's that two quid?'

'I'll get it for yer right away.'

She turned to go towards the bedroom door, and then the knock came. A loud, reverberating double knock.

Tommy Swann went quickly to the gas bracket and turned the light out.

'Who is it, Rose? Who is it?'

In the dark Rose shook her head. Her lips moved, but no words came forth. Her bosom heaved under the flower-patterned pinafore.

'Who is it, Rose? Who is it?'

'It must be . . . them.'

'Who d'yer mean – *them*?'

He heard her gulp in the dark.

'The perlice, of course.'

''Ow d'yer know? 'Ow d'yer know?'

'It can't be nobody else. It can't be. 'Oly Muvver, what am I gonna do?'

'Don't let 'em in, Rose. Don't . . .'

''Ow can I stop 'em. I'll 'ave ter open the door, Tommy. I'll 'ave ter!'

Her voice rose to a piteous wail.

'Wait; they might go away,' he whispered.

'They won't. They must 'a' seen the light. They must 'a' seen the light. Oh, Tommy, what am I gonna do? Oh, I wish you ain't never come 'ere! Oh, what you wanna come 'ere for, bringing me all this trouble? Oh, oh, oh! . . .'

'Shut your bleedin' row. Keep quiet an' they'll go away.'

He had caught her by the arm and was shaking her, as if to shake the hysteria out of her system.

'They won't never go away!' she wailed. 'They won't never . . .'

And then the knock came again. *Rat, tat! Bang, bang!*

'There, d'yer 'ear it? I told yer they won't never go away. They'll keep on banging and banging and . . .'

'All right, you damn cow, open the door. I'll go out the back way. Same as I came in.'

She burst into tears.

'That's a nice thing to call me. After all I done.'

He heard her whimpering in the dark, and even his mean soul knew contrition. He put his arm round her.

'I'm sorry, Rose. I didn't mean it. 'Onest, I didn't. On my liberty I didn't.'

'That's a nice thing ter swear on, yer liberty. Yer ain't got none.'

She dabbed at her snivelling nose.

'We'll see, we'll see,' he spoke through clenched teeth. 'We'll see. All right, you go down an' open the door. Keep 'em talking if yer can. I'll try ter get aht the back.'

'What about the money? Don't yer want the two quid? You won't get nowhere if you ain't got no money.'

'Yerce, I forgot. Fer Gawd's sake 'urry up and get it.'

'It's in me purse in the kitchen. Come down wiv me.'

She unlocked the door and they emerged from the darkness of the bedroom on to the gas-lit landing. They were halfway down the stairs when they heard the street door open.

'Somebody's opened the door!' There was amazement in Tommy's frightened whisper.

Rose looked down over the banisters. Standing at the open street door in his nightshirt was little Alfie Sandigate. He was staring up at the man who stood on the doorstep. Rose could not see the man's face. Just a mackintosh, a hand with a cigarette burning between the fingers and a foot sliding on to the doormat. Then she heard the man speak.

'Is your mother in, sonny?'

Little Alfie Sandigate's voice drifted up the stairs.

'I don't know. I fink she's asleep.'

'Go dahn, Rose,' Tommy Swann whispered. 'Go dahn an' keep 'em talkin'. I'll find yer purse.'

Rose Sandigate went to the door. Against a background of teeming rain she saw a strange young man wearing a mackintosh and a soft hat. She could only presume him to be a detective. She tried to speak, but could not form the words. Her lips moved soundlessly. The street seemed to be spinning round her. She saw not one young man, but a score of young men, all with the same pale, sleuth-like face and the same sinister smile as they all raised their hats and said: 'Good evening, madam. Are you Mrs Sandigate?'

Lips slackly apart, paralysed with fear, she just nodded.

'I'm making a few inquiries about a man named Tommy Swann,' said Slopey Collins, 'and I was wondering if . . . Hey, what's the matter?'

Rose Sandigate had fainted.

Slopey stepped inside the passage, half-closed the street door, and knelt down beside the slumped-up figure of Rose Sandigate. He loosened her clothing at the neck.

Little Alfie Sandigate, standing nearby in his nightshirt, stared at him.

'What you doing to my mum?' he asked.

'Go and get some water,' said Slopey.

'Who are you?' the child persisted.

'Never mind who I am,' said Slopey angrily. 'I'm a policeman. Can't you see your mother's fainted? Go and get some water – quick!'

The child edged away up the passage. Slopey watched him go, a cross-eyed little brat in a nightshirt, ungainly bare feet splayed out at the ends of his bony little legs. With a last scared look, he disappeared down the kitchen stairs.

Slopey waited for the child to come back with the water. Mrs Sandigate showed no signs of recovering. He wondered whether Tommy Swann was still in the house or if he had skipped out the back way. Could he dare risk a search of the house? He ruled it out as being a bit too risky; even a policeman couldn't do it without a warrant. But there would be no harm done in carrying the woman into her own room. And what better room to carry a woman who had fainted than her own bedroom? It was probably the upstairs room, the room in which he had seen Mrs Sandigate reaching upwards to pull down the blind, with Tommy Swann in the background. He kneeled down, put his arm round the recumbent, pinafore-clad mountain of flesh that was Mrs Sandigate, and tried to lift her. It was an impossible task.

He stood up, a crick in his back, and looked along the narrow passage, illuminated by a fishtail jet of gaslight which jumped and fluttered in the draught from the street door. The little house seemed to hold an ominous stillness. At the top of the kitchen stairs an inquisitive black cat was rubbing its arched back against the banisters, its tail erect, its eyes looking like two yellow sixpences in a disk of black paper.

It was only a few seconds since Mrs Sandigate had collapsed on to the doormat. To Slopey Collins it seemed an eternity. He went to the top of the kitchen stairs and looked down.

'Hey!' he shouted. 'Where's that water?'

Then things began to happen. First there came a scream of terror from little Alfie Sandigate. The kitchen door was flung open, and Tommy Swann came hurtling up the kitchen stairs. Slopey Collins braced himself for the combat. It was not the first time he had been in a rough and tumble, but Tommy Swann's methods of combat were strange to him, extremely fierce and extremely unscrupulous. A terrific kick caught Slopey at a vulnerable spot between the legs. With a grunt of pain, the reporter sank down on to his knees, and as he did so, Tommy Swann kicked out again and the boot landed full in Slopey's face. He felt the hot, sweet rush of blood in his mouth before the boot landed again, this time at the side of his ear. The last kick sent Slopey headlong down the kitchen stairs, and before he had recovered sufficiently to get to his feet, Tommy Swann was out in the backyard and scrambling over the wall into the alleyway that ran parallel with Coronet Grove.

Meanwhile, Rose Sandigate was opening her eyes. She blinked at her own front door, but failed to recognise it. She had never seen it from this angle before. Then she put out a podgy, coldly perspiring hand and felt the rough, mud-caked bristles of the doormat. She was dimly aware that something terrible had happened, but exactly what she could not immediately recollect. Her voice came back to her in a husky, tremulous whisper.

'Where am I? Where am I?'

Then she heard a footstep, and she saw a young man coming slowly along the passage. He was walking as if in great pain, his shoulders bent forward, arms clasped round his middle, his face streaming with blood. He did not seem to notice her, but walked right past and out into the street, leaving the front door open. As if watching some strange apparition in a silent film, in which she neither knew the beginning nor the end, she saw him groping his way down the steps. By the gate, he half-turned and looked up at her but he did not speak. His features seemed contorted in an agonised mask. Then she remembered, and in the terror of her recollection she wished she had never regained consciousness.

'Oh, Gawd,' she sobbed. 'Oh, Gawd!'

Slowly she got to her feet. She saw a car pulling up in the kerb-way outside, the brakes squealing. Two men were getting out of the car, and they came towards the gate, talking in matter-of-fact voices. Panic-stricken, Rose Sandigate shut the door.

Only then did she become conscious of little Alfie tugging at her pinafore and whining, 'There was a man 'iding in the kitchen, Mum, and 'e kicked that policeman what just went out. What's a matter, Mum? What is it? What's a matter, Mum?'

Mrs Sandigate leaned against the door, her face ashen under her tousled, copper-coloured hair, expecting any second to hear once more a peremptory *rat-tat-tat*.

'What's a matter, Mum? Was it a burglar in the 'ouse? What's a matter?'

She looked down at her child. He, too, was white with fear, but he was also tense with excited curiosity. His bare legs were frail and bony under the flannel nightshirt, his feet splayed out on the worn, green linoleum. His voice rose to a more shrill, an even persistent wail. '*Mum, what's a matter?*'

She shook her head.

'Nothin', son, nothin'. Go back ter bed, go on wiv yer. You'll catch yer deaf a cold. Go back ter bed, go on wiv yer.'

IV

While Mrs Sandigate was falling in a heap on the front doormat of number 26 Coronet Grove, Mr George Sandigate was standing in the public bar of The Two Compasses. He was consuming his fifth pint of old and mild.

Mr Sandigate was not a heavy drinker. He liked his pint and he could take his pint. He liked his drink just as he liked his pipe and his game of darts. He had other thoughts on his mind. He was worried. Genuinely worried.

Rose had shown her tantrums many times in the past, but they had been short-lived affairs. They had been of no lasting consequence. Never had he known a scene as ugly, as distressingly unpleasant as the scene in the house earlier that evening.

He was by no means a sensitive individual. He had lived all his life in a rough, tough world, but physical violence always upset him, particularly when it was shown by the womenfolk of his own household. A household of which he was proud. A household which, despite occasional quarrels and Rose's bad language, was quite respectable.

A nasty situation might have developed on the stairs that evening if he had not interfered, and the respectability of the house would have been shattered for ever. A brass stair-rod would be a wicked enough weapon in the hands of a child, let alone grown women. It might have resulted in a hospital job, and the police calling to make inquiries. Coppers on the doorstep. Coppers in the front parlour. A nice thing. And all over a silly squabble about a locked door. Funny, though, Rose had never locked that door before. Why she should suddenly take it into her head to do so was beyond his comprehension.

'What's the matter, George? Down in the dumps?'

He looked up to see the landlord of the Compasses surveying him from the other side of the bar.

'No, Joe. I'm all right. Got a bit of 'eadache, that's all.'

'Ah, nasty things, them 'eadaches. Shall I ask Edie if she's got an aspirin?'

'No, thanks. Don't believe in patent medicines. Oh, and 'ere's the dollar I owe you, Joe. Much obliged.'

'Pleasure,' said Joe Barker, pocketing the two half-crowns.

He drew up a pint and pushed it across to Mr Sandigate.

It was not often that the landlord of The Two Compasses stood drinks, and when he did it was only to the privileged few.

'All the best, Joe,' said Mr Sandigate.

The landlord glanced over at the dartboard.

'Shall we take the winners on?' he asked.

Mr Sandigate had not intended to play that night, but as the guv'nor so seldom played, in spite of being a remarkably good player, it would have been churlish to refuse. He turned to the chalker.

'Put an 'S' down, mate.'

'Where's the missis tonight, George?'

'Er – she ain't well tonight.'

'She got an 'eadache too?'

At that moment Edie came across from the saloon side to get some change from the public bar. Her voice floated cheerily as she ran up a *No Sale*.

'Good evening, Mr Sandigate.'

'Evening,' he replied.

'What d'yer think of that Tommy Swann?' she called out.

On the saloon side, Detective-Sergeant Fothergill heard Edie's exclamatory question. He did not see to whom it was addressed, neither did he hear Mr Sandigate's reply, but when Edie came back to the saloon bar, he emptied his glass and asked for another bitter.

Edie smiled.

'Would you like it in a tankard this time, sir?'

'Just as you like,' said Fothergill. 'I didn't know you kept tankards.'

'That's just our trouble. *Keeping* them.'

She turned her smile on again, hoping he would appreciate this gentle witticism. She knew Fothergill as a 'Plain Clothes Man'. Apart from that, she found him physically attractive.

Her taut skirt went tighter as she reached for a pewter tankard.

'Have a drink yourself,' said Fothergill.

She looked up as she jerked at the beer pump.

'O-oh, that's nice of you, sir.'

'What'll it be?'

She came back with the tankard overflowing.

'I think I'll 'ave a port, sir. A small port.'

'Good. Any special kind?'

'No,' she giggled. 'Any port in a storm.'

'Any port in a storm,' he concurred. 'But make it a large one.'

'Oh, shall I 'ave a Guinness?'

'Okay. It's good for nursing mothers, they say.'

'But I ain't a nursing mother.'

'You may be one day.'

'Some 'opes. I think I'll 'ave the port after all.'

She uncorked a bottle of red port and poured out a dock glassful.

'Cheerio, sir. All the best.'

'All the best,' said Fothergill.

'H'm.' The up-curling, pink tip of her tongue moved in circles around her lips in an exaggerated gesture of appreciation. 'A drop of all right, that, sir.'

Detective-Sergeant Fothergill watched the circling motion of the barmaid's tongue for a minute and then said, 'By the way, did I hear you talking about Tommy Swann just now?'

Thumb and finger curled round the glass, Edie paused to consider.

'Why, yes, I believe I did say somefink to Mr Sandigate about it in the public just a minute or two ago.'

Fothergill sipped his beer.

'Did you know Tommy Swann?'

Edie sipped her port, put the glass down, and then leaned forward confidentially, the neck of her dress sagging down and her raw, red elbows resting on the counter. She lowered her voice.

'Well, I can't say as 'ow I ever knew Tommy Swann, not really *knew* him, if you get my meaning; but Rosie – that's the girl who was 'ere when I first started 'ere – she knew 'im all right. Rosie was a bit of a lad, I can tell you.'

Fothergill sipped his beer.

'Is that so?'

Edie winked and adjusted the strap of her brassiere. She then scratched the back of her leg and, having looked around to ascertain that nobody was waiting to be served, returned to the absorbing topic.

'Did you know Rosie?' she asked.

'No,' said Fothergill. 'I can't say that I ever had the pleasure of meeting Rosie.'

'A doubtful pleasure at times, I can tell yer.' Edie leaned forward again. 'Although I wouldn't say as 'ow Rosie isn't one of the best, cos she is. Got a 'eart of gold, that girl has.'

Fothergill sipped his beer.

'So Rose is a nice girl, is she?'

Edie studied her port and then leaned so far forward that Fothergill couldn't but help seeing rather more than what Hollywood has called 'the cleavage'.

'Yes and no,' said Edie.

'By which you mean that Rose is sometimes a nice girl and sometimes she isn't a nice girl. Is that it?'

'If by a nice girl yer mean a refined girl,' said Edie, 'I'd 'ave to say "no", because Rose isn't at all what you'd call refined. But she's a sort of . . .' Edie paused to capture the inspiration, and, having captured it, added breathlessly: 'She's a sort of *rough diamond*.'

Pleased with the phrase, she could not resist repeating it.

'She's a *rough diamond*, that's what Rose is. D'you get my meaning, sir?'

Fothergill nodded, but not quite certain yet if he did get her meaning. The barmaid was prattling on.

'She was too good fer Tommy Swann, anyway, and I was glad it didn't come to anyfink. I told 'er in this very bar one night after closin' time, after he'd been in chucking 'is weight about in a flash suit, I told 'er: "Rose," I said to her, "he ain't no good to yer."'

'They were very friendly, were they?'

'Friendly!' Edie folded her arms. 'Why, do you know, 'e used ter take 'er to all sorts of lowlife places up West where girls danced naked and things.'

'And things, eh!' said Fothergill, trying to look duly shocked. 'D'you ever see Rosie now?'

'Oh, reg'lar,' said Edie. 'Reg'lar as clockwork she comes in 'ere – every Sunday night.'

'Then she'll be in tonight?'

Edie turned her ten-and-sixpenny perm to look at the clock.

'S'funny. She's usually in by this time. Reg'lar as clockwork she comes in with 'er old man.'

'Her husband or her father?'

''Er 'usband, of course. Mr Sandigate, that is. Him what I spoke to in the public just now.'

'Oh, so he's left Rose at home tonight, has he?'

'Looks like it,' said Edie. 'Funny, though. Sunday nights they come in together, reg'lar as clockwork.'

'Well, I must be getting along home.'

Fothergill pushed the empty tankard across the counter and buttoned up his mackintosh. Edie smirked at him as she rinsed out the tankard.

'Going to show a wife a good 'usband?'

'Oh, no. I'm not married.'

'Really, now! Fancy that! And you look the marrying kind, too.'

'Well, I suppose it's never too late.'

'What for?' asked Edie. 'To marry or mend?'

Detective-Sergeant Fothergill made no reply to the last verbal inanity. He just knocked the ashes out of his pipe and said 'good-night'.

'Goodnight, sir,' said Edie, and she grimaced as she put her hand beneath her skirt to scratch somewhere in the vicinity of a suspender clip.

V

A few minutes later a dark-blue police car was threading its way from Leman Street station out into the intersecting, maze-like lines of East End traffic, like a little blue spider speeding towards a fly that has foolishly attempted to escape its meshes.

'I'm fed up with this bloody manhunt,' said Leech.

'Think there's anything in this tip?' asked Nicolson.

'It's Fothergill's idea. Apparently he knows some barmaid who knows this woman Rose Sandigate, and she says Tommy Swann used to run around with her.'

'What's the address?'

'Coronet Grove.'

'Christ.'

'Exactly,' said Leech, lighting a cigarette.

'You know,' said Nicolson, 'sometimes I wish I were an American cop.'

'Aw, you've been reading too many magazines.'

'Maybe. But this job is positively degrading. What have we been doing all day – from eight o'clock in the morning to nine o'clock at night – we've been touring kip-houses and pubs and stinking tenements – kip-houses, pubs and stinking tenements.'

Leech chuckled.

'And now Coronet Grove.'

'Do we get a promotion if we catch this bastard?'

'Not if Fothergill knows it. He'll take the credit.'

'D'you know what I think?'

'What?'

'I'll give five to four this bastard Swann isn't in London or any other big town. I don't suppose he's more than fifty miles away from the Moor.'

'That's what my missis said. Was she annoyed when I had to report for special duty today! You see, I'd promised to take her and the kids to Whipsnade.'

'It's been a lousy day for looking at lions, anyway.'

'Yeah. I must tell her that when I get back.'

'When you get back.'

The car turned into Coronet Grove.

CHAPTER 8

I

Thus a Sunday night in Stepney. Rain falling. Cinemas crowded. public houses crowded. Cymbal-banging, red-jerseyed Salvationists. Grey-haired apostle of the Lord tramping the gutters between sandwich boards. Warm odour of good food from *Strictly Kosher* restaurants, the double triangle of the House Of David in gilt stencil on the steam-clouded windows. A hundred tattered communists, rain-soaked but still vociferous, marching back from Hyde Park yelling, '*Arms for Spain!*' Youths playing on pin-table machines. Lovers in dark doorways. Trams and buses thundering and screaming down the main roads. Roads garish with neon and a hundred different sights, sounds and smells. And back of the main roads a wilderness of grey streets, little dwelling-houses, rows and rows and rows of them, intersected by gaunt blocks of tenements. Against the sky a filigree tangle of swaying aerials. Streets silent as the grave, except here and there the blare of an exceptionally loud wireless set from somebody's kitchen; or a piano played with hideous mixed harmonies at somebody's front-parlour birthday party; or a teetering, sexless creature singing in the doorway of a public house, hat in hand, ignored by the crowd within; or a crying baby that refused to be hushed.

A night not so very different from a thousand and one previous nights. A night of rain and relaxation; a night of beauty and beer drinking and bawdiness; a night for young lovers and old harpies; a night of communal laughter and lonely tears. A night for comedy. A night for tragedy. A night for the sublime. A night for the ridiculous. Tomorrow was Monday.

Blissfully unaware that a police car had just pulled up outside his house, Mr Sandigate was in the public bar of The Two Compasses getting slowly but surely intoxicated. His daughter, Vi, was sitting on a divan bedstead three floors above Lisle Street. Slopey Collins was clinging to the railings of Coronet Grove. Tommy Swann was running breathlessly down an alleyway that led to Coronet Square. Whitey Williams chewed the damp end of a Woodbine as he came out of The Duke Of Teck, a raw whisky burning pleasantly inside him as he went forth to 'do' Mr Caleb Beasley – to 'do him good and proper'. Morry Higham was driving down to Brighton. His wife, Sadie, sat on a bedside trying to console her youngest baby. And Lou Hyams was looking not a little surprised as he gazed first at Doris Sandigate, then at Bessie Weinbaum, then back at Doris Sandigate.

'Well, fancy that!'

'Fancy what?' Bessie Weinbaum answered.

'Fancy you knowing Little Dolly Daydream!' he replied, smiling at Doris.

'Yes, she's just been telling me about you,' said Bessie. 'But I didn't know her name was Daydream.'

'Oh, that's just my pet name.' Lou grinned as he threw his hat on to a bookshelf and sat down. 'Mind if I smoke a cigar?'

Doris had been silent until now, feeling acutely sorry that she had spoken so enthusiastically to Bessie about Lou Hyams. It would be pretty awful, she reflected, if he turned out to be Bessie Weinbaum's *fiancé*. But, of course, the daffodils! The daffodils! Lou Hyams must have bought them.

'I – I – didn't know you knew Miss Weinbaum, Mr Hyams,' she blurted.

Lou grinned at Bessie this time and pointed his cigar at Doris.

'You've got very formal company tonight, Bessie.' He turned to Doris. 'Can that *Mister* and *Miss* stuff, kid. We're all friends here.'

'So it seems,' said Bessie. 'So there's no need for introductions.'

Doris shifted her feet awkwardly.

'Well, I s'pose I'd better be getting t'wards home now.'

'Not on your life,' said Lou. 'Don't you go running away because I'm here. How did you two meet, by the way?'

'At the ARP classes.'

'At the what? Oh, you mean that air-raid stuff?'

'Yes, we're doing first aid.'

'So I'm in good hands if I should fall and break my neck tonight?'

Doris smiled.

'You are a one, aren't you?'

Just then Mr Weinbaum came back into the room, spectacles on nose, Sunday paper crumpled in his hand. He pointed the crumpled paper at Lou, who was leaning back in exaggerated ease, legs stretched out showing a good length of his striped silk socks.

'You see, he's here. He kept his promise.'

Lou bit off the end of his cigar.

'I always keep my promises.'

'Perhaps,' said Bessie. 'But we didn't expect you to keep this one quite so promptly.'

Mr Weinbaum shrugged his shoulders.

'Such a boy he is! We don't see him once in six years, and then he comes twice in one day! Can you make that out?'

Lou swung round to face him.

'What d'you mean – *six* years?'

Mr Weinbaum shrugged his shoulders again and, head on one side, extended his hands, palms uppermost. The wrinkles around his eyes multiplied.

'All right, all right!' he said. 'Six years or six months. What's the difference? We don't see you once in six months, then we see you twice in a coupla hours.'

'Have a cup of coffee before you smoke your cigar,' said Bessie.

'No, he won't,' said Mr Weinbaum. 'He'll have a glass of wine. I know he likes it because he used to pinch it when he did the paper round.'

'I did no such thing.'

'Oh, yes, you did,' said Bessie. 'Because I watched you once.'

'You mean you used to pinch it, and then tell your father it was me.'

'Bessie,' said Mr Weinbaum, anxious about the niceties of polite behaviour, 'have you introduced your young friend to Lou?'

'No need to, father. They've already met.'

'That's right,' said Lou, grinning. 'Doris is one of my business acquaintances – aren't you?'

Mr Weinbaum pushed his steel-rimmed spectacles up on to his forehead.

'Business acquaintance! What sort of a business?'

'She's a customer of mine.'

'A customer, eh?'

'Sure. She plays on my pin-table machines.'

At this there was mild laughter. Doris felt more self-conscious than ever.

'And what's more,' Lou went on, 'she always walks out with half a dozen prizes.'

'I'm glad somebody wins a prize occasionally,' said Bessie. 'I always feel there's something not quite honest about those places.'

Lou crossed his legs, looked at Mr Weinbaum significantly and jerked his thumb towards Bessie.

'You see, Mr Weinbaum. Ever since your daughter's gone into politics she's been trying to reform everybody around here. Thinks she's too good for us.'

He looked back at Bessie.

'Keep that stuff for the Toynbee Hall, will you!' he bantered.

Mr Weinbaum shuffled out to get wine glasses. At the door he paused to say, 'You should worry, Lou! Why, she even tries to reform *me* at times.'

'That's not true,' Bessie protested.

'I'll lay six to four it is true,' said Lou.

'Must you always talk like a bookmaker?' Bessie asked in her sweetest voice.

'Well, you told me once I dressed like a bookmaker,' he cracked back. 'Besides,' he added, 'I am a bookmaker, aren't I?'

'Are you?'

'Oh, sure! Would you like me card?'

'Not interested.'

'No? Well, perhaps you could recommend me to some of your friends. We pay out on the nail. No arguments, and the best odds.'

There was something more than good-humoured raillery in Lou's words. Beneath it all, he was trying to annoy Bessie, to upset her complacency, even to slight her. Of this he was conscious, and wondered why he found himself doing it. He had always liked her. And yet now he found himself alternately attracted and then repelled by her. It was her confounded 'bookishness' he objected to, and it was all the more aggravating because he considered her physically desirable. He would have preferred her to have grown up into a woman with more human weaknesses, even an empty-headed film fan with a passion for clothes and having a good time. He couldn't help feeling that it was something of a pose. She wasn't a brilliant girl. She was just trying to appear intellectually superior. It was as if she no longer belonged to this part of the world, and her very act of staying here seemed to him to be a condescending insult. And yet, with all this, it was the woman in her that attracted him, and attracted him more than a little.

'Say, Bessie, why don't you move out of this dump?'

'Where to?'

'Stamford Hill.'

'Why, are you in the removal business as well as bookmaking and pin-tables?'

There it was again. That odour of snobbery. That implied criticism. That rank, suburban respectability, beloved of school teachers and bank clerks and shorthand typists who loved to call themselves 'secretaries'.

'What's that about Stamford Hill?' asked Mr Weinbaum, coming in with a bottle and a tray of glasses.

'I was suggesting Bessie would be more at home out there than here.'

'Stamford Hill! Oi, yoi!' Mr Weinbaum was contemptuous. 'I got a brother lives there. A great big 'ouse like a castle, and a great big motor-car like a charabanc. He hasn't paid for either of 'em.'

'Have a sandwich with the wine, Lou?' Bessie asked.

'No, thanks. I'll have *strudel* cake.'

'I didn't make any.'

'So! You got me here on false pretences, eh?'

'How's your brother getting on, Lou?' Mr Weinbaum asked as he handed him a glass of wine.

Lou made a derogatory gesture with his left hand as he took the glass with his right hand.

'He's a bad boy. A bad boy.'

'I sometimes see his wife shopping in the Lane.'

'Sadie's a sweet girl,' said Lou. 'The worst thing she ever did was to marry my brother.'

'A nice way to talk about your brother,' said Bessie.

Lou's voice became a shade louder.

'So he's my brother! All right, he's my brother! So am I to say he's a good feller just because of that, when I know damn well he isn't? Besides, he's a *schlemiel*.'

'What you mean is, he hasn't got your *chutzpah*,' said Mr Weinbaum, as he handed a glass of wine to the silent, tongue-tied Doris. She attempted to refuse it.

'Go on!' said Lou. 'Do you good.'

With half a smile she accepted it.

'Cheerio,' said Lou. 'All the best, Mr Weinbaum!'

'*Mazel tov*,' said Mr Weinbaum.

'Cheerio!' said Bessie.

'All the best,' said Doris, in a scarcely audible voice.

'D'you think there's going to be a war?' Mr Weinbaum asked suddenly.

'Who knows?' said Lou. 'Who can tell?'

'What does he know about it?' said Bessie. 'Ask him about dogs or racehorses and he might be able to tell you something. Of course there's going to be a war.'

'Who told you?' said Lou. 'Hitler?'

'My own common sense.'

'There was a bit in the papers about the Government making four 'undred thahsand steel shelters in case of air raids,' said Mr Weinbaum. 'They say you fix 'em up in your backyard, just like a chicken-house.'

'If you've got a backyard,' said Bessie.

Doris had taken a deep gulp of the wine and found it warm and sticky, cloying and pleasant. She realised she was unduly quiet, and decided to show that she did take an intelligent interest in world affairs.

'But,' she ventured, 'didn't Mr Chamberlain say last September that it was goin' to be peace in our time, didn't 'e?'

'Yes,' said Bessie scornfully. 'Like Sir Samuel Hoare, speaking at Swansea, said the Government was hoping for peace and pre-paring for war.'

'Perhaps they're only hoping for peace,' said Mr Weinbaum. Lou lit his cigar.

'You know,' he said, 'this conversation's getting a little too serious for me.'

'What shall we talk about, then?' asked Bessie. 'Pin-table machines?'

'Do me a favour,' Lou pleaded. 'Leave my machines alone.'

'I certainly shall. You'll never find me playing on them.'

'I should worry!' Lou retorted.

'Have another glass of wine,' said Weinbaum.

'I certainly will,' said Lou.

'And you, young lady?'

Doris fluttered a polite refusal.

'No, thanks. Really, not now. I'd better be getting along now.'

'Don't be silly,' said Bessie. 'Lou will run you home in his car. Won't you, Lou?'

Lou gave Bessie a searching glance and then grinned.

'A pleasure. It's parked just round the corner.'

'No, no. Please don't bother. Besides, I've got an umbrella.'

'All right, all right!' said Mr Weinbaum. 'Have another glass of wine. The umbrella only keeps the rain off. A drop more wine will keep the cold out.'

'Yes, but I'd sooner walk, really I would.'

'All right, walk, walk! But drink first.'

'Well, just 'alf a glass, then.'

It was still drizzling with rain when Bessie accompanied Doris to the street door. The pavements, black and shiny, reflected the lemon splutter of light from an overhanging streetlamp.

'Thanks for a nice evening,' said Doris. 'Thanks, ever so much.'

'Thanks for coming,' said Bessie. 'Come again, soon.'

At that moment they heard a car starting up rather noisily. It backfired several times and then there came the groaning, harsh chatter of roughly handled gears – gears in the hands of a driver unaccustomed to them. The next second a large Hudson Terraplane flashed past the house.

'O-oh, that's something like Lou's car, isn't it?' said Doris.

Then Lou himself came running to the door. He ran past them on to the pavement and into the roadway. He looked to the right and to the left.

'Which way did that car go?' His voice was loud, vibrant on the night air.

'That way,' said Bessie. 'Why?'

'Because it's my car, that's why!' said Lou.

'But how do you know – you didn't see it.'

'No, but I heard it,' Lou answered. 'And I'd know my car anywhere, blindfolded.'

And turning up his coat collar he ran in the direction of the nearest telephone kiosk.

'Where are you going?' Bessie shouted after him.

'Phone the police,' he shouted back.

II

When Detective-Sergeants Leech and Nicolson stepped out of their car in Coronet Grove, the first person they saw was Slopey Collins, doubled up against the railings, obviously in great pain, blood pouring from a chalk-white face.

He looked up as they got out of the car and came towards him. He could not see the uniformed driver, but he knew instinctively that they were police officers.

'You've just missed Tommy Swann,' he said, and turned his head to spit out a clot of blood.

'How do you know? And who are you?' Leech sounded suspicious.

'My name's Collins. I'm a newspaper reporter. I got a tip Tommy Swann was in that house.'

'And was he?'

'Yes; but you'll have to look nippy. I think he's scrammed out the back way.'

Leech turned to the uniformed driver who was still sitting in the car.

'Bert, you'd better drive round the block – see if you can head the bastard off. Freddy, you'd better go with him.'

'Excuse me,' said Slopey, spitting again.

'You're in a bad way, son,' said Leech. 'Would you like an ambulance?'

The reporter shook his head. Nicolson was just getting back into the car. 'Hey, you!' he called to Slopey. 'How is he dressed?'

'I didn't have time to notice,' said Slopey. 'But I know he's wearing a bloody heavy pair of boots, and I think he had a blue shirt on.'

'Was he wearing a hat?'

'For Christ's sake get going,' said Leech irritably.

The small blue car shot off towards the other end of Coronet Grove. Leech was genuinely concerned about Slopey.

'Sure you wouldn't like an ambulance, son?'

'No, I'm all right, except for a kick.'

'Okay, but you look pretty sick to me.'

'I'd look a damn sight more sick if Tommy Swann was picked up around here tonight and I was parking myself in an ambulance.'

'You're quite sure it was Tommy Swann?'

Slopey winced and spat blood again.

'Look,' he said. 'I'm a newspaper man. I recognise a face the first peep I get, see?'

'Got any credentials on you?' the detective asked.

'Here's my card and my police pass, complete with photography. Any more questions?' Slopey answered angrily.

'No, that's okay. One has to make sure, that's all. Now tell me briefly what happened.'

Slopey told him. Then they went up the steps together, the reporter moving slowly, step by step.

'We'll see what the luscious Mrs Sandigate has got to say about all this,' said Leech, as he knocked at the door. A thunderous double *rat-tat-tat* boomed down the rain-drenched street.

'I believe she took *me* for a 'tec,' said Slopey. 'Because she fainted as soon as I spoke to her.'

Leech gave his cocky little grin.

'I *am* a 'tec,' he said. 'But nobody ever fainted because I spoke to 'em.'

He lifted the knocker again and brought it down in another thunderous double *rat-tat-tat*. 'Nothing like a good bash of the old knocker to scare the pants off 'em,' he explained.

'Got a search warrant?' Slopey asked.

'Mind your own bloody business,' said Leech amiably.

They stood on the top doorstep, waiting. Waiting with that inexorable, illimitable patience characteristic of policemen and newspaper reporters. Opposite them and on either side stretched the little grey houses with their stained-glass fanlights, their spearhead rows of railings, their rows of whitened and unwhitened steps, here and there a lighted window. Rain dripping from the bluegrey roof slates, the smoke from the squat chimneys curling up to a pale, crescent moon, a skyful of mountainous clouds and weeping stars. Leech bit his lip.

'The old cow seems to be giving us the runaround.' Once again he gave the door knocker a 'good bash'.

'She's not so old,' said Slopey, leaning against the railings that divided the steps from the basement area. 'Fortyish, I should say.'

They were still standing on the doorstep when the car came back again. Nicolson came up the steps. He turned his thumbs down.

'Not a sign of the bastard.'

'All right, Freddy,' said Leech. 'And look, you'd better call up the Old Man. Tell him where we are, and tell him a man believed to be Tommy Swann has been seen at this address within the last fifteen minutes.'

'Right,' said Nicolson, and clattered down the steps.

'Now we'll see how far Mr Bloody Swann gets.' Leech knocked at the door again, louder than ever. To Rose Sandigate, sitting on Alfie's bed, every knock on the door seemed like a blow on her own body. With every knock she trembled more violently, until her trembling became a continuous shiver, and the shiver communicated itself to little Alfie Sandigate, who was sitting up in bed staring at his mother. His voice rose in a frightened, baffled but curious wail.

'Mum, why don't yer open the door? What's a matter wiv yer, Mum? Who's that knockin' at the door? Why don't yer open the door?'

Mrs Sandigate just shook her head. She was conscious only of this terrible, chilling fear. A fear she could not bring herself to face. Yet she knew she could never escape. In this moment she felt that she was the fugitive and not Tommy Swann. He had gone out into dark streets, and even if they never caught up with him, she knew that for her, Rose Sandigate, there could be no escape. 'I'm not a crim'nal,' she told herself. 'I'm not a crim'nal.' Rose Sandigate might have been a terror to her neighbours, and her language might at times be reprehensible, but she had never before committed any action likely to involve her with the police. Even when she had been a barmaid she had never 'fiddled' the till, and that was unusual. Now the police were on her own door-steps, hammering with a cruel insistence, demanding the entry which eventually they must obtain. BANG! BANG! BANG! went the knocker again. Her small son clutched at his arm.

'Mum! Why don't yer open the door?'

She looked at him. Then she stood up. She smoothed his pillow.

'Go ter sleep, son.'

'I can't! I can't! Why don't yer open the door?'

'They'll go away soon, son. You jes' go ter sleep.'

Then she went out of the room and down the stairs, a big, fat, white-faced woman in a coloured pinafore, untidy hair coiling down her neck, lips parted, eyes staring blankly like those of a sleepwalker. Thus, she went down to the kitchen and locked the door from the inside. But even here there was no peace. No escape. BANG! BANG! BANG! went the street-door knocker. And little Alfie was calling down the stairs, 'Mum, why don't yer open the door?'

III

From the CID, Leman Street police station, two circulars went out almost simultaneously for radio and general transmission. The first was that a man believed to be Tommy Swann had been seen leaving a house in Coronet Grove, Stepney. The second reported the loss of a 20 hp Hudson Terraplane car, licence number XYP 2351. It was quite possible that the two incidents were linked up. All officers were therefore instructed to keep a particularly keen lookout for the stolen car.

A few seconds later, over the sprawling city, at every main road junction the blue lights began to flicker over the police boxes. The officers taking the call wrote down the number and the description of the missing car. The mobile police were already peering through the windscreens at the number plates of every car they saw. The 'flatties' pounding the side streets had the car's description and number in their pocketbooks. And on the fringes of the town, on the junctions of the great arterial roads, every AA and RAC patrolman had the number.

It was thus unfortunate for Tommy Swann that Lou Hyams had reported the theft of his car so quickly. At the worst, Tommy had figured that the owner would not discover the theft for, say, twenty minutes, long enough to enable him to get to the outskirts of London. He was unaware that the theft had been reported before he had travelled half a mile. It was not until he got to Canning Town Bridge that he became aware that the car he was driving was already 'hot'. A policeman standing outside Canning Town station ran into the road waving his hands. Tommy Swann changed into top gear and swerved to avoid him almost in one movement. The tyres sang on the wet roadway. Then he heard a crash of glass and guessed that the flattie had thrown his truncheon at the car, smashing the side window.

Tommy grinned. Okay. If it was going to be a battle, let it be a battle. He swerved again and skidded across the traffic into Silvertown Way. The broad highway to Dockland was deserted except for an occasional lorry and a trolley bus. Tommy looked into his driving mirror and saw that the flattie had jumped on to the side of a private car, a Morris 12 it looked like, and was urging the driver to give chase. But the Hudson just leapt ahead, and made the smaller car look silly. It was lucky he'd pinched such a fast 'jam jar', he reflected. She was a beauty. As sweet as a nut. Even so, he knew regretfully that he'd have to abandon it at the first opportunity. In the pocket on the offside door he found a half-smoked cigar and a box of matches. He jabbed the cigar end into his mouth and lit it.

As he drove, his eyes flashed quickly to left and right looking for a stationary car which he could exchange for this 'hot number'. It was near the Graving Dock that he saw a public house, well back from the main road, standing more or less in a *cul-de-sac*. A bicycle was propped up outside near the door. Tommy Swann didn't hesitate. He swung the car round, drove up alongside, slipped out of the driving seat and on to the saddle almost without touching the ground.

A less wily man would have pedalled on in the same direction. Not so Tommy Swann. He turned the bike round and began pedalling back in the direction whence he came. He was glad of that decision, for a few minutes later a Flying Squad car flashed past him going all out down the Silvertown Way towards the Graving Dock. They didn't even notice the cyclist.

Back over Canning Town Bridge he went, grinning to himself as he passed the same flattie who had thrown his truncheon at him. Nearing Blackwall Tunnel he got another shock. Without warning, a policeman suddenly stepped off the kerb and held up a gloved hand.

There was no alternative but to apply the brakes. The policeman was a big man, and if he had tried to run him down, both Tommy and the bicycle would have bounced off him on to the hard, wet granite. And even if he had tried to swerve, the copper could have just swung one of his long arms and knocked him spinning. There was nothing for it but to pull up, but, even as he pulled the brake lever, Tommy Swann was looking for his getaway. No mug of a flattie was going to march him off meekly to the nick. No, sir. Not Tommy Swann. This flattie was due for the surprise of his life, and he wouldn't wake up until he was in hospital.

But as he dismounted it was the constable himself who dispelled Tommy's worst fears.

'Your light's gone out, mate,' the bobby said in quite a friendly voice.

'Oh – er – thanks, officer,' Tommy mumbled, keeping his head down and fumbling in the pockets of Mr Sandigate's old overcoat. He had left the matches in the Hudson.

'I don't seem to 'ave any matches,' he said nervously.

'Here.' The policeman's gloved hand rattled a box under his nose.

'Thanks,' said Tommy Swann, still keeping his head down and even venturing to give a tweak to the brim of Mr Sandigate's ridiculous old cap, so that it came down farther over his eyes.

The convict's hand trembled as he applied the flame of the match to the wick of the lamp. The first attempt proved unsuccessful. Tommy had to strike another match.

'Those oil lamps are out of date,' the policeman chatted pleasantly. 'You should get yourself one of those electric sets.'

'Yerce, I s'pose I ought to.' Tommy was bending over the lamp, adjusting the smoky wick. 'When I can afford it, that is.'

'Pay you in the long run,' said the flattie.

'Yerce, I s'pose so. Well, thanks for not pinching me, any'ow.' He gave a nervous laugh as he handed the matches back, swung his leg over the saddle and pedalled on furiously.

The constable stared after him, scratching his chin. Was the guy just nuts or what, riding a bicycle in those ridiculous baggy clothes – no collar, no tie, no socks, and yet smoking a fat cigar! And he said he hadn't any matches. Only when Tommy Swann was out of sight did the constable realise that he had not even caught a brief glimpse of the face of this strange, cigar-smoking, match-less cyclist.

The policeman walked on, deep in thought.

IV

When Doris Sandigate arrived back at Coronet Grove that night, she saw a small blue car parked in the kerbway outside the house. Three men were standing on the doorstep. What on earth could they want? They all stared at her as she mounted the steps. One of them was smoking a cigarette and had a bloodstained handkerchief clasped in his hand. But they didn't look rough men.

One of them raised his hat and said politely, 'Good evening, miss.'

'Good evening,' she said, putting her umbrella down and shaking the raindrops out. 'Did you want somebody?'

'Yes, I'd like a word with Mrs Sandigate, please.'

He reminded her somehow of the insurance man, but insurance men never came on Sunday nights. They sometimes came in pairs, but never in threes, and they didn't clasp bloodstained handkerchiefs in their hands.

'Mrs Sandigate is in, isn't she?' said another of the men.

'I think so. I'll tell 'er.'

Her hand was not too steady as she inserted the key in the lock. What on earth could three strange men want with her stepmother at this time of night? She turned to face them as she opened the door.

'What name shall I say?'

'Leech. Detective-Sergeant Leech.'

So that was it! She looked past them down at the car parked in the kerbway, the rain beating a tattoo on its shiny, dark chassis. She looked at Leech again. She looked at the other two. A small lump rose in her throat.

'You're policemen!'

'That's right,' said Leech cheerily. 'Just a few formal questions. Nothing to worry about.'

'Oh, all right. I'll tell 'er.'

'Thanks. Don't mind if we stand just inside the door, do you, out of the rain?'

'Oh, no,' said Doris. 'Oh, no.' She hurried down the stairs to the semi-basement kitchen, her heart thumping.

'Not a bad-looking kid that,' said Leech, as he watched her go.

'Nice legs,' said Nicolson.

'Nice all over,' said Slopey.

Downstairs Doris found little Alfie sitting outside the kitchen door.

'Alfie, what on earth are you sitting out 'ere for? Why aren't you in bed?'

He looked up at her, the same child who had made her feel so acutely embarrassed in Coronet Square earlier that evening, but a rather more wan-looking child, a pale, tousle-haired urchin in a flannel nightshirt.

'What's a matter wiv Mum?' he whined. 'What's a matter wiv 'er?'

'What do you mean – what's a matter with Mum?'

'There's bin people knockin' at the door and she won't answer it, and there was a p'liceman 'ere and he 'ad a fight wiv a man wot was 'iding 'ere, and Mum shut the door an' she wouldn't open it, and she tol' me ter go ter sleep. Then she came down 'ere and shut 'erself in the kitchen an' she won't come out.'

Doris tried the handle of the kitchen door. It was locked. She rattled the handle to and fro.

'Mum!' she called out. 'Mum!'

No reply came. She rattled the handle again.

'Mum!'

'Yer see,' said Alfie, 'she won't answer yer.'

Once more she rattled the door handle. Then she felt like jumping out of her skin with fright. For she heard a voice from the top of the stairs. It was Leech.

'Anything wrong, miss?' he called down.

'N-no, I don't think so. My stepmother must 'ave fallen asleep.'

But Leech was already down the stairs.

'Phew!' he said. 'Can't you smell the gas?'

Shoulder first, he hurled himself at the door.

CHAPTER 9

I

Midway between Coronet Grove and Stepney Highway is a depressing, factory-surrounded thoroughfare which is cross-sectioned at intervals by a number of railway arches, above which, at all hours of the day and night, lines of trucks are shunted, rattling and squeaking, to the goods depot of the LNER. Between these arches is a big, wooden gate which the railwaymen use as a quick cut-up to the sheds and sidings. There are two signs on the gate. One says *Trespassers Will Be Prosecuted*, the other says *Commit No Nuisance*. The latter instruction is frequently flouted. For this gate forms a most convenient recess which the sparse light of the streetlamp fails to penetrate.

In the daytime it is a desolate enough spot, and it would be even more desolate were it not for the fact that the brick walls of the railway arches are adorned with multicoloured advertisement hoardings, transforming this urban patch of industrial wilderness into a flowering gallery of commercial art. A fine, bearded sailor tells you that *Player's Please*, while a desirable wench in a tight swimsuit retaliates that *Craven A Do Not Affect The Throat*. A pink cherub is sound asleep, *Thanks To Nestlé's*, and we learn that *Mary Had A Little Lamb With Lots Of HP Sauce*. From the off-white pinafore of a little girl, and the superior smirk of her companions, it is obvious that *Somebody's Mother* – we presume to her everlasting shame – *Isn't Using Persil Yet*. The drinking fraternity, admonished for being vague, are told to *Ask For Haig*, but in spite of this a most foolish-looking fellow is running frantically after a bottle of beer, crying, *'My Goodness, My Guinness!'*

That, at any rate, was more or less the pictorial set-up of the railway arches which Whitey Williams surveyed as he stood in the dark recess of the big wooden gate. He was not there to commit a nuisance. He was there to commit a felony, to wit, robbery with violence. Or to use Whitey's own inimitable phraseology, he was going to do Caleb Beasley – do him good and proper.

Every Sunday evening, fine weather or foul, Caleb Beasley went for a walk – after the church service. Whitey knew this, and he waited for him in Coronet Square, a useful strip of iron railing tucked into his coat pocket. He wasn't going to muck about with old Beasley, no mucking fear. But when Mr Beasley did emerge from his house, Whitey's courage had evaporated. It would have been easy enough to give Beasley a crack on the skull, but there were too many people about at the time. So he tailed Beasley, and not ten minutes since he had seen him go, strangely enough, into a public house just beyond the railway arches. Probably the diabolical old liberty-taker had some business on hand. Either buying or selling. Whatever it was, he was bound to return this way eventually, and Whitey was prepared to wait for him all night. He needed money badly. He was hungry for money and the pleasures money could buy, and with that feeling was mixed the desire to cause Caleb Beasley the maximum of physical pain. Oh, yes; he'd do him all right – do him good and proper . . .

A train thundered overhead. What an ideal spot this was for giving Beasley what was coming to him! Even if he did cry out, nobody would hear him. He'd got it all worked out, Whitey had. When Beasley came along he'd creep up behind and crack him on the head so that he'd never know who hit him. Then when he was unconscious he'd give him the boot in the face. And then he'd go through his pockets. Whitey fell to speculating as to how much the crafty old fence would have on him. Maybe, as much as fifty pounds. You never knew. And then his lot, that gold watch and chain must be worth another thirty nicker. The saliva rose pleasantly in his throat in eager anticipation. He felt the reassuring hardness of the broken railing-end in his coat pocket.

Overhead some trucks rattled. Further along the line a shunting engine let off a shuddering whistle of steam. Whitey looked across at the posters on the opposite wall. *Player's Please. Thanks To Nestlé's. 'My Goodness, My Guinness!' Don't Be Vague, Ask For Haig*. He curled his lips. People got paid money for writing that sort of tripe, eh? Some people got easy money, a fact they did. He felt in his pocket for a Woodbine and was about to light it when he heard a footstep. This might be Beasley now. He flattened himself against the wooden gate, scarcely daring to breathe. He felt the raindrops dripping off the rusty iron stanchions on to his neck. The footsteps were nearer now. He wrapped a handkerchief round his hand and grasped the piece of broken railing. It is coming to yer yet, Beasley; it is coming to yer. Any minute now. First he saw a shadow. Yes, this was him. This was the moment. His fingers tightened on the broken railing and in preparation. He drew it slowly from his pocket.

But the passer-by was not Beasley. It was a rain-soaked lascar in a battered felt hat and drab blue dungarees, carrying a fibre attaché case, which was probably full of gaudy neckties. Whitey had often seen him hawking his wares around the Stepney and Poplar pubs. The coloured man shuffled past without appearing to notice Whitey.

Peep, peep, peep! went a distant engine. *Crash!* went a line of trucks. Then silence, except for water dripping everywhere. Whitey relaxed and felt in his pockets for the crumpled Woodbine. Five age-long minutes went by, a red Royal Mail van, a prowling tabby cat, and Whitey's heart stood still as a policeman sauntered past on the opposite side of the road. But he didn't see Whitey in the shadows and he went on.

Whitey was beginning to feel damp and cold. He pulled the knot of his muffler tighter under his chin, tilted his black hat over one ear and spat into a puddle. Another five minutes went by. In the distance a church clock chimed. Then two women came along. They stopped against the wall a few yards along, under the archway. One of them pulled her skirts up and kneeled down almost on her haunches. Then she got up and straightened her clothes and the other one kneeled down. Then they went on their way, talking loudly, thinking themselves unobserved. Their voices dwindled into the distance. Silence again. Whitey was beginning to feel restless.

Another five minutes. Then footsteps again. Once more Whitey flattened himself in the shadows against the wooden gate. Once more he wrapped the damp handkerchief round his fingers. Once more he grasped the hard, cold end of the broken railing.

The footsteps were nearer. A shadow under the lamplight. Then the man came into view. Yes. No mistake about it this time. It was Caleb Beasley, alone.

He didn't see Whitey. He walked past the gate, close to the wall, a thin, spare figure in black with slightly rounded shoulders. Whitey braced himself for the supreme moment, stepped out and without hesitation brought the broken railing down on to Beasley's head with a sickening crack.

Perhaps Beasley had an unusually hard skull. Or perhaps Whitey had been so nervous that he hadn't hit hard enough. Whatever the reason, the first blow did not completely stun Mr Beasley. He reacted in an odd way. For a second he seemed paralysed, but he did not fall. He put his hands up to his head and said quite mildly, 'Oh!' He repeated this several times and then, without looking round, teetered forward and leaned drunkenly against the curved wall of the railway arch, a pathetic, black, beetle-like figure silhouetted against the gigantic pink legs of the bathing damsel advertising Craven A cigarettes.

If nervousness had caused Whitey not to hit hard enough with the first blow, it caused him to hit all the harder the second time. He made no mistake about it this time. Beasley's skull seemed to go soft, and the broken railing to sink into it. Without a sound, Beasley crumpled forward on to his knees and fell face downwards in a puddle, the puddle into which Whitey had spat. A trickle of blood wound down over Beasley's forehead, across his face and into the puddle, transforming it from a muddy sepia into a pool of purple crimson.

Whitey wasted no time now. He ripped open Beasley's clothes, tugged his watch and chain out and then felt for his wallet. Elation filled him, joy swelled through his whole being as his fingers closed on that wallet. It had a comfortable fat feel. One glance was sufficient to show that it was filled to even beyond the dreams of Whitey's avarice. One side contained pound notes. The other side held a wad of very thin, white notes printed in black. Fivers and tenners!

There was no time to waste now. His heart thumping, Whitey dragged the recumbent, slumped-out form of Beasley into the recess forced by the wooden gate and turned to hurry away. He must get away from here as quickly as possible – miles away. He half-ran into the roadway, intending to take a quick cut down by the side of the railway sheds, and as he stepped into the road he collided with a cyclist. They both fell to the ground.

Whitey swore, got to his feet, ready to make a dash for it, but the cyclist caught him by the tail of his coat and swung him round.

The man holding his coat was a slim, vicious-looking fellow rather older than himself – a pale, unshaven face, upturned nostrils and narrow eyes and sooty black brows, meeting over the bridge of his nose. He was dressed in shapeless clothes, the peak of a grey cap pulled down low over his forehead. He wore a frayed blue shirt, without collar or tie, and stuck between his thin lips was a cigar stub. He took the cigar end out of his mouth and said, 'No 'urry, mate, is there?'

Then Whitey recognised him. Yes, he had seen this face before. He had seen this face in public houses and in the billiards hall over Burton's, at dog-tracks and coffee stalls. He had seen this fellow in smart clothes, and he had seen him in shabby clothes, although never quite as shabby as he was now. And he had seen his picture in the *News Of The World* that very morning. It was Tommy Swann.

'I've seen you before, ain't I?'

'Yeah?'

'Yeah; you're Tommy Swann.'

'That's right – right first time. I reckon you're one of the boys, too. Who's the mug?'

'What mug?'

Tommy Swann was still holding on to his coat tail. With the other hand he made a gesture towards the wooden gate.

'The mug you just done.'

'I dunno what yer talking about.'

The face under the grey cap sneered.

'Uh, come orf it. Don't give me the fanny. I saw yer do 'im.'

'All right,' said Whitey. 'I done 'im, so what?'

'And done yerself a bit of good, eh?'

It was Whitey's turn to sneer, but he looked apprehensively

up and down the street. At any minute somebody might come along. At any second Mr Beasley might recover consciousness, stagger to his feet and recognise him.

'All right, I done meself a bit of good. What are you gonna do about it?'

'Nothing, mate, nothing.' Tommy Swann's eyes were cunning, astutely expectant under the brim of the grey cap. 'I'm in trouble, mate. That's all. I'm in trouble. I need dough, I do.'

'Look,' said Whitey, opening the wallet. 'Here's –'

'I'm looking,' said Tommy, softly. 'I'm looking.'

'Here's a nicker, if it'll 'elp yer.'

Tommy Swann's hand closed over the crisp pound note.

'Thanks,' he said. 'What am I supposed ter do with it – buy jelly babies?'

Whitey frowned.

'Ain't it enough, then?' he demanded aggressively.

'I ain't sayin' it ain't enough,' said Tommy smoothly. 'I ain't saying that. But I'm in trouble, I am. And what's a nicker, after all? You can knock a nicker out in the boozer, can't yer?'

Whitey was beginning to feel scared now. For a fleeting second he considered poking Tommy Swann with a left under the chin, but it was a chancy business. It was neither the time nor the place for a rough and tumble.

'All right, all right, if yer in trouble, I'll 'elp yer,' he said. 'But let's git a move on. I don't wanna be 'ere when that mug wakes up.'

Tommy Swann let go of his coat tail. 'Come on, then.' They walked up the road together, Tommy Swann pushing the bicycle, Whitey Williams glancing over his shoulder every few yards. They turned into a narrow street near the railway sheds, leading down to the Minories. After walking for ten minutes, Whitey stopped. He was determined to get rid of Tommy Swann at any price.

''Ow much d'yer want?' he asked.

''Ow much can yer give me?'

'If a fiver's of any use –'

''Ow many fivers did yer say?'

'What yer tryin' ter do?' said Whitey, indignantly. 'Put the black on me, yer greedy bastard?'

'Put the black on yer, mate?' Tommy replied mildly. 'Now, I arst yer, do I look that kind of a feller?'

'Yerce, yer do,' said Whitey. The prospect of having to part with any more of these crisp new notes hurt him intensely.

'Oh,' said Tommy. 'Feelin' nasty, eh?'

'Look!' Whitey retorted. 'I ain't feelin' nasty to nobody, see? I've given yer a nicker and I've offered yer another five. If yer don't like it, yer can lump it, see? I can't 'elp it if yer on the run, can I?'

'Don't start rorting, now,' said Tommy. 'Don't start rorting. Somebody might 'ear yer. Sure I'm on the run, and so are you.'

'I ain't on the run.'

'You will be when they find out who did that mug under the arches.'

'Yeah?' said Whitey. 'Well, they ain't goin' ter find out, see?'

'I've seen you before somewhere, ain't I?' Tommy spoke in a soft, insidious voice.

'Maybe you 'ave. Maybe you 'aven't.'

'Didn't you do a stretch in the Scrubs?'

'Maybe I did. Maybe I didn't.'

Far down at the other end of the street Whitey saw a policeman's helmet. The constable was just sauntering on his beat in the normal way, but the sight of a blue uniform glimpsed under a streetlamp was enough to put panic into Whitey's heart. He pulled the rubber band off the packet of virgin-white banknotes and peeled a handful off, then he took some pound notes from the other side of the wallet.

''Ere, take this.'

A smile spread over Tommy Swann's unshaven face.

'Thanks. You're a pal.'

He took the notes with both hands. Then, as an afterthought, Whitey Williams put the watch and chain on top of the notes. Under his tilted black hat the perspiration of fear was glistening on his forehead.

'Take that as well. It's worth at least a pony. Now, for Christ's sake, leave me alone. There's a flattie coming up the road.'

Tommy Swann wrapped the notes round the watch and chain.

'Thanks; you're a china, you are, a regular china. I'll pay yer back some day.'

He swung his leg over the saddle and rode away. Whitey breathed a sigh of relief. He glanced over his shoulder. The policeman was still a couple of hundred yards away trying the lock of a warehouse. Whitey tightened the knot of his muffler and walked on as quickly as possible without inciting suspicion.

Reaching the Commercial Road he hailed a taxi-cab, instructing the driver to take him to the Shimmy Club in Lisle Street. He sat back in the cab, put his feet up on the opposite seat, lit a Woodbine and began to count the money. He counted it three times to make certain. It was incredible! Such good fortune simply didn't exist! It was more than he had ever dreamed of getting. He was lucky – stone lucky. Altogether he had two hundred and fifteen pounds on him, more money than he had ever had in his life. Oh, what a good time he was going to have with this! Just fancy, that diabolical old liberty-taker, Beasley, carrying all this money about with him! An enchanted vista of good things swam before Whitey's eyes. Women. Lovely, luscious blondes. Red-lipped, big-breasted brunettes. He'd sleep with two every night for a month. Whisky, champagne, cigars, new clothes. Half a dozen smashing suits. Gambling. Dog-tracks. He'd be able to try out that system he'd thought of. He was sure it was infallible. Life was good. His luck had turned all right. He saw it all in the cloud of smoke from his Woodbine. Woodbines! Pah! He hurled the cheap, offending cigarette out of the window. He leaned forward and spoke to the driver. 'Stop at the first pub yer come to. I want to buy a cigar.'

'Yes, sir,' said the cabby.

II

Mr George Sandigate had spent a pleasant evening, so pleasant, in fact, that his brain was now considerably befuddled with drink. This in itself was a rare enough occurrence. George Sandigate enjoyed his pint, but he could also take his pint. In fact, he could take a good many pints and remain, if not quite as sober as a judge, at least as sober as the next man. On this Sunday night, however, he had entered The Two Compasses in that frame of mind which is so often the phase preliminary to alcoholic excess – profound gloom. Consequently, closing time at The Two Compasses found Mr Sandigate profoundly happy – and drunk.

He was among the last knot of stragglers to leave the bar, while the potman was shouting, 'Your glasses, please! Long past closing time! Now, please! Come along there, now, *please!*'

Mr Sandigate rolled rather than walked out of the public house. Cap aslant on his head, one arm embracing a lamp-post, he began to sing in a strong, tuneless voice:

> *'By the ol' mill stream,*
> *Where we used ter sit an' dream,*
> *Nellie Dean . . .'*

He was still indulging in his one-man singsong some ten minutes later when the rest of the stragglers had departed homewards, and Edie, the barmaid, came out, also on her way home. She stopped and stared. The sight genuinely distressed her.

She was not distressed because she saw a man embracing a lamp-post and singing old-time music-hall ditties in a drunken, drawling voice. She had seen so many men do that sort of thing, and she had seen so many women do it, perhaps more women than men. She saw it almost every weekend after closing time. It was the natural aftermath to her working hours. She was distressed because the man she saw clinging to the lamp-post was Mr Sandigate, and Mr Sandigate was not the sort of man who clung to lampposts singing boozy songs.

Everybody knew that Mr Sandigate was no public-house loafer. For one thing, he worked for a big brewery, and breweries didn't favour that kind of employee. Mr Sandigate was a hard-working man, up at the crack of dawn, winter and summer alike, proud of the fine horses he drove for the brewery, proud of his little home, and yes, proud of his wife and daughters. Proud of his respectability. Edie walked across to him.

'Oh, Mr Sandigate, I'm surprised at yer! Don't yer think you ought to go 'ome now?'

> *'Jus' a song at twilight,*
> *When the lights are low,*
> *And the flickerin' shadders . . .'*

He broke off and peered at her. Who was this young woman in a mackintosh and a black beret with a feather in it? He touched the feather with unsteady fingers and mumbled, 'Stick a fevver in 'is 'at an' call him Macaroni.' But he knew this girl, didn't he? Yes, he knew that smile and that whiff of scent.

'Why, it's Edie. 'Ullo, Edie! 'Ave a drink?'

He fumbled in the pocket of his overcoat for the bottle of brown ale he had bought just before closing time. He tore at the sticky paper label over the screw stopper.

'Open it for me, will yer, Edie? I'm all fumbs.'

'Oh, Mr Sandigate!' Her voice rose in reproach. 'I've never seen you like this before. I'm surprised at you, really I am.'

With the bottle still clasped in one hand, he lurched, swung halfway round the lamp-post, recovered his balance, and then grinned at her.

'Never seen meself like it, gal,' he replied, looked at her hat, and burst into song again:

> *'Where did yer get that 'at,*
> *Where did yer get that tile?*
> *Isn't it a nobby one, just the latest style;*
> *I should like ter 'ave one, jus' the same as that . . .'*

He fumbled with the screw stopper of the brown-ale bottle again and looked surprised, hurt, when Edie pulled it roughly from his hands.

'Now I'm going ter see you 'ome,' she said. 'Right this very minute.'

'Open the bottle, Edie. There's a good gal!'

'I'm going ter see you 'ome, right this very minute.'

Tightening his embrace round the wet corrugated iron of the lamp-post, Mr Sandigate frowned and appeared to consider this prospect.

'Whoa!' he said. 'You gonna see me 'ome! What'll the missis say ter that, eh?'

'She's going ter say enough, in any case,' Edie retorted.

Mr Sandigate appeared to recollect something, as if in an inspired flash he saw the reason, the primary reason for his own alcoholic excesses.

'That's jus' the trouble,' he blurted. 'That's the root of the whole bloody trouble. She says too much. Too bloody much.'

'Now, Mr Sandigate. You shouldn't say such things. You know Rosie is a good wife – one of the best.'

Mr Sandigate appeared to straighten up and then held up a finger which wavered before Edie's eyes.

'An' my kids are good kids,' he said. 'Are they, or are they not?'

'Of course they're good kids,' said Edie patiently. 'Nobody denies it, does they?'

'They 'ad a good mother,' Mr Sandigate mumbled.

'Well, isn't Rose a good mother, too?'

'Ah, ah!' Mr Sandigate held his finger up again. 'But she ain't like their own mother.'

'Well, I s'pose she does 'er best.'

'We all got ter do our best, ain't we, Edie? We got ter give an' take, ain't we?'

Edie nodded. Encouraged, Mr Sandigate proceeded, getting into a sentimental mood. He wagged an admonishing finger.

'That's what we all got ter do. Give an' take. If we all did that, it 'ud be 'appy world, wouldn't it, Edie?'

'I s'pose so,' said Edie. She was now getting somewhat tired of the duologue. Playing the role of a Salvation Army lass, urging drunken men to return to the bosom of their families, wasn't her strong point.

'Look,' she said. 'Don't yer think you oughta be going 'ome now? Think of yer kids.'

'Ah!' said Mr Sandigate. 'That's jus' what I am doing. Thinkin' of me kids. Gawd bless 'em.'

Edie sniffed.

'You're showing it in a nice way, I must say.'

Mr Sandigate appeared to consider this thrust. He shifted his stance and put his other arm round the lamp-post.

'Don't worry, gal. I know I'm drunk. I'm staying 'ere till I sober up, see?'

'Staying 'ere till yer get pneumonia, yer mean,' she retorted.

'Staying 'ere till I sober up,' he reiterated. 'I got two young daughters at 'ome, yer know.'

'And a wife.'

Mr Sandigate frowned. His shaggy eyebrows came down low over his small, pale-blue eyes. He pushed his cap back, revealing the bald patch on his head. He was suddenly angry, flamingly angry with the swift unaccountable temper of the inebriated.

'Gawd stone the crows! Are you trying ter preach ter me? I'm old enough ter be yer farver.'

At this Edie took offence. It was quite humiliating enough to stand and argue with a drunken man; and what did she care, anyway, if he stayed out all night? She tossed her chin.

'Oh, all right,' she said. "Tain't none of my business I'm sure.'

And she walked away – trim, neat, efficient and curved in her mackintosh and black beret, the feather bobbing up and down as she walked. With his back to the lamp-post, Mr Sandigate watched her go. Suddenly, he recollected something.

'Hi!' he called out. 'You got my bottle o' beer!'

She made no reply, and Mr Sandigate was about to shout after her again when he heard a crash, an unmistakable, glassy crash. Edie had dropped his bottle of beer into the gutter.

Left alone, Sandigate pushed his best blue Sunday cap farther back on his head, so far back that it fell with a splosh into a puddle. Cursing, he bent to pick it up, and then proceeded to wipe it carefully on the sleeve of his best overcoat. Then he turned towards home. He was no longer in a singing mood. The night air and the rain were dispelling the fumes of alcohol. He no longer felt happy. The exhilaration was oozing away with amazing rapidity, leaving a feeling almost of physical nausea. He felt almost ashamed. Yes, he *was* ashamed that he, George Sandigate, could cling to a lamp-post and sing boozy songs. If a bobby had come along he might have run him in, and that would have meant goodbye to his job at the brewery. For drunkenness was the one sin his employers would not tolerate in their staff. At any rate, they didn't mind how much a man drank, so long as he didn't show it. Then, again, what would Rose have said if a policeman had knocked at the door of number 26 Coronet Grove, to tell her that her husband had been locked up for being drunk and disorderly? A nice thing.

With such things occupying his still somewhat hazy mind, Mr Sandigate walked steadily homewards. He turned into Coronet Grove and made a mighty effort to walk straight. He nearly succeeded. He lurched only once.

Turning the corner, he became dimly aware that something was happening quite near his own house. A small crowd of people had collected near his front gate, and the centre of attraction appeared to be a white LCC ambulance. Funny, he couldn't recollect that anybody in the Grove was ill. At least, Rose hadn't told him, and she was usually pretty well informed on such matters. Illnesses, births, deaths, miscarriages and marriages, Rose Sandigate always seemed to have inside information of every domestic upheaval affecting those around her. Perhaps it was a diphtheria case. He wouldn't be surprised at that either, what with the drains and one thing and another.

Wait a minute, though! Two uniformed men were coming out of the front door of number 26. Yes, it must be 26, and they were walking slowly down the steps. The crowd was stirring now, some of them standing on tiptoe. Christ! The men in uniforms and peaked hats were carrying a stretcher. He hurried forward and pushed through the crowd. People spoke to him, but he did not hear them. He was just in time to get a fleeting glimpse of the person on the stretcher. It was a woman's face. A face he knew he should recognise, but, for all its intimate familiarity, it was a strange face. Strange in a distorted, ghastly way. The texture of that face wasn't flesh at all. It was lead. And the lips were so blue. And yet that hair. Good God! It was Rosie!

'Hi!' he called out to the ambulance man. 'Hi, just a minute! Hi, just a minute!'

The ambulance doors closed silently. The driver went round to the front, took his brake off, pushed in the self-starter, and the ambulance moved off. Mr Sandigate began to run after it. 'Hi, hi! Jus' a minute! That's my wife in there. That's my missis! Hi! . . .'

At the end of the Grove the ambulance slowed down, and Sandigate increased his pace, thinking it was going to stop. But the driver had only slowed down to turn the corner – the white, wraith-like ambulance had vanished from sight.

He stood stupidly in the middle of the road, fear and confusion in his eyes. Water from his puddle-drenched cap dripped down his neck. In the distance he heard a bell ringing. The quick, urgent peal of an emergency ambulance. *Tring! Tring! Tra-tring, tring!*

What could he do? What should he do? Attempt to follow an ambulance now nearly half a mile away? He turned and ran back to the house. He arrived at the front gate panting, hoping an insane hope that he had made a fantastic mistake, that he was suffering from some form of alcoholic hallucination. Hoping with a desperate hope, a childish hope, that the woman he had seen on the stretcher was not his wife. No, no. It simply couldn't be Rose. She was waiting for him in the kitchen, and his supper was there on the table. Cold meat, cheese and pickles. No matter what tantrum she had been in during the day, Rose always had his supper ready at night. Suddenly he became aware that a police constable was stopping him from entering his own front door. This was monstrous.

'Me missis. What's 'appened to me missis?'

'Are you Mr Sandigate?'

'Course I'm Mr Sandigate. That was my missis on that there ambulance. What's 'appened? What are yer starin' at me for? What's 'appened?'

'The Inspector will tell you.'

The Inspector! What was all this? Mr Sandigate followed the policeman along the passage and down the stairs as if he were walking in a strange house. His kitchen seemed full of strange men. Actually, there were only three. Detective-Sergeants Leech and Nicolson, and Divisional Detective-Inspector Cherry.

The Inspector had arrived only a few minutes previously from Leman Street. His name was eminently unsuitable. He looked more like a turnip than a cherry. A great, big, white turnip in a sombre grey suit, his hair parted loosely over his head and looking like two decayed brown leaves.

'Mr Sandigate, sir,' said the constable, and went back up the stairs. The Inspector held out a flabby white hand.

'Good evening, Mr Sandigate. My name's Cherry. Divisional Detective-Inspector Cherry.'

'Me missis. What's 'appened to 'er? What are you blokes doin' 'ere?'

The Inspector spoke in a bland, soft voice which was intended to be sympathetic, but all his conveyed sympathy could not lessen the shock.

'Your wife attempted to commit suicide tonight.'

Although Mr Sandigate had seen his wife on the stretcher, although he had even chased the ambulance so desperately, although he had shouted so hoarsely as it had turned the corner, he was not prepared for this. Incredulity showed in his small blue eyes. His shaggy moustache seemed to pouch up under his nostrils as he gulped, 'You're makin' a mistake, ain't yer? My wife wouldn't commit suicide.'

'I said she *attempted* suicide. You can thank Detective-Sergeant Leech here for the fact that she's still alive. He broke the door down.'

Mr Sandigate looked at the kitchen door, the old familiar kitchen door, and sure enough it was splintered all the way down. Watched narrowly by the three detectives, he gazed dumbly round the room. Gazed as if he were seeing the place for the first time. There was the old-fashioned dresser, with the odd cups hanging on the small brass hooks. There was the teapot with the broken spout, and the Coronation souvenir milk jug. There was the old tin tea-caddy which had belonged to Rose's mother, a faded picture of Queen Victoria on the lid. There was the fireplace and the old black fender; the whitened hearth, now untidy with the accumulation of a day's ash and cinders. He looked back into the yellow-white face of Divisional Detective-Inspector Cherry. Old Turnip Face.

'No, no. You're makin' a mistake, mister. I don't care if yer did 'ave ter bust the door in. My missis wouldn't ever try to commit suicide. She ain't that type, see?'

The Inspector shrugged his broad shoulders and appeared to sigh.

'Mr Sandigate,' he said, 'have you any sense of smell?'

Smell? Smell? Sandigate was so dazed at first he failed to realise the drift of the question. What the hell was this big, fat copper talking about? Then, instinctively, he sniffed. He sniffed again and he felt the sickly tickle of coal gas in his nostrils and then oozing like a gaseous treacle into his throat.

'Oh, Gawd.' He moved like a blind man towards one of the Windsor chairs and sat down – inert, beaten.

'Oh, Gawd,' he said again. 'She did that? My Rose did that?'

The Inspector nodded.

'That's why we've got all the doors and windows open.' He took a large packet of Player's out of his pocket. 'Have a cigarette, old man? I think it's safe to strike a light now.'

Mr Sandigate shook his head. 'No, thanks. No, thanks.' He was staring at the gas stove. The old familiar gas stove on which Rose had cooked so many Sunday dinners. He now noticed that its heavy black door was wide open. The sight made him wince. He pointed to it. 'Was she there?'

'Yes,' said Leech. 'All the taps were full on.'

'But Rose 'ad no cause ter do a thing like that.'

He sat on the Windsor chair, cap on the back of his head, a head that shook to and fro with the meaningless detachment of a ventriloquist's dummy.

'Rose 'ad no cause ter do a thing like that. No cause at all.'

'That's what I wanted to talk to you about, Mr Sandigate,' said Inspector Cherry. 'In fact, it's my reason for being here. Are you sure you don't know why your wife attempted to take her own life?'

Sandigate looked up at him.

'We 'ad a few words this afternoon, but that wouldn't make Rose do a terrible thing like – like that . . .' He completed his sentence by nodding towards the open door of the gas stove.

The Inspector drummed his fingers on the cigarette carton. 'You mean you had a quarrel this afternoon?'

'Yerce, we 'ad a quarrel. But we've 'ad quarrels before, and – and – well, nothing more'n that.'

'What was the quarrel about this afternoon, Mr Sandigate?'

He made a physical effort to recollect the details of the scene on the stairs earlier that day. Rose, Vi and Doris. The thin strip of brass stair-rod whirling to and fro. Thin female screams. But what connection could that have with this – *this?*

'One of the kids wanted ter go into our bedroom ter powder 'er nose or somethin', and me missis wouldn't let 'er, that's all.'

'In fact, the bedroom door was locked?'

'Yerce, I believe it was; but 'ow did you know?'

'Mr Sandigate, we have already questioned your daughter. She says the door was locked.'

Sandigate looked baffled, indignant, and yet pitiful in his anger.

'All right, the door was locked. What's that got ter do with Rose doing a thing like that?' He nodded towards the gas stove. 'She had no reason. No reason at all.'

Inspector Cherry thrust his hands deep into his trousers pockets, appeared to sway forward a little from the hips, and then back on to his heels. He took his hands out of his pockets and folded his arms.

'It seems pretty conclusive, Mr Sandigate,' he said, 'that your wife *did* have a reason.'

George Sandigate stood up. He kicked the kitchen chair back and faced the Inspector aggressively, chin out. 'What d'yer mean? What reason?'

The Inspector's voice was bland, casual, almost ingratiating. 'Mr Sandigate, were you aware that this house was harbouring a criminal – a man who was wanted by the police – a man who had recently escaped from prison?'

Sandigate's frown deepened into bewilderment. Mentally, he seemed to be repeating the Inspector's words, attempting in the recesses of his brain to make some sense out of what seemed to be nothing less than sheer fantasy.

''Arbouring a criminal!' he repeated. ''Ere, just what the bloody 'ell are you talking about?'

'Mr Sandigate, do you know a man named Swann – Tommy Swann?'

George Sandigate sat down again. He sat down abruptly. Tommy Swann! The three detectives were watching him narrowly.

'Tommy Swann? No, I don't know 'im. I mean – well, in a sort of way I do.'

'You mean you do know him?'

'Well, yerce. I met 'im once or twice yers ago – yers ago.'

'When was the last time you saw him?'

'Must be five or six yers ago. 'Ere, but what's all this got ter do with my missis and – and –'

He broke off, too bewildered to talk coherently. Inspector Cherry placed a hand on his shoulder.

'Look, Sandigate,' he said. 'We're here to help you. Why don't you tell us everything? Was it your wife who persuaded you to allow Tommy Swann to hide in this house?'

George Sandigate had already received one severe shock that evening, but as the full implication of the Inspector's words became apparent to his bemused mind, the accusation struck him as being too preposterous, too outrageously silly for contemplation. He jumped to his feet again.

'Are you bloody daft, or what? Tommy Swann 'ere in my 'ouse! Gawd stone the crows! Where d'yer get that one from?'

'I'm afraid, Mr Sandigate, it happens to be true. A newspaper reporter saw him tonight, your own child – the boy – saw him, and a number of fingerprints found in the upstairs bedroom are undoubtedly those of Tommy Swann. Isn't that so, Leech?'

Leech nodded. 'Quite true.'

Sandigate now looked at the three detectives just as narrowly as they had been surveying him. A menacing, distrustful note crept into his voice.

''Ere, are you blokes trying ter frame me, because if so –'

Inspector Cherry held up his hand. 'Look, Mr Sandigate, we're not trying to frame you, as you put it. We're trying to help you.'

''Elp me!' Mr Sandigate's voice became a shout. 'That's a joke, that is. 'Elping a bloke by accusing him of 'arbouring criminals. That's a laugh, that is.'

'Now, take it easy, Mr Sandigate.'

'Look, I don't care what you blokes think or what you say. I know nothin' about Tommy Swann being 'ere, and I don't think he ever was 'ere. I'm going to the 'ospital ter see me wife. You ain't gonna stop me, either.'

'As a matter of fact, Mr Sandigate, I was going to offer to drive you to the hospital. But I doubt if you'll be able to see your wife just yet.'

'Why not? She's all right, ain't she?'

'Yes; but she's in a very critical condition – very critical. I want you to understand that. Come on, I'll drive you to the hospital now.'

Mr Sandigate moved towards the splintered kitchen door, paused as he looked up at the Inspector. ''Ere' – his voice was querulous – 'I ain't under arrest, am I?'

The Inspector placed a reassuring hand on his elbow, but Sandigate found it far from reassuring.

'Of course you're not under arrest,' said Cherry pleasantly, 'but when we've been to the hospital I'd like you to come to the station to sign a statement.'

'Oh!'

They went up the stairs to the front door, down the steps to the waiting car. A uniformed driver opened the car door for them. 'London Hospital,' said Cherry as they stepped in.

'Yes, sir.'

The car moved forward, swung out of the Grove and across Coronet Square. Divisional Detective-Inspector Cherry took the large Player's out of his pocket.

'No, thanks,' said Sandigate.

'Rain seems to have eased off a bit,' said Cherry as he lit a cigarette.

'You know,' he went on, 'we've had quite a busy evening. We've got a murder on hand as well.'

'Murder?'

'Yes. You know Beasley, the builder? We've just passed his house –'

'Yerce, I know 'im.'

217

'Well, he was picked up under the railway arches tonight – dead. His head was bashed in, bashed to pulp. Nasty job – a very nasty job.'

The Inspector sat back in the car, stretching his legs, hands deep in his trousers pockets, his lips tugging at the cigarette and continuously emitting wreathing clouds of smoke. Mr Sandigate sat next to him, leaning forward a little, silent, taciturn, afraid, bewildered, his blue serge cap on the back of his head, revealing the bald patch, his eyes surveying but not seeing the wet streets that flashed past the car, the public houses now closed, the rows of little shops, brass balls of the pawnbroker's insignia, and a *News Of The World* contents bill flapping outside a paper shop. Blue letterpress on the white double-crown, *Dartmoor Gaol Break*. The Inspector flicked a spiral of ash out of the car window.

CHAPTER 10

I

No chaste virgin could have been more horrified than Vi Sandigate when she realised that Lulu Blair, her next-door neighbour,
had mistaken her for a woman of the streets. For a long time she
sat on the divan bedstead, smarting under the insult. She sat
there with her knees drawn up under her chin, her hands clasped
round her shapely legs, a cigarette twitching in her mouth. The
cheek of it! She made up her mind to tell Lulu Blair a thing or
two the next time she met the platinum-headed, flabby-fleshed
old haybag. And wait till she saw Morry again, just wait, she'd tell
him a thing or two, too. What did he take her for, she'd like to know.
What next! It was a pity he wouldn't be calling until tomorrow.
Otherwise she'd pack up and leave this place right this very night.
Inwardly, she seethed with indignation, and, being unable to give
vent to this indignation, the corners of her mouth puckered with
suppressed fury, and with each twitch of the lips a cascade of
cigarette ash floated down on to the knees of her artificial silk
stockings. And as each cigarette burned down to a lipstick-coated
stub, she would extract another one from the packet beside her
on the bed. It was just as she was about to light a fresh cigarette
that she felt something crawling on the back of her neck, just above
the hem of her frock. She flicked it off and, as it fell on to the divan,
she jumped to her feet shuddering with revulsion. It was small
and round and red, rather like a tiny berry. It crawled leisurely.
An examination of the walls and bedclothes revealed that this
was no stray adventurer. The room was teeming with them.

Hurriedly she got her things together, straightened her hair,
painted her lips once more, snapped the locks of her attaché case,
put her hat on and ran quickly down the uncarpeted stairs. It was
on the second flight down that she collided with Whitey Williams,
who was on his way up to the Shimmy Club, a room on the first

floor. The collision knocked the attaché case out of her hand and the cheap locks sprang open, scattering the contents on to the stairs.

'Oh – sorry!' she said, breathlessly.

'Don't be sorry,' said Whitey, feeling quite the gentleman and remembering how soft her body had felt in that brief, accidental contact. 'I like it.'

He stooped to help her pick up her garments.

'In a bit of 'n 'urry, weren't you?' he asked.

'Yes. I'm getting out of 'ere.'

'What's a matter, kid? In trouble?'

'Oh, no; but there's bugs in my room.'

Whitey laughed. He couldn't help it. Vi Sandigate flushed.

'I don't see anything funny,' she began.

'No,' he agreed. 'But from the way yer came running down the apple and pears I should a thought the bloody things were chasing yer. Haw, haw, haw!'

'Damn this case,' she said, trying to close the lid on the heaped-in garments.

''Ere, let me 'elp yer.'

'No, I can manage.'

'Yer can't see prop'ly on the stairs,' he persisted. 'Come inter the club and do the thing in comfort.'

'Club?' She looked up. 'What club?'

'Strewf,' said Whitey. 'Yer mean ter say yer live 'ere and yer don't know the Shimmy Club? Come on in. I'm a member. I bet you could do with a drink, couldn't yer?'

Vi hesitated. The word 'club' was magic in her ears. She had heard a lot about West End clubs, but had never been in one. Whitey's fingers were on the fleshy part of her arm. 'Wouldn't yer like a nice drink, eh, kid?'

'That's jus' what I could do with,' she said. 'A nice drink.'

And they went into the tawdry little room above the Italian-owned café in Lisle Street, a little room with a bar in one corner and a piano in the opposite corner, between the door and which were several fruit machines, a sofa and an easy chair. Reclining in the easy chair, placidly smoking his pipe, was Detective-Sergeant Fothergill.

There were a number of people in the club, and Whitey failed to see the detective. He swaggered towards the wooden flap which constituted the bar, black hat tilted towards his left eyebrow, white scarf knotted under his chin, a stale cigar purchased in a public house jutting from his mouth. The proprietor of the club, a fat little man in a pinstripe suit, seemed surprised to see Whitey.

'You've got a nerve coming 'ere,' he said.

Theatrically, Whitey folded his arms.

'What d'yer mean – nerve? I'm a member, ain't I?'

'Coming back 'ere after knocking me for two quid,' said the little fat man.

Whitey unfolded his arms and flapped the fingers of his right hand up and down rather in the manner of someone waving goodbye.

'Shut up, shurrup! I don't do nobody for nothing, see?'

'Well, where's my two nicker, then?'

'All right, all right! I got it 'ere.' Whitey tapped the breast pocket of his tight-fitting overcoat and then turned to Vi. 'What are you 'aving, kid?'

'I think I'd like a gin and lime,' said Vi.

'We're out of gin,' said the little fat man.

Whitey clicked his tongue in disapproval. Folding his arms again, his head went to an angle of forty-five degrees as he sneered at the proprietor. 'A nice dump you got 'ere. A nice bloody dump ter bring a lady friend.'

'We've got whisky. We've got brandy. We've got beer. We've got port. But we've run out of gin,' said the proprietor aggressively. 'If some people would pay us the money they owe we'd be able to get a bigger stock and then we wouldn't run out. We 'ave ter pay cash, we do. Cash.'

'Okay, okay. Yer 'ave ter pay cash. Stop crying, will yer!' Whitey turned to Vi again. 'What'll 'ave, kid?'

'O-oh, anything'll do,' she said.

'I know.' Whitey held up his right index finger in the manner of a man who is visited by divine inspiration. 'You'll 'ave a brandy and ginger ale. You'll like that. Two large brandies and a split ginger ale.'

The little fat man poured out two large brandies and divided a ginger ale between the two.

''Ave one yerself,' said Whitey, magnanimously.

Whitey Williams with money in his pocket was a superior relation to that Whitey Williams who had stood in the saloon bar of the Compasses. As a flower blossoms in the sunshine, so Whitey Williams blossomed when money came his way. And tonight he had more money on him than he had ever had in his life. He was convinced that his luck had now changed. No more small-time villainy for him! He was a Big Money Boy now. By comparison, Alfie Price and Dicey Perkins were small fry. Breaking into warehouses, risking their liberty to steal a gross of roller skates and then getting three quid for their trouble. Thinking of it, Whitey's lips curled in contempt. He had completely forgotten that the job in Great Mansell Street had been undertaken at his instigation, that he had informed them that there was eight hundred pounds in the safe. To him, Alfie and Dicey were just plain mugs, afraid to have a go. If they had been wide boys they might even now have been sharing in his good fortune. As it was, well, so much the more for Whitey. He had taken the risk, and he was going to lap up the gravy. It was a pity he had had to give so much to that son of a bitch, Tommy Swann, but in retrospect Whitey was inclined to see it as a good deed. It pleased his vanity to think that he had assisted a man who had made a notorious gaol break. The few notes he had given away did not seem to make the fat wad in his pocket much thinner, and as for the red lot, the watch and chain, how much would a fence give for it? Peanuts. What would have been a fortune to Whitey in the morning he considered peanuts at nightfall. Besides, there was always a risk in getting rid of that sort of thing. And Whitey couldn't afford to take any chances.

'That'll be nine bob,' said the proprietor. 'And two quid makes two pahnd nine. Come on, let's see the colour of yer coin.'

Whitey made a lordly, magnificent gesture. His voice rang loud. 'Got change of a tenner?'

'No, I 'aven't.'

Whitey sighed. 'A fiver, then?' And he said this in a manner which the average person might use in referring to a threepenny bit.

'I might just be able to manage it,' said the little fat man.

'Okay.' Whitey tossed the note on to the counter. 'G'luck, kid.'

'Cheerio,' said Vi, and sipped the brandy and ginger ale. 'O-oh, isn't it lovely! Ever so nice.'

Whitey looked as flattered as if the drink were his own creation. 'Best drink there is,' he nodded. 'Stick around wiv me, kid, and you'll learn a fing or two. By the way, ain't I seen you before somewhere?'

'I don't think so,' said Vi.

'Ain't I seen you in the East End?'

'Oh, no. I come from Streat'am.'

Vi Sandigate had never been to Streatham, but she had a vague idea that it was one of the nicer suburbs. She had seen that wad of notes in Whitey's hand. Why, he must be a very rich man. Stone rich. She had never even seen a five-pound note before, let alone a wad of them. He wasn't bad-looking, either, and under the tilted brim of his black hat she could see that he had the beginnings of what is commonly known as a 'cauliflower ear'. Perhaps he was a champion boxer. How thrilling. As if divining her thoughts, Whitey suddenly pointed his brandy glass at a photograph on the wall.

'See that picture?' he said. 'It's me.'

So it was. A photograph of a much cleaner-looking Whitey Williams wearing only boxing gloves and a brief pair of dark tights about his middle. His left arm was extended in fighting stance. Across the photograph was written in an illiterate hand, *To my old pal, Monty.*

Whitey suddenly turned to the little fat man, not at all in the manner of a man addressing an old pal, and said, ''Ere, what about my bleedin' change?'

Monty pushed it across the counter. 'Here yah, two pounds one.'

Whitey appeared to be making an intricate mental calculation. 'Is that right?'

'Sure it's right,' said Monty. 'I don't short change nobody.' He smoothed out the five-pound note, held it up to the light, then folded it and was about to put it in his waistcoat pocket when another voice spoke, a mild, rather slow voice, which made Whitey spill his brandy and look round as if he had been stabbed.

'D'you mind if I look at that note?' said Fothergill.

Monty's flat little hand closed tight over the crisp white paper. He looked suspiciously from Fothergill to Whitey, whose face was now even paler than the banknotes in his pocket. Monty looked at Fothergill again. The detective's baby-blue eyes were smiling through a cloud of tobacco smoke.

'D'you mind if I see that note?' he said again.

Whitey Williams felt himself shrinking like a pricked balloon. The swagger, the bombast was oozing out of his feet. How did Fothergill come to be in the West End? What was he doing in this place? The bastard seemed to be everywhere. Had Caleb Beasley reported the assault and robbery? Had he given the police the numbers of the stolen notes? Whitey found himself perspiring as he had never perspired in any boxing ring. He saw Monty handing the note to Fothergill.

'What's a matter?' Vi said softly, moving closer to Whitey.

Vi's voice and her proximity gave him an idea. He put down his drink and suddenly embraced her. She was so surprised that she made no attempt to resist him as she felt his body against hers and his mouth pressing down on her own. But it did seem a bit sudden and rather too public, and then she felt his hand under the neck of her frock. ''Ere, wait a minute,' she gasped. 'What sort of caveman are you?' But nobody heard the words. His own mouth smothered them and his hand went deeper. She felt it warm and perspiring against her breasts.

'Don't make a rort abaht this,' he whispered fiercely. 'I'm in trouble 'ere. I've just stuck two 'undred quid down yer neck. Get out of 'ere quick an' wait for me at the Corner 'Ouse. Go on, be a china. 'Urry up, fer Christ's sake.'

Dazed, scarcely believing that she really had two hundred quid nestling in her bosom, Vi Sandigate went out of the club and down the stairs into the street. Detective-Sergeant Fothergill looked up as she went out.

'Is your girlfriend leaving us, Whitey, so soon?'

Fear made Whitey adopt a truculent attitude.

'Look,' he said. 'What d'yer want wiv me?'

Fothergill was still studying the five-pound note. He looked round at Whitey, smiling over his pipe.

'What makes you think I want anything with you, Whitey?'

Whitey swallowed the remains of his brandy and, although he was trembling inwardly and globules of perspiration were shining behind his ears, he stepped up to Fothergill, and his voice became a snarl. 'Listen, copper, you bin tailing me about all day.'

Fothergill blew a cloud of tobacco smoke so that it wreathed about Whitey's face. 'You flatter yourself, sonny boy. What makes you think I've been tailing you – unless, maybe, a guilty conscience?'

Behind the bar, Monty was watching Fothergill folding the banknote. He gulped.

'Say,' he said. 'That fiver's all right, ain't it?'

'Yes,' said Fothergill. 'Quite all right.' He handed it back to Monty, who lost no time in thrusting it into his waistcoat pocket.

'Of course it's all right,' said Whitey, feeling a great sense of relief. 'He's just trying ter be funny.'

'Where did you get that note, Whitey?'

Whitey looked indignant again.

'Why, what's a matter? Yer just said yerself that it was all right, didn't yer?'

Fothergill nodded. 'Sure I said it was all right, meaning that it wasn't spurious currency. But I'd still like to know where you got it.'

'A feller give it to me.'

'*Gave* it to you?'

'A feller what owed me some dough paid me back.'

'You're quite sure you didn't get it by selling some roller skates?'

'Roller skates! I don't know what yer mean. What would I be doing wiv roller skates?'

'Suppose you tell me.'

'I don't know what you're talking abaht.'

Whitey was feeling brave again. Fothergill wasn't after him for doing Caleb Beasley. He knew nothing about that, and even if he did know, he couldn't possibly suspect him. Even Beasley himself didn't have a chance to see who cracked him. The only person who could possibly testify against him was Tommy Swann, and *he* wasn't likely to turn stool pigeon. He'd got quite enough on his plate already without incriminating himself further. After all, he had been an accessory after the fact, Tommy Swann had. Whitey Williams squared his shoulders, tightened the knot of his scarf. He felt very much better. Fothergill hadn't got a thing on him. He was just a dumb dick.

'Give us another brandy.' Whitey rapped on the counter. 'A large one.'

'Better make it a quick one,' said Fothergill quietly.

With a theatrical gesture Whitey folded his arms. An inch or two taller than Fothergill, he tilted his chin so that he looked down his nose at the detective-sergeant.

'And why should I make it a quick one?' he asked, his mouth curling insolently.

'Because I'm in a hurry,' said Fothergill. 'I've had a long day. Come on, Whitey. There's a car waiting for you downstairs.'

Just then there came a tinkle of silver from one of the fruit machines. A miniature cascade of sixpences pouring into the hands of the lucky player, a woman, who was so delighted that she screamed, 'Whoopee! Whoopee!'

II

After telephoning the police to report the loss of his car, Lou Hyams went back to Weinbaum's house to collect his hat and coat. He found Bessie Weinbaum still standing at the door, her wavy hair disarrayed in the breeze.

'You'll catch a nice cold standing there,' he said.

'Not half the cold that you'll catch, running out in the rain without even a hat on. Did you phone the police?'

'Yes. They're circulating the description right away. I came back for my hat and coat.'

'Oh!'

Lou got his hat and coat and they again stood at the street door together. The doorway was narrow. Their arms were touching.

He felt her pulse beating against his own. A stray wisp of her hair touched his ear. Her perfume was in his nostrils. He looked at her, the soft curve of her neck, the upward thrust under her blouse. She was a woman to be desired. She did not meet his gaze, but stared before her into the street.

'I hope you get your car back, Lou.'

'Oh, yes; I'll get it back. I expect it was just some kids having a joyride.'

'They might have an accident.'

'That's possible.'

'The car might get smashed.'

'If they smash the car, they'll smash themselves, too.'

He walked to the kerb and kicked at something in the gutter. She stared at him.

'What are you doing?'

He made no immediate reply, but walked back to her and said with a grin, 'I'm sorry your old man doesn't like my cigars.'

'What do you mean?' she asked.

'Oh, nothing. Goodnight, Bessie.'

She turned to look at him. 'Goodnight, Lou. I – I suppose I'll be seeing you sometime?'

'Oh, sure, sure.' He nodded vigorously. 'Well, goodnight, Bessie.'

'Goodnight, Lou.'

She watched him go. Broad-shouldered, swaying slightly from the hips as he walked, his American-style hat slightly tilted, his well-polished shoes glinting every time he passed under a street-lamp. She felt curiously dry in the throat. At the corner he looked back and waved his hand. Then he was gone. Gone. Tomorrow was Monday. She went in and closed the door.

III

The public houses had closed. The Salvationists had packed up their cymbals and marched back to their righteous abodes. The fried-fish shops were in darkness. The last audiences had filed out of the cinemas, leaving the interior a dark, blank-screened, paper-strewn cavern. The rain had abated, but the wind, gathering strength, tore round corners, playing havoc with unpinned hats, lifting skirts thigh-high, turning cheap umbrellas inside out, and making the young green leaves on the smoke-blackened trees in the Mile End Road shiver in vain protest. Here and there a neon sign still gashed the night with a whirling crimson wound, and way up in the sky a pale moon had slipped out from behind the mountainous clouds and, surveying the scene below, smiled wanly, cynically.

In the London Hospital a woman opened her eyes and muttered, 'I'm not a crim'nal. I'm not a crim'nal.' Whitey Williams sat in a police car, cursing Fothergill, cursing all humanity, cursing all policemen, but secretly glad that those incriminating notes were not in his possession. He had given them to a strange girl. It had been a good hunch, a brilliant hunch. Could he trust her? He thought he could. The girl sat at a table on the ground floor of the Coventry Street Corner House and waited, waited, waited. The last buses, the last trams roared East and roared West. At the Underground stations the lifts and the escalators went up and down, and long, red, illuminated monsters hurtled under the earth, swallowed humanity here, spewed them out there.

An old blind beggar tapped his way towards Spry's Hotel and stopped as he heard somebody calling his name softly.

'Tim! Tim!'

Tommy Swann stepped out of a doorway and held him by the elbow. 'Look, Tim, I want you to do something for me.'

'What can I do for anybody? I'm just a poor blind man. I can't do nothing for nobody.'

'But I've got money, Tim. Here's a pound. Here, take it in yer 'and. It's yours.'

'God bless you, sir. God bless you, whoever you are.'

'You don't know me, Tim, do you?'

'No, sir. But God bless you, whoever you are.'

'But I know you, Tim – see? You sleep at Spry's, don't yer?'

'That's where I rest my weary, tired old bones, sir.'

'You're going back there now, aren't yer?'

'Yes, sir. To rest my tired old bones. I shall say a prayer for you, sir, so that the Lord may be kind to you.'

'Thanks; but there's something else yer can do for me.'

'What can I do for anybody, sir? I'm just a poor, blind man.'

'Yer know 'Enry, the big nigger at Spry's? Well, tell him a friend of his wants to see him. An old china what's in trouble. Tell him it's an old friend what's just passed by. Tell him I've got ter go on a journey, but I can't go by train because of me train sickness – see? An' tell 'im I've got some gelt, see? Don't ferget to tell 'im that. And tell 'im ter 'urry, because I'm liable ter catch a cold 'ere, see? Tell 'im where I am and tell 'im ter 'urry. Will yer do that for me?'

Tommy Swann paused, breathless after such a long speech. He looked anxiously at old Timothy, who nodded. 'I understand, my son, I understand. I will do as you ask. God bless you.'

And tapping his white stick he went off down the street towards Spry's Hotel, a bent figure in a long khaki overcoat, a tin box under his arm, grey rats-tail wisps of hair flowing from beneath his stained, shapeless hat. *Tap, tap, tap.*

Tommy Swann crouched in the doorway of an empty shop, waiting. Hurry up, you old bleeder, hurry up. I haven't got all night. Here he was with more than fifty pounds in his pocket, and yet he had to crouch in this doorway just like any tramp. The watch and chain, too, was worth at least another twenty-five nicker. What a stroke of luck that he had come along at the right moment. Dead lucky. He'd certainly scared the pants off that mug. Who was he? He'd seen him before somewhere. Hadn't he done a stretch in the Scrubs? Whoever he was, he was going the right way to get ten years' penal, plus the cat. He was a dead villain all right though. Bashing an old man over the nut like that and lifting his poke. A right mug all the same. Risking his liberty to give another guy the gravy. It had been easy. Perhaps it was fate. Perhaps there was a God after all. Perhaps He had said, 'There's a lag named Tommy Swann in trouble. I'll see he's coming along under the railway arches just when this mug bashes the other mug, so that when this mug cops, Tommy Swann can cop, too.'

All the same, in spite of the money and the red lot in his pocket, here he was standing like any tramp in a doorway. He was afraid to go to a coffee stall to get a cup of tea, because he knew all the coffee stalls would be watched. He was afraid to get on to a bus, because there would be dicks at the bus stops. Afraid to go into a railway station, because they would be there, too. Afraid to venture near the main road. Afraid to stay in the back streets. Afraid to go here, afraid to go there, afraid to stay. There have been men of great resolution and ingenuity who have tried the break from Dartmoor. Tommy Swann was not one of these. He was no Thurston. Desperation and a little luck had got him so far, but what now? Where to? Henry, the nigger, would be able to help him. Yes, big black Henry would do anything for money, especially if it was something to spite the flatties. Henry had seafaring acquaintances, rummy skippers of dirty little cargo boats who'd do anything for a little palm oil. When *was* Henry coming? Hurry up, you black bastard, hurry up!

Somewhere in the distance a church clock chimed. Then he heard the sound of a car. It was cruising along slowly on the opposite side of the road. Then he heard the sound of another car. The second car was coming from the opposite direction, but it was also cruising. 'Ere, what was this? Had that little blind bastard tipped the cops off? And was this a trap? He blenched. His heart seemed to be turning somersaults. Yes, there was no doubt about it. They *were* police cars, and they were turning their flash-lamps into every doorway. There was no escape. There was no escape. But there must be an escape. There must be a getaway. There is no getaway. But there must be. Then think of something quick. They're here. They're almost on top of you. I can hear their voices. I can see the rays of their flash-lamps splayed like searchlights over the wet pavements and into the doorways. Any minute now it'll be *this* doorway, and I'll stand here blinking, with all their flashlights shining into my eyes, and they'll come and grab me, and I'll go back to the Moor. No, no. I won't let them take me. But what can I do? If I walk out of this doorway they'll grab me. The cars are on top of me. They'll run me down. The whole place must be lousy with cops. That flashlight, it's right next door now. It must be, and it's moving up. It's stopped; it's wavering. It's coming on again. A white light; now it's on my feet. Now it's – crash! As the beam from the flash-lamp picked out Tommy Swann crouching in the doorway, he made a desperate leap upwards, clasped the top of the shop door and crashed headfirst through the glass fanlight into the shop.

Simultaneously with the crash, the two police cars pulled up, and plainclothes men and uniformed constables seemed to be pouring from all directions.

Farther up the road, at Spry's Hotel, an old blind beggar sat in the kitchen drinking a cup of cocoa made with condensed milk which he had salvaged from the bottom of a tin which some wasteful person had thrown into the dustbin.

Big Henry, the negro, stretched his feet and threw a lump of coal on to the fire. 'You had a good day today, Mistah Timothy, eh?' he asked, white teeth grinning in his black face. 'I bet you sure 'as, eh?'

Timothy shook his head and shuffled up the stairs to his bed in a corner of the long room, a room redolent of many smells and many sounds, coughing and spitting, and sounds more vulgar; odour of wet socks and unwashed blankets; men sitting up in bed smoking cigarette stubs. And as Timothy shuffled into the room the man with a strawberry mark on his face cheered ironically and mocked him by shouting in a nasal voice, *'Box o' matches! Box o' matches!'*

And big Henry, the negro, opened the door of Maria Spry's room and said, 'Would yuh like a cup of tea, Maria?'

To which she muttered drowsily, 'No, 'Enry; jus' come in and shut the door, come on.'

IV

Vi Sandigate sat at a table on the ground floor of the Coventry Street Corner House until long past midnight. She sat there so long and saw so many different people come in and go out, so many interesting-looking people, that she was beginning to feel less agitated about the money that had been thrust upon her. Even now, with the notes in her handbag, she could not entirely comprehend it. Such things just did not happen. And yet it *had* happened. She squeezed her handbag and felt the bulge of the notes. Yes, they were still there. But fancy a man trusting a complete stranger with all that money! Perhaps she had an honest face. Yes, of course I've got an honest face. I am honest, aren't I? I've never stole anything. But suppose that young man never comes back? What does he expect me to do – wait here forever? And suppose I never see him again. What am I to do with all this money? If it was my money I could buy a lovely fur coat with it. I could buy some jewellery, too, and a couple of nice dresses and several sets of underwear, and a dozen pairs of stockings, pure silk, fully fashioned. And I'd still have money left over. I could even go and stay at an hotel. I might meet a rich man there, a rich, good-looking man. She opened her handbag for the twenty-third time in the last two hours. How beautiful and crisp these notes are. This is adventure.

She yawned. How much longer must I sit here? I'm so tired. I'd like to go to a really swanky hotel and get into a lovely, soft, clean bed instead of that room in Lisle Street, with bugs crawling all over the place. And my skin's so sensitive, too. I've got enough money to go to a hotel, too. I could go to the best hotel in the land I could. Shall I? I'm so tired. No, I mustn't. I'd be afraid to. This money isn't mine. But I didn't steal it, did I? I didn't ask him to push it down my neck. And I've waited here for him, haven't I? What does he expect me to do, wait all night? And I'm so tired. I could go to sleep. Go right off to sleep, I could. She closed her bag and put it on the seat beside her. She yawned. Ten minutes later she opened her eyes. There were still people coming in and going out, well-dressed people and people not so well-dressed. Half-a-dozen dance-band musicians carrying their instruments and all laughing very loud at some joke as they sauntered towards the tables. And there, just going out, was Lulu Blair. Fat people, thin people, well-fed people and hungry-looking people. Pretty girls and ugly men. Ugly women, too. Who were they all? Did they never go to bed? She reached for her bill, got up and walked to the door. At the cash desk she found that her handbag was open and the money – the money – it wasn't there.

V

WhiteyWilliams kicked a cell door in Leman Street police station and shouted, 'I want bail! I want bail!' Nobody answered him. So he kicked again and he shouted again, 'I want bail! I want bail! I wanna talk ter my mouthpiece. I want bail!You can't keep me in 'ere.'

For twenty minutes this had been going on, twenty minutes of kicking and shouting. Whitey Williams was keeping up his reputation of being an awkward prisoner. Besides, he was thinking of his two hundred pounds nestling in a strange girl's bosom. If the two hundred nicker was still there. If, in fact, the girl was still there. The more he thought about it, the more worried he got.What would she do when he didn't turn up? He was more worried about his two hundred pounds than the charge that was hanging over him, a charge of being concerned in the robbery of a gross of roller skates. He was sure he could beat that rap. Luckily, they had said nothing about the attack on Caleb Beasley.They couldn't possibly associate him with that. Perhaps Caleb Beasley had just picked himself up and gone home, deeming it more prudent not to report the matter to the police. On the other hand, if he *had* gone to the dicks he would have given them the serial numbers of the notes stolen from his wallet. But perhaps Beasley himself didn't know the numbers. How many people troubled to memorise banknote numbers? Besides, Fothergill had seen the fiver he had changed at the Shimmy Club, and he hadn't come a tumble. He kicked at the door again.

'I want bail!You can't keep me 'ere! I want bail!'

Presently he heard footsteps and a jingle of keys. Encouraged, he shouted all the louder.

'Pipe down, will you?' came the voice of the gaoler. Then the cell door opened and Fothergill stepped in. He looked strange without a hat or mackintosh on. His baby-blue eyes smiled. He was enjoying this.

'Now listen,Williams,' he said. 'You're not making it easier for yourself.'

'What yer want me ter do, then?' Whitey retorted. 'Make it easier for you?'

Fothergill actually laughed.

'All your kicking and shouting doesn't worry me, son. I don't sleep here.'

'And I ain't sleeping 'ere, either. I want bail!' Whitey's voice rose to a shout again.

'Look, Whitey, why don't you be a wide boy?'

'I'm too bleedin' wide for you, Fovvergill. You ain't got nothing on me.'

'Look, you want bail, don't you?'

'Yus, I want bail.'

'Well, that's easy. Come clean about that job in Mansell Street, and I'll see what I can do for you.'

Whitey's lip curled and he burst into song, or, rather, into a hymn. 'Tell Me The Old, Old Story'.

Fothergill looked mildly amused and leaned against the cell doors.

'I might as well tell you, Williams, that your two pals, Alfie and Dicey, have talked. They've talked good and plenty.'

Whitey's sneer became a snarl. 'Garn, don't tell me Alfie or Dicey 'ave come their guts, because I know better, see!'

Fothergill shrugged his shoulders.

'Would you like to see their statements? They say the whole job was your idea. You put them up to it.'

Whitey wheeled round. 'Then they're damned liars, because . . .' He broke off, realised his slip, and said, 'Don't 'and me that dishwash. They couldn't say a fing like that, because we didn't do the job, see! And, besides, if you've done Alfie and Dicey, why ain't they down 'ere in the floweries?'

'Alfie and Dicey aren't down here in the cells, because at the moment they are upstairs in the charge room. Isn't that so, gaoler?'

'Quite right, sir,' said the big, bald-headed gaoler, who was standing just outside the cell.

Whitey stuck his chin out over the knot of his white muffler and put his thumbs into the armholes of his waistcoat. 'All right, so what? You've done 'em. But you ain't got nothing on us, Mister Clever Dick Fovvergill, you ain't got nothing on us. You ain't got no evidence.'

Fothergill's blue eyes twinkled. 'We found a pair of skates.'

'Yeah, well stick 'em up yer –'

'Oh, no,' said Fothergill. 'That might spoil the fingerprints.'

'Fingerprints? What fingerprints?'

'The dabs on the roller skates we found, silly boy! They're yours.'

'I ain't left my dabs on no roller skates,' Whitey retorted.

'Well, if they're not yours, they're Alfie's, and if they're not Alfie's, they're Dicey's. We'll soon find out.'

'Don't give me that bull. You ain't found no roller skates.'

The detective chuckled and turned to the gaoler.

'Got any cigarettes on you, gaoler?'

'Yes, sir.'

'Give this villain one, will you?' he said, indicating Whitey. 'He's going to need it.'

Whitey took the cigarette, wondering what was coming next. He puffed on it hungrily.

'Now, Williams,' said Fothergill. 'A pair of skates similar to those stolen from the warehouse in Mansell Street were found tonight in a house in Coronet Square.'

Whitey tautened inwardly, but he gave no sign. He drew the cigarette smoke deep into his lungs, but he did not speak.

'A house in Coronet Square belonging to a Mr Beasley,' the detective went on. 'Or perhaps I should say the late Mr Beasley.'

A muscle twitched in Whitey's face.

'What d'yer mean – the late Mr Beasley?'

'Oh, didn't you know?' Fothergill was smiling at him again. Curse his light-blue eyes. 'Mr Beasley was murdered tonight.'

Murdered! Murdered! Murdered! The word kept coming back at Whitey like vicious left and right hooks to the body, and he wanted to gasp. Murdered. Murdered. Murdered. No, I ain't murdered Beasley. You couldn't kill a man as easily as that. Of course not. Murdered. Murdered. They hang murderers, don't they? Yes, he remembered them hanging a murderer when he was doing a stretch at the Scrubs.

He said nothing. He made no sign. Not by a flicker of an eyelash did he reveal the ice-cold fear within him. He opened his mouth, and the smoke rolled out, then his lips closed on the cigarette again, and then the smoke rolled out of his nostrils.

'Well,' said Fothergill. 'Aren't you going to say anything?'

Whitey whipped the cigarette out of his mouth and frowned. ''Ere, I 'ope you ain't saying I murdered that old sod?'

'I'm not saying anything of the kind, Williams. In any case, I don't think you'd have the guts to commit murder. But if Beasley hadn't been murdered, we wouldn't have called at Beasley's house. And if we hadn't called at Beasley's house, we wouldn't have found that pair of roller skates. And that pair of skates is going to get you about three years. Unless you want to be a good boy, and perhaps we'll let you off with eighteen months.'

Whitey sat down on the wooden form, tugging at the cigarette. The ice-cold fear was beginning to evaporate. They didn't suspect him of killing Caleb Beasley. But anything might happen. Anything might happen. Suppose they discovered that Beasley had been carrying a lot of money, and suppose they traced the serial numbers? And suppose Fothergill remembered the number of the note that he, Whitey, had changed in the Shimmy Club? What then? Or, worse, suppose they caught Tommy Swann? Yes, that was the real danger. Tommy Swann would come his guts all right. A certainty he would. He'd do a deal with the cops. 'Treat me right,' he'd say, 'and I'll tell you who killed Caleb Beasley. I saw him do it.' Ten to one that's what Tommy Swann would do, rot his guts. Whitey Williams stood up.

'Look, Fovvergill, there's something I ought to tell yer.'

'Yes?'

'You know I'm a crook, don't yer?'

Fothergill laughed.

'Well, I suppose I must agree to that also. What's the point?'

'I was in on that Mansell Street job.'

'I knew you were; but I'm glad you've admitted it, son.'

'But look, Fovvergill, you'll do yer best fer me, won't yer? I mean, if I could do something fer the perlice, they ought ter do something fer me, eh?'

'Such as?'

'Well.' Whitey gulped and loosened the knot of his muffler. He stretched his neck. 'I know the bloke what killed Beasley.'

'Who was it, Whitey?'

'Tommy Swann. I saw 'im do it.'

'You're quite sure of this, Whitey?'

'On my liberty, Fovvergill, on my muvver's life, I saw 'im do it. It was under the railway arches. I saw 'im crack 'im over the 'ead with what looked like an 'ammer or a piece of iron. I ran up ter try ter stop 'im, but it was too late, although I didn't know he'd killed 'im, of course, and that fiver you saw me change in the club, it was what Tommy Swann give me for keeping me mouth shut. And I suppose I would 'ave kept me mouth shut if you 'adn't told me about Beasley being dead. I may be a crook, but I draw the line at murder. That's the troof, Fovvergill.'

From upstairs came the sound of a telephone bell ringing.

VI

'Keep away from me, copper! Keep away from me, copper!'

Tommy Swann crouched on the parapet of a factory rooftop and watched the uniformed constable edging up from the other side of the parapet. Down below, despite the late hour, a crowd had collected, eyes turned skywards, fascinated, thrilled to the marrow.

'Keep away from me, flattie, or you'll go over the side. I warn yer.' The policeman didn't reply. He edged nearer, nearer, nearer.

'Keep away, yer silly barstid!' Tommy Swann shrieked. 'I've warned yer, ain't I? You'll go over the side with me. They ain't gonna take me to the Moor alive. They ain't. Keep orf, will yer, keep orf!'

The constable paused, legs dangling over the side. The crowd below held its breath as they saw the two dark figures silhouetted against the skyline.

'Have a cigarette, Tommy.' The policeman's voice was coaxing.

'I don't want no cigarette. Don't you come near me or you'll go over the side. I've warned yer.'

But Tommy Swann's eyes were fastened hungrily on the cigarette packet. He could do with a cigarette. How he could do with it.

'Look, help yourself.' The policeman tossed the packet on to the parapet between them.

Tommy Swann looked at it. 'Don't you try no tricks, flattie.'

'I won't try no tricks, Tommy.'

Tommy Swann reached forward and his hand closed on the packet, and as it did so the policeman's hand closed on his wrist. Tommy tried to twist it free, but the grip was like iron. 'Lemme go, you barstid, lemme go!' He gave a tug, and down below a woman screamed as the two men were seen to sway, first to the right and then to the left. For an age-long second it seemed inevitable that they would come crashing down to the pavement. They swayed out and they swayed back, out and back. And then they were gone – they went over backwards on to the safe side, the factory roof. They rolled over and over, Tommy Swann punching, biting and swearing like a madman. More policemen came squeezing through the skylight on to the roof, and then it was only a matter of time. A truncheon rose and fell twice – crack, crack. The policeman lifted his truncheon again, but it was unnecessary. Tommy Swann was out. They slipped the handcuffs on him. They searched him and found more than fifty pounds in notes and a gold watch and chain. There was an engraving on the back of the watch: *'To CR Beasley, presented to him on the occasion of his fiftieth birthday by the –'* The constable put the watch away. 'He won't have any more birthdays,' he commented. Then he looked down at the inert, manacled figure of Tommy Swann, who was groaning in his stupor, his face badly lacerated from his jump through the shop fanlight. 'And you're one lag that won't go back to Dartmoor,' the constable added. 'You're going to swing, Tommy, me boy.'

VII

Doris Sandigate lay, face downwards, on her bed. She had not undressed, except for kicking off her shoes. Dark-blue, high-heeled shoes. One of them was on the bedspread. The other had fallen on to the floor. Her hat was clenched in one hand, a damp handkerchief in the other. The room was in darkness.

Outside, the wireless aerial swayed in the wind, causing the dangling earth-wire to tap rhythmically on the window. She paid no attention to this noise. She did not hear it. Neither did she hear a distant clock strike three. Her father was still at the hospital. Would he never come back? Would he never come back? Should she have gone to the hospital? She had; but at the gates she had turned back and returned home. What use could she be at the hospital? What could she do? What could she say? Nothing.

Once before she had waited for her father to come back from the hospital. That was years ago, years ago. She had been just a baby, but the recollection was as vivid to her now as if it had only happened yesterday. She remembered hearing the street door open, and she had gone out on to the landing and looked down through the banisters. She saw her father come in. Heard him sigh. Then he had walked along to the end of the passage to turn out the light, and as his face was tilted up under the gaslight she saw something she had never seen before. She saw two tears on his face, one on each side of his nose. Then he turned the light out and the passage was in darkness. And she knew that her mother was dead.

A distant clock struck the half-hour. She sat up and shivered. How cold it was. I am cold all through. My hands are cold. My feet are cold. My heart is cold. Everything is cold. But that is not true. There is warm blood in my body. I am young and alive. I want somebody to love me. But there is no love – anywhere. Shall I make myself a cup of tea? No, I'm too tired. Besides, I might awaken Alfie, and it was a terrible job getting him to go to sleep as it was. He asked so many questions. I hate that child. But I shouldn't hate him. He is my half-brother. Why is there such a thing as hate? And where is Vi? Yes, where is Vi? Just then the gate creaked and there was the sound of a key being inserted in the front door. Perhaps this is Vi now. I must tell her.

Doris Sandigate got up quickly from the bed and went out on to the landing. Still holding her hat in one hand and a damp handkerchief in the other, she looked down over the banisters. Mr Sandigate was just closing the door. Then he came along the passage, not noticing her looking down from the landing above.

In the flickering light from the gas-jet on the wall bracket he looked old, very old. His blue serge cap was lopsided on the back of his head, revealing the bald patch. And there was a smear of mud on his cap. She heard him mutter something to himself. She saw him pass his hand across his eyes. She wanted to speak, but knew not what to say. Then, at the end of the passage, he stopped to turn out the light, and the house was in darkness.